P9-DNW-239

RAGE

RAGE

BY PHILIP FRIEDMAN

BASED ON AN ORIGINAL SCREENPLAY BY

PHILIP FRIEDMAN & DAN KLEINMAN

NEW YORK 1972 ATHENEUM

Library of Congress catalog card number 72–84261
Published simultaneously in Canada by McClelland and Stewart Ltd.
Manufactured in the United States of America by
Kingsport Press, Inc., Kingsport, Tennessee
Designed by Harry Ford
First Edition

TO

ARLENE

BENNETT

FRED

AND MORTY,

WHO MADE IT POSSIBLE,

AND TO

GEORGE,

WHO MADE IT REAL

The author wishes to thank for their unfailing willingness to answer questions and to be generally helpful and encouraging: Milton Eisen, M.D.; Barry Keller, M.D.; Walter Newman, M.D.; and Joseph Ransohoff, M.D. The author trusts they will forgive him for whatever distortions he has visited on the accurate information they so freely provided. Special thanks as well to John Briggs, for reasons too numerous to list.

ONE

1

Alone in the cloudless, late afternoon sky, the jet fighter leveled off and began its run over the bleak, barren ground three thousand feet below.

In the plane's cramped cockpit, Captain Roger Liefler pressed a small black button, opening the spray-release valve of the tank slung under the fighter's belly. He glanced briefly over the rows of dials that told him he was following the right flight pattern, and then he returned to his thoughts, which were the same as they always were on these flights: mostly a rehash of the reasons why he should get the hell out of the air force or at least get a transfer to someplace where he could get some better duty.

When Liefler's wrist chronometer had ticked off thirty seconds, he reached out and hit the red button that closed the spray valve. Then he hauled back on the stick and pulled up and around to begin the long sweep that would put him in position for the next pass. The empty, deep-blue sky and the lifeless terrain of the target zone flashed by the clear bubble of the cockpit as he came around.

It was not until he was leveling off again, ready to start his second pass, that he happened to look at the level indicator for the silver tank and notice that its needle was resting steadily on zero, which it wasn't supposed to do for another three runs.

Which meant that he had somehow mistakenly released three hundred pounds of experimental nerve gas into the air above the Wyoming countryside.

2

Dan Logan finished tightening a hose connection on his pickup truck's radiator, then gave the hose a tug to make sure it was fastened tightly enough. Satisfied, he straightened up, pushed his Stetson to the back of his head, and wiped the sweat from his forehead.

"O.K.," he said, "start it up."

In the cab of the truck, Logan's twelve-year-old son, Chris, turned the ignition key, and the starter cranked over the truck's engine until it caught. Logan poured some water into the radiator, then slammed the hood closed and walked back to the cab of the truck, followed by Emily, his black-and-brown mongrel sheepdog. When Logan opened the truck door, Emily jumped onto the seat next to Chris.

Logan stowed the water can behind the seat and got into the truck. "We're going to need some of that hose," he said to his son. "Let me have the pad and I'll mark it down."

As he wrote himself a reminder about the radiator hose, Logan said, "You want to camp out tonight?"

Chris made no attempt to hide his excitement. "Sure,"

he said, grinning broadly.

Logan, pleased by his son's reaction, smiled. He put the truck in gear and started along the dirt road that cut across the northeast corner of his ranch. In spite of his care to avoid ruts and potholes, Logan could hear the gas cans and tools and his small trail motorcycle shaking and rattling in the back of the truck.

After a short drive, he pulled up in front of a small, rough corral. The truck had barely stopped when Chris and Emily were out the door, running toward the pump that stood near the corral gate. Logan watched his son prime the pump from the bucket that had been hanging from its spout and then begin pumping enthusiastically, sending water gushing and splashing into the bucket. Emily stood next to the boy, her tail wagging.

While Chris carried the full bucket into the corral, Logan got out of the truck and walked over to the corral fence. The small corral held only four sheep, which Logan and Chris had separated from the others soon after they were born the previous spring, setting them aside to be raised and cared for by Chris, without help from his father or the hands he sometimes hired. The boy was proud to have his own livestock. Almost the first thing he had done after they had chosen the sheep was to get an old, worn piece of shelf board and carve into it the legend, "These sheep belong to Chris Logan." The sign had weathered a bit in the five months since he had nailed it up, but it still hung proudly at the corral gate.

In the corral, Chris emptied the bucket into a small concrete watering trough. He smiled at his father, who was watching from near the fence, and went over to the sheep, which cowered in a corner of the corral, regarding

Emily warily. One by one, Chris examined the sheep, running his hands through their wool, peering at their skin, lifting their legs to look at their hooves, doing everything carefully and deliberately to make sure that he got it all right. Leaning on the corral fence, watching, Logan was happy to see his son working with such care, and enjoying himself.

Logan worried about the boy more than he usually would admit to himself. It was hard for a boy Chris's age to be without a mother and to have so much responsibility: the boy did a lot of chores around the ranch, besides going to school. Logan did what he could for Chris, but he knew he wasn't a talkative man, or very demonstrative about his feelings. He thought, sometimes, that the boy might withdraw under the weight of all that, and become bitter and sullen. The miracle was that he hadn't. He was well liked at school, he enjoyed working around the ranch, and mostly, if you encouraged him a little, he tried hard at whatever he was doing. Logan didn't know how to account for it, but he thought Chris was likely to turn into a pretty fine man.

When Chris was finished with the sheep, he picked up the bucket and led Emily from the corral, latching the gate carefully. His father walked over to meet him. "They look all right?" Logan asked.

"Yep. Fine," Chris answered.

Logan tousled his son's hair, and the boy smiled. They got back into the pickup truck and drove back down the dirt road.

3

EYES ONLY
HAND DELIVER
TO: COL WM FRANKLIN
FROM: MAJGEN RONALD PHILLIPS
RE: FORT HOWARD

Bill—

The attached just came in on the top wire. I think you'd better red-phone it to your boss right away.

R. P.

A4DX329–P982
TOPSECRETCLASSQSCRAMBLE
CODEDESIGRADARFOURAUGHTTWO
MAJOR GENERAL RONALD PHILLIPS
PENTAGON6E2962
PRIORITY BLUEBLUEYELLOW
BEGINS: 1554 HOURS TODAY TEST MX3 RELEASED ESTIM THREE HUNDRED POUNDS BEYOND LIMIT TEST ZONE. DISPERSION PATTERN NOT DETERMINED THOUGHT TO INCLUDE UNCONTROLLED AREAS. FULL SAMPLING UNDERWAY. BLUE BOOK PHASE TWO INITIATED 1602 HOURS. ALL ELEMENTS AVAILABLE. RED BOOK PROCEDURE ON STANDBY. ADVISE.

COL ALAN A NICKERSON
COMMANDING OFFICER
FORT HOWARD WYOMING

4

TO: ALL PERSONNEL, FORT HOWARD

FROM: COMMANDING OFFICER

All personnel are hereby ordered confined to the post. There will be no communication of any kind with any person not currently assigned to Fort Howard, except on direct order or authorization of the commanding officer. Normal duties are suspended until further notice. SECURITY PROCEDURE FOUR IS IN EFFECT AS OF 1900 HOURS.

5

EYES ONLY

HAND DELIVER

TO: MAJGEN RONALD PHILLIPS

FROM: COL WM FRANKLIN

RE: FORT HOWARD

Ronny—

The boss thinks we'd better sit on this one hard. There's some question about the locals' ability to get it right. Word is that CO Fort How is mostly a desk jockey, waiting for his pension. A good administrator, but no imagination. Also, there's some worry about the current mood. The boss thinks this is definitely our hot potato, so I'll be taking it off your hands. The boss will give you the direct order when he gets around to it, but meanwhile we don't have time to wait for the technicalities. I'll be in the CBW library boning up, so I'd appreciate it if you could bring anything you think I'll need and meet me there.

Bill

6

Colonel William Franklin looked up from the abstract he was reading as Major General Ronald Phillips eased his bulky frame into the chair across the table from him. "Well, how does it look?" Phillips asked in his best I'm-glad-this-is-your-mess voice.

Franklin paused a moment before answering, leaning back and running his hand through his prematurely steel-gray hair, then said, "I think we'll be able to get out of it whole. From what I've been able to tell, there doesn't seem to be anything serious. Even so, I want to get out there right away. You know how the boss feels about bad publicity."

"Yes, I've heard that little lecture. I even give it myself sometimes," Phillips said. "You think this'll be all right, then?"

"I've seen worse. A lot depends on how hard the wind

was blowing. And how alert they are out there. You know anything about the CO? He must report to you."

"He's one of my people, but we haven't had much contact. I don't know much more than you do. I knew he was waiting for his star, but it'll be a gift if he gets it. That's not much of a job, you know, just nursemaid and traffic cop to a bunch of technicians. A lot of paper shuffling and riding herd on that tag-end air force detachment that does the test flights."

"Well, he's got something big to handle now," Franklin said with a shrug of distaste. "If he can keep his head long enough to do it right. What's this Blue Book Phase Two he's put in effect?"

"The Blue Book is our emergency operations manual. Phase Two is a testing procedure to be used if there's suspected leakage or an accidental overspray like this one they had at Fort Howard this afternoon. We've got other procedures for the same thing. Phase Two is covert: minimum contact with civilian population, maximum security. He wouldn't be using it if he thought there was continuing danger of civilian exposure. At least he's not supposed to."

"So presumably he feels that if damage is going to be done, it's too late to help it."

"Either that or he's so concerned about publicity that he hasn't thought about it. It's hard to tell from that one wire, and I haven't queried him. I wanted to see how you people were going to handle it."

Franklin thought for a few seconds, then closed the cover of the file he was reading. It bore the label "ATOM: MX3." He said, "I think we'd better get more details right away. I can't get out there until tomorrow morning, and

I want to be sure I understand what the situation is before I get on the plane. I want to be sure that they understand, too." He stood up decisively. "Let's go over to the communications room."

7

FILE NO: A459–3401–AXFHOW9
DESIGNATION: MX3
DEVELOPMENT: CHIVINGTON, WYO
TYPE: Nerve agent, modR, contact.
DELIVERY: Air.

Aerosol distribution. Droplet size, spray rate, optimum altitude and weather not determined.

NOTE: Preliminary testing indicates mid-range droplet size, dilution with standard delivery medium estimated 10:1. Details monthly test bulletin 124–J–6, Fort Howard, Wyoming, pp. 124–212.

ACTIVITY: Highest.
PERSISTENCE: Moderate. Estimated half-life two weeks.
ANTIDOTE: None.
DEACTIVATOR: Rn42 or V-6. Partial effectiveness only.
CRITICAL DOSE: Not determined.

NOTE: Agent developed to have widely varied effects depending on dosage. First successful "radiomimetic" (modR) agent to date. Symptoms similar to those of radiation poisoning; severity varies markedly with concentration and length of exposure, although these two factors not yet isolated. See Progress Report 4: ATOM Program, Rocky Mountain Arsenal, Colorado, pp. 72–119.

8

Dan Logan stopped chopping wood for a moment and let his gaze wander downhill past a cluster of grazing sheep to the broad winding creek and rolling land beyond. The late afternoon sun turned Logan's ranchland into a relief map of light and shadow traversed by a crooked ribbon of glistening water.

It had been a good afternoon. He and Chris had gotten a lot done and enjoyed themselves, too. Logan felt unusually content, pleased with his world. He turned to look at Chris, to include the boy in his contentment. These days, Chris reminded him more and more of JoAnn. Logan knew Chris favored him in speech and manner, down to even the smallest gestures, but the boy had none of his own massiveness; he was slight and trim and wiry, like his mother had been.

Logan could think about JoAnn now, finally, could accept her absence as just another of those things the world did to you. He could feel the hollow place in his life, in his soul, but it didn't ache any more in the old way, it was just something he always carried with him.

So he accepted it, and for a moment enjoyed the sunset and the sight of his son, their son, hammering the pegs around the edge of the little mountain tent, enjoyed, too, the sounds of the hilltop and the approaching twilight and the sheep, enjoyed even the smells and the textures. All of this in a brief moment, then he went back to chopping dead branches into firewood.

After a few minutes, Chris ran over, excited, holding something.

"Hey, Pop, look at this," he said, holding out his cupped hands. "It's a thousand-legger."

Logan looked close to watch the millipede crawl over his son's hands. "He's a real monster, all right."

The boy grinned up at his father. "Look at the way his legs wiggle." The two of them watched the bug for a moment, then Chris set the bug down in the grass and went back to putting up the tent.

By the time the sun was all the way down, but long before it was really dark, the two Logans had their camp set up for the night. Dan stirred the hash and beans he had thrown in a frying pan over the bright, hot fire, while Chris filled a food bowl for Emily. Then the three of them sat around the fire, each eating in his own style: Logan, slowly, deliberately, attacking his food, like everything else, with quiet concentration; Emily, gobbling hungrily; and Chris, playing with the food a little, pushing his fork around the plate to line up a row of beans, looking around at Emily and his father, and at the line of orange that still lingered in the sky.

9

Colonel Alan Nickerson left the Fort Howard teletype room even unhappier than he had been when he entered it an hour before. His communication with General Phillips, who was his immediate superior at the Pentagon, had only increased his conviction that hc was in the middle of the worst pickle he had been in. And now it seemed that there were aspects of this particular pickle that he hadn't even known about. There had been a second person on the Washington end of the line—a Colonel Franklin—and, whoever he was, General Phillips seemed to be deferring to him. This was odd, because it was unlike Ronny Phillips to defer to anyone, least of all someone he outranked. Very odd, and a little ominous, it seemed to Nickerson.

For the hundredth time, Nickerson wished that there was a telephone line secure enough for a conversation like the one he had just finished, so that he could pick up some cues from the other party's tone of voice, instead of being faced with abbreviation-and-jargon-ridden pieces of paper fresh from the unscrambler and the decoder. As he turned down the corridor toward his office, he gave a small mental shrug. Why worry about that one now? The teletype machine was unavoidable, and Colonel Franklin would present himself in person all too soon anyway. All Nickerson could hope for was that he would be able to get things into presentable shape by the morning. And pray that there wouldn't be any human casualties.

In the office, Nickerson found Major John Reintz, his second-in-command, waiting impatiently. He nodded to Reintz and pushed on into the inner office. Reintz followed and closed the door behind him.

"What do you have, Jack?" Nickerson asked.

"The second batch of test results are in, sir. The maximum reading this time was eighteen micrograms. That's down from twenty in the first readings. And our average outside the Fort is only fourteen. Maybe we'll luck out after all."

Nickerson shot him a sharp glance. "We'll need more than luck this time, Jack." Then, changing tack, "What about the local hospitals? Have you checked?"

"Well, sir," Reintz said, "I didn't really know how far you wanted me to go. There's the Rawlins Clinic, and Carbon County Hospital, of course, but I wasn't sure where else to cover."

"Goddam it, Jack, cover the whole damn state if you have to. Whatever else happens, we can't let this get out. I don't imagine I have to tell you what it will mean to your career if this gets screwed up any worse. You have a lot further to go than I do."

Reintz squirmed a little under Nickerson's barrage, and Nickerson, watching him, thought: If only the ambitious little bastard were smarter, we might get out of this all right. At least I've got him worried. That should sharpen him up a little.

10

It was without enthusiasm that Major Bertram Holliford, M.D., answered his phone at the Fort Howard Bachelor Officers' Quarters. Not having seen the general order confining all personnel to the Fort, he was just about to go out to dinner and then to a movie—one of his rare excursions off the post—and he didn't want his plans disturbed. He even considered not answering at all and just leaving the room, but he got so few calls that he had to assume any call was likely to be important.

It was Jack Reintz, which didn't please Holliford at all. It pleased him less that Reintz was calling to tell him to get right over to Conference Room A, where Colonel Nickerson had just called an urgent meeting. Something big must be up, Holliford thought, if Nickerson is calling meetings at this hour, and inviting an ivory-tower experimenter, to boot. And it is probably not a bunch of loose monkeys they're worried about.

11

Major Stonewall Jackson Cooper, on the other hand, was neither mystified nor annoyed by his call from

Major Reintz. If the CO was calling an urgent meeting during his dinner hour, it had to mean a security problem. Otherwise the old goat would have waited for morning. And while a security problem meant that Stoney Cooper's head would be on the line, it also meant that he would finally have something to do besides write and check guard-duty rosters. He was looking forward to getting off his ass for a change.

12

In the Pentagon, supper for two was served in a small dining room not far from room 6E2962. Major General Ronald Phillips and Colonel William Franklin walked the short distance from Phillips' office in silence. Neither was unaccustomed to eating at nine o'clock at night, and neither was unaccustomed to being kept at work long past normal quitting time. In spite of their worries about the problem they had to deal with, they were both going to enjoy their meals, taking out a half hour or so to slow down and let their minds relax before getting back to work.

This ability to put their work out of their minds was something that General Phillips and Colonel Franklin had in common with each other, although it wasn't shared by the bulk of their fellow officers at the Pentagon. Phillips had come to it late, after almost being laid up permanently with a particularly painful ulcer, which had led him to two years of very surreptitious visits to a psychiatrist. Franklin, on the other hand, had always had the talent, and it was one of the reasons why those who knew him called him—in private conversation—the Pentagon's Young Man Most Likely to Succeed, not an unreasonable title for a man who in two years of special assignment had become number-one trouble-shooter for the Joint Chiefs of Staff.

13

OFFICIAL MINUTES
SECURITY BRIEFING
FORT HOWARD, WYOMING
12 OCTOBER, 1850 HOURS, CONFERENCE ROOM A

PRESENT: Col. A. A. Nickerson, CO; Maj. J. Reintz; Maj. S. J. Cooper; Maj. B. Holliford; Capt. R. Liefler.

MINUTES TAKEN BY: N. Johnson, SP/4

TOPIC: TEST A4–MX3–SSQi3/003/6

PROCEEDINGS: 1. Captain Liefler reported details of test flight SSQi3/003/6 as normal in all respects. Preliminary checklist procedure carried out as per standard orders. Test pattern established and initial run made to determine reference points. Weather check green prior to initiation. First run normal. At point zero, run two, spray tank volume gauge registered empty. Cancellation procedure four initiated.

2. Questioning by Colonel Nickerson and Major Reintz centered on time between endpoint run one and point zero run two. Captain Liefler: spray-tank function normal during run one, tank-function termination at thirty seconds after point zero, specified endpoint. Expected volume reading 0.75 at point zero run two. Captain Liefler dismissed, confined to quarters pending further investigation.
3. Ground crew findings reported by Major Reintz. (a) test plane—normal function throughout. (b) automatic log indicates proper flight path, tank-function initiation at point zero run one as specified, tank-function termination as specified. (c) examination of tank and sprayer (type 318) by ground crew and laboratory test team indicates spray-valve malfunction.
Conclusion: At endpoint run one, spray valve locked in open position.
Analysis and projections: Calculations based on data in automatic log and examination of malfunctioning spray valve indicate approx 325 lbs. MX3 dispersed at constant rate over linear path length 5 miles ± 1 mile alt. min. 3,000 feet max. 15,000 feet.
4. Summary by Major Reintz of air-sampling procedures: present results indicate maximum readings of twenty-two micrograms per cubic meter over controlled areas, with uncontrolled areas having a maximum of eighteen micrograms, except for a single reading of twenty in

one area. As of last readings, 1800 hours, average over uncontrolled areas at twelve micrograms. Present estimates place effective military concentration in mid-range droplet dispersion pattern at thirty-five micrograms per cubic meter.

5. In response to questioning by Colonel Nickerson, Major Holliford unable to give firm estimate of probable casualty rate. Data insufficient on both present conditions and on effects of MX3. Suggests reliance on estimated effective military concentration as basis for first order calculations.

6. Meeting terminated 1945 hours. Major Holliford, Major Arnold, Captain Atherton, Captain Eisen to confer on medical precautions, report by 2100 on proposed course of action. Major Reintz to report 2030 on latest air test results. Major Cooper to draft security recommendations, report by 2130.

TWO

1

When the alarm went off, Colonel Nickerson was already awake. He hadn't slept much, even though he knew that the four hours he'd had in bed might be the most he'd get for the next few days. Nickerson found that it wasn't easy for him to sleep when his whole career was going down the drain.

As he went wearily about his morning routines, Nickerson tried to close off the anxiety that was taking big, tearing bites at his insides, but his attempt to clear his head just intensified the problem. What made the whole situation so intolerable was that he was in danger, as he saw it, of losing the fruits of a life's work in the army not because of any mistake he had made or could have prevented, but because of some damn chance mechanical failure. If it was anybody's fault, it was somebody on the assembly line in whatever company had the contract to make those valves. Of course, that didn't matter: whoever was at fault, Alan Nickerson was going to have to suffer for it. He wondered, on his way to the office, whether there was even a chance he could get out of this with a whole skin, much less a general's pension.

Shortly past 6:00 A.M., a few minutes after Nickerson had finished his first weary cup of coffee laced with the brandy he always kept in his desk, there was a brief knock on the office door, and Jack Reintz let himself in, saluting perfunctorily.

"Morning, Jack," Nickerson said without enthusiasm. "Report?"

"Yes, sir," Reintz said, and he thought: The old bastard is feeling sorry for himself. Reintz poured himself a cup of coffee. "I've got the readings from the five-thirty run. They look pretty good."

Nickerson nodded, but he showed no sign of relief.

"We've got zero readings virtually everywhere. Nothing at all outside the Fort." Reintz put his coffee cup down on Nickerson's desk and pulled up a chair.

"What about the roadblocks?" Nickerson asked him.

"I just called the State Police and told Captain Petrone to have them removed. The road was clear all night over the stretch that runs along the west perimeter, and we dusted it twice, so I didn't see any point in keeping it closed. There doesn't seem to have been any comment about it."

"That's good. I only hope we can keep it that way."

"Well, we shouldn't have to worry much about the locals. They've always seemed to be very happy about having us here, and as long as they know we're important to the national security, I don't think they care what we do."

"That's well and good, Jack, until we start spraying their ranches with nerve agents. I don't know how long we could keep the good will of the community if that got out." Nickerson fell silent, brooding about the specter he had just raised.

From across the desk, Reintz watched him, wondering how Nickerson had managed to stick out nearly thirty years in the army. The small, bespectacled colonel sometimes looked as if he couldn't manage the rigors of even a file clerk's life—in spite of his rugged face and mania for fitness—and yet here he was, just a hairsbreadth from getting his star. If nothing else, it gave Reintz hope for his own career.

Nickerson looked up. "And it's not only the damn town we have to worry about, either," he said. "There's Washington, General Phillips, and the Joint Chiefs of Staff into the bargain." He reached into the humidor on his desk for a cigar. "Have you made arrangements for our guest from the Pentagon?"

"Yes, sir," Reintz answered. "There's a helicopter meeting his plane. He should be out at strip one by about 0815."

"Good. You'd better meet him there yourself. I'll have to stay here and make sure everyone's ready for the briefing."

Reintz grimaced and thought: Another dirty job for Jackie Boy. He said, "Yes, sir. Is there anything else?"

2

Dan Logan awoke more slowly than usual, feeling stiff and achy, with a dry taste in the back of his mouth. The dawn sunlight filtering through the green cloth of his small mountain tent made him blink and rub his eyes. Gradually, he became aware of what had awakened him: Emily was just outside the tent, whimpering and tugging at the tent's closed flaps.

Still groggy, Logan pulled back one of the flaps. Emily barked sharply and ran away from the tent a short distance, then came back and barked again, impatient. Logan sat up and quickly pulled on his boots, pushing the other flap out of the way so he could slide out of the tent and stand up.

As soon as Logan was standing, breathing deep lungsful of the cold morning air, Emily ran away from the tent again, to the edge of the campsite, where Chris had spread his sleeping bag the night before. Logan started after her, wondering what could have her so upset. When he was about halfway to the boy, he sensed that something was wrong with Chris and broke into a run.

The dog stood nearby, watching, as Logan crouched beside Chris's sleeping bag. The boy was flushed and sweating, his nose bleeding, the whole upper part of his body shaking with intermittent tremors. Logan felt the boy's feverish forehead, then shook him gently, saying his name, trying to wake him. Chris's head, hanging limp, rolled back and forth, and his eyes began to open slowly. He seemed to be trying to look at Logan, but his eyes were blank, glazed, unfocused. His mouth worked feebly, as if in an attempt to speak, and then he lapsed back into unconsciousness.

Logan, more worried now, reached down for the zipper of Chris's sleeping bag, fumbling with it, his fingers made clumsy by his concern. Finally, he got the zipper started and opened the bag in one hurried motion. He saw at once that the boy's clothes and the bag were soaked with sweat and urine. He scooped his son up in his arms and ran the few yards to where he had left his pickup truck. He put Chris in the passenger's seat and closed the door. Then, as an afterthought, he ran to his tent, snatched out his sleeping bag and threw it over the sick boy.

Logan, his mind fixed only on the need to get help for his son, got into the truck and started the motor. As he was about to drive away from the campsite, he reached out and banged the side of the truck.

"Emily," he snapped, "get in back."

The dog jumped into the bed of the pickup truck, and Logan let out the clutch pedal. The truck lurched into motion, spraying dirt and stones behind it, weaving unsteadily over the rough ground as it accelerated down the hill and away from the campsite. Logan fought the wheel to keep the truck angling down the hillside toward a small dirt causeway he had built across Medicine Creek.

He looked over at the boy, slumped on the seat next to him. Chris's nose was still bleeding, and the shaking had gotten worse. Logan slowed the truck a little so he could get Chris into a better position, then speeded up again, heedless of the rocks and potholes over which the truck was bouncing, building up momentum for the run across the causeway.

The truck plowed across the loose dirt of the causeway, wheels spinning and digging in, barely carried across by the speed Logan had built up.

Once he was across the creek, Logan turned up the narrow sheep path toward the old corral, and something caught his eye. He slowed down, staring out the window at two sheep lying by the side of the path, looking at them long and carefully before he speeded up again, wondering about them lying there: their legs twitching, stuck straight out from their heaving bodies, fresh blood trickling from their nostrils across older, dried blood that matted the wool around their muzzles. He had never seen anything like it in all his years of ranching, any more than he had ever seen, or heard of, anything like the thing that had hold of Chris.

He shut the worry and questions out of his mind and concentrated on driving, on getting across the ranch to a decent road as quickly as he could. When he came to the turn onto the gravel-covered county road that ran along one edge of his ranch, he felt a touch of relief. The route to the hospital from here was a familiar one, and a lot less chancy than the sheep paths and dirt roads he had just traveled over.

As Logan came into sight of the gate to the neighboring ranch, he slowed down and turned in at the gate. Driving up the dirt lane toward Bill Parker's house, Logan leaned on the truck's horn, hoping that it would get Parker, normally a slow mover, into high gear.

The strategy worked. When Logan pulled into the Parker yard, Bill was coming down the porch steps. He recognized Logan's truck immediately, and his expression changed from belligerent curiosity to concern.

"Morning, Dan," Parker said as he hurried over to the truck, "Something wrong?"

"My boy is sick," Logan was keeping his voice steady, but there was an unmistakable edge of anxiety in his tone. "I have to get him to the hospital right away."

"Sorry to hear it," Parker began, but Logan cut him off.

"Can you call Doc Cardwell? Tell him to get right

over to the hospital. The boy's got some kind of convulsions, and he feels like he's burning up."

Parker, shaking his head, peered into the truck to see the boy as Logan continued, his agitation becoming more evident.

"He was all right yesterday. I don't know what it is. We camped over by the creek last night, and this morning he was sick. You better call Spike Boynton, too. There's a couple of sheep he ought to look at over by where we were camped. They were lying there twitching, with a lot of blood around the muzzle. Tell him halfway between the old line shack and the creek."

Parker nodded. "I'll tell him, don't worry." He paused to look over toward the house, where his wife was coming down the porch steps. "You want Sarah to come with you?"

"We'll be all right, thanks," Logan said, anxious to be back on the road. "Can you look after Emily?"

Almost without waiting to hear Parker's reply, Logan thumped the side of the truck and called to Emily. When the dog jumped from the truck, he told her "Stay here," put the truck in gear, and sped up the Parkers' drive toward the road, glancing quickly at Chris to see that he was still propped up on the seat. As he made the turn back onto the road, Logan reached out to keep the boy from falling over, then turned all his attention to the task of reaching the hospital as quickly as he could.

3

TO: ALL PERSONNEL, FORT HOWARD
FROM: COMMANDING OFFICER
Pursuant to Regulation 2304.07 *all* activities at this post have been placed under SECRET classification. Anyone discussing his assignment or duties without the express order of the commanding officer will be liable to severe penalties. This regulation is in effect until further notice.

4

Bill Franklin would have thanked whoever was responsible to have sent a car for him instead of a helicopter. He had never particularly liked or trusted helicopters, and his last assignment hadn't made him any happier about flying in them. He had spent three weeks on a helicopter training post in Texas trying to find out why rotors kept falling off the training helicopters in mid-flight. In the process, he had learned a lot about the untrustworthiness of helicopters and helicopter ground crews, and he had seen a lot of badly mangled and burned trainees and pilots. But he was a fatalist, so he climbed into the second row of seats in the chopper Fort Howard had sent for him and strapped himself in. Major Russel Kagle climbed in next to him, and Franklin indicated to the pilot that he could take off.

Franklin hadn't been sure whether he'd need either an aide or a medical officer on this one, so he had decided at the last minute on Russ Kagle, because in one previous job they had been on together, Kagle had proved himself to be bright, alert, and generally useful. Franklin had figured that with Kagle along he had both an aide and a medical officer, or if he wanted neither, someone smart enough to stay out of the way. One thing Franklin was sure of: Kagle knew how important it could be to have Colonel William Franklin think he was a good man in a pinch.

After ten noisy, unpleasant minutes, the helicopter came down at the edge of a medium-length runway, near a cluster of olive-drab, prefabricated buildings. Franklin and Kagle climbed out of the helicopter and started across the concrete toward the buildings. They were met about halfway by a jeep. As it pulled to a stop in front of them, a tall, blond major jumped from the front passenger's seat and saluted smartly.

Franklin groaned inwardly. He had just arrived, and he could already see that he was in for trouble. As a result of previous sad experience, he could tell from his first impression that this young major was cocky, self-interested, and career-oriented, just the kind to be so involved in looking for angles and advantages that he would have neither the time nor the energy to do his job properly. The major's attitude was an indication that his CO wasn't all he should be either, which in turn boded ill for the whole operation. As he returned the major's salute, he thought, I suppose it was too much to expect this to be easy.

"Colonel Franklin, I'm Major Reintz," the major said.

"Major," Franklin said dryly, and then inclined his head and, by way of introduction, said, "Reintz, Kagle." The two men nodded at each other, and then Reintz stepped aside so that Franklin and Kagle could get into the jeep.

Reintz said, "I'll show you to your quarters, sir. Colonel Nickerson has a briefing planned for you as soon as you're ready."

Sitting in the back of the jeep as it crossed the Fort, Franklin thought: I wonder if I was like that when I was his age. The idea bothered him for a moment, then he dismissed it as ridiculous.

5

Pressing the gas pedal to the floorboards, Logan managed to keep the pickup truck at seventy-five, except on long upgrades, where it fell off gradually to about seventy. It wasn't as fast as he wanted to be going, but it was faster than the truck was meant for, and he could feel it protesting, shuddering and shaking even on the smooth surface of the Interstate. He could hear, too, the motorcycle banging in the back, trying to break free of its support. He ignored all this, except to register it in the back of his mind along with the flow of traffic and the other things that affected his speed on the way to the hospital. From time to time, he reached across the seat to steady Chris, or to wipe the sweat from his forehead. The boy was even more feverish than he had been when Logan found him in the morning, and the shaking was worse.

Then, finally, he saw the sign that marked the Rawlins city limits, and the truck was speeding past the first signs of the town: a feed lot, a small railroad freight yard, some gas stations. A limited-speed-zone sign warned Logan to cut his speed to fifty, and then another said thirty-five, but he kept his foot on the floor, pushing the truck along at seventy-five, paying no attention to speed limits or to the fact that the traffic was getting heavier, and slower.

Just into town, and only a few blocks from the hospital, he ran a red light. A car was entering the intersection, across the path of the pickup truck. It skidded to a stop barely in time, so that Logan, who saw it only at the last minute, could swerve just enough to miss a bad collision. Even so, he nearly turned the pickup over fighting to stay on the road. He ran up on the curb and then, overcompensating, swung back across the road to the other side, narrowly missing a head-on collision before he swerved back into his own lane and got the truck back under control.

At the big white sign that said "CARBON COUNTY HOSPITAL," Logan made a left turn and then, not bothering to go around to the hospital's driveway, bounced over the curb and across the hospital lawn to the emergency entrance. He jumped out of the truck and ran around to the passenger's door, pulled Chris gently but quickly from the seat, and with the boy in his arms ran to the pair of heavy doors marked "Emergency." Barely slowing down, he hit one of the doors with his back and pushed through into the hospital.

The only person in the Emergency Room was a nurse, who looked up from the admitting desk to see a tall, burly rancher standing near the doors, panting, with an obviously sick child in his arms. She called for an attendant and got up from the desk as the rancher took a few uncertain steps in her direction.

"Yes, sir?" she asked, keeping her voice soft and soothing.

"It's my boy," Logan said.

An attendant came into the room, wheeling a stretcher.

"Why don't you lay him down here," the nurse suggested to Logan, "and I'll get a doctor. Bill will help you."

The nurse hurried from the room, and Logan and the attendant laid Chris on his back on the rolling stretcher.

The nurse returned with a doctor, a bulky, florid man in hospital whites. He went immediately to the stretcher, ignoring Logan, and began to examine the boy, who was still unconscious, although his convulsions had subsided somewhat. The nurse put a reassuring hand on Logan's arm.

"That's Doctor Thompson," she said. "He'll take real good care of the boy. Don't you worry a bit."

Logan nodded absently and watched as Thompson

felt Chris's head and then squeezed his upper arm and his thigh. Logan noticed, for the first time, that Chris's arms were bent sharply at the elbows, with his clenched fists almost touching his still shaking shoulders. Gently, Dr. Thompson took hold of one of Chris's wrists and tried to straighten the arm. Finding that he couldn't, Thompson let go, and the arm was seized by a sudden series of sharp convulsions that shook the boy violently. When the convulsions subsided, Thompson felt the glands under Chris's chin and then pulled one of his eyelids back, exposing the red, unseeing eye. Abruptly, he looked up and spoke to the attendant, still standing nearby.

"Get Dr. Holliford. Tell him there's a boy here he should look at." And then, to the nurse, "All right, Joyce, get him ready. I'll be right there."

The nurse wheeled the stretcher to the rear of the Emergency Room, where she pulled a curtain around herself and the boy. Dr. Thompson turned to speak to Logan, whose increased worry was evident in the way his eyes followed Chris until the curtain was closed.

"How long has he been like this?" Thompson asked, his voice and manner professionally reassuring.

Logan pulled his attention away from Chris to answer the question. "I don't know for sure. I found him that way this morning."

Thompson nodded. "Did he seem all right yesterday?"

"As far as I could tell, he did."

"Did he complain of anything before he went to bed last night?"

"Nosir."

Thompson thought for a moment. "Well, there's a

chance it might be food poisoning. What did he eat last night?"

Logan didn't answer at once. "I can't think of anything," he said tentatively. "We both ate the same things. Just a can of hash and some beans. And some coffee . . ." His voice trailed off as Thompson turned from him to greet Bert Holliford. Holliford's uniform was securely locked in a closet in the hospital basement, so Logan saw only a brisk, efficient-looking man of about thirty-five, dressed like Thompson in hospital whites.

"Dr. Holliford, this is the boy's father." Thompson said.

Holliford took charge immediately, putting Thompson virtually in the position of an assistant. He nodded briefly to Logan, and then asked Thompson, "What are the symptoms?"

Thompson listed them quickly: "Fever. Nasal hemorrhage. Hypertonus of the biceps and the upper leg. Convulsions."

Holliford turned to Logan.

"Has he been vomiting?" he asked in a crisp, clinical tone.

Logan, anxious to be as helpful as possible, considered this carefully. "Nosir. I don't think so."

"Was there any involuntary urination?"

"Uh, yes . . ." Logan began, starting to answer.

Holliford, impatient, cut him off. "Did he wet himself?"

"Yes, I think so."

"I see. Was he outside any time last night?"

"He was out the whole night. We camped out."

Before Logan had finished his sentence, Holliford

turned to Thompson and pointed to the closed curtain at the back of the room. "Is that him?"

Thompson nodded, and Holliford started toward it. "I'm going to need a glucose I.V.," he said over his shoulder.

Thompson left to arrange for the required intravenous feeding equipment. Logan stood there alone for a moment, then walked slowly to a wooden bench at the side of the room and sat down. The tension and worry of the morning were beginning to weigh heavily on him. He sat motionless, his shoulders slumped, his forearms on his thighs, his work-worn hands clasped, staring at the closed curtain, beneath which he could see Holliford's feet as he moved around the stretcher examining Chris. Logan's hands began to work at each other: rubbing his knuckles, then twisting on his finger the wedding ring he still wore, as if by touching the ring he somehow could summon some of JoAnn's warmth and calm reassurance.

6

Spike Boynton had been a veterinarian for twenty-two years, and he thought he knew what there was to know about sheep. Looking at the sheep on Dan Logan's ranch, though, he had some second thoughts. He ran over in his mind the whole catalog of ailments that sheep were subject to, and then what he knew about diseases of cattle and horses. Nothing he came up with made any sense when he looked at Logan's sheep.

When Bill Parker had called and described his strange visit from Dan Logan, Boynton had decided he'd better get over to the Logan place and take a look right away. Dan Logan wasn't the kind of man who called on Boynton very much, so he figured that if Dan was as upset as Bill seemed to think, there might be something up. Just on the off chance that the something was virulent enough to cause an epidemic, Boynton wanted to see it as soon as possible.

Now that he was looking at it, though, he had no idea what to do. It was pretty clearly not bluetongue or anything like that. That much was obvious right away. And it wasn't anthrax, either. Whatever had killed Dan Logan's sheep had done it quickly and thoroughly and, Boynton felt, unpleasantly. It didn't look like any kind of ordinary poisoning, and it didn't look like the diseases Boynton knew about. He was puzzled by it, and worried.

As he stood near the creek, looking at a sheep in the last throes of death—twitching and shivering and foaming at the mouth, blood streaming from its nostrils—a vague thought began to form in the back of Boynton's mind. He was beginning to remember something he had read about, he didn't know exactly where, that was vaguely similar to what he was looking at. He tried to dislodge the thought, to bring it up where he could work with it, but it stayed just out of reach. Nothing to do, he decided, but go back home and search among his piles of journals and magazines and books and pamphlets. And, he thought, I'd better stop off and see Bill

Parker on my way out.

Boynton sighed and shook his head. The rest of his patients would just have to wait.

7

Notes and Impressions/Fort Howard
Day One—arrival
This is the kind of post we don't like. Signs of isolation all over, no contact with army mainstream, emphasis only on regular schedule of duties and lousy leave in the sticks. Badly habit-ridden, some even bored. This only on first glance, but heavily probable that experience will confirm. 2nd in command (Reintz, John R., Maj., USA) a climber, probably incompetent. Briefing scheduled 0830, likely to be a whitewash for our benefit.
Prognosis: inferior.
First guess strategy: smokescreen.

8

When Bert Holliford finished examining the boy, he knew things had worked out badly. Everyone was in for one hell of a time about this, because there was no doubt in his mind that the child had been exposed to MX3. Holliford thought there might be one chance in a thousand that the boy would survive: He was already well into the advanced stages of deterioration, at least by comparison to the animals Holliford had been able to study.

Holliford took a deep breath. The next part was what he didn't want to have to face. The boy's father was out there, waiting, and Holliford knew that he had to go out and talk to him, ask him questions about the boy and himself, without revealing anything. He'd never liked talking to people about their ailments, and now, when it was so important, it made him particularly uncomfortable. He thought about how to go about it for a moment, then decided that it couldn't be very different from getting a history from an experimental subject and pushed aside the curtain that separated him from the rest of the Emergency Room.

Logan saw Holliford coming toward him and started to stand, but the doctor waved him down.

"You can just sit there, if you want," he said. Then, "Your son will have to be admitted to the hospital." He spoke quietly, and Logan took the tone to be one of reassurance.

"What is it?" Logan asked. "Is he all right?"

"It's nothing to worry about," Holliford said in the same even voice. To forestall further questions on the subject, he took a pad from his pocket and made a few notes about the symptoms he had observed in the boy.

As Holliford wrote, he said, "I'll have to ask you a few questions." It came out a little more brusquely than he would have liked, so he looked up from the pad.

"Does your son have a history of asthma?"

"Nosir." Logan was pretty sure he knew what asthma was.

"Has he ever had rheumatic fever?"

"No."

"Any blood disorder?"

"No." Logan didn't see any sense in all these questions. Chris had always been the healthiest boy around. "He's never been sick at all," Logan said. "Except for when he had his tonsils out."

Holliford nodded absently at this. It seemed to Logan that the doctor might have expected him to say it.

"When did you first notice the symptoms?"

"He was sick when I got up this morning. Just like he is now."

"What time was that?"

"A little after six."

"When you found him, did he speak to you at all?" Holliford was sure the answer would be no. If the boy had been this sick for the last couple of hours, he had been past any possibility of control over the speech centers for at least twice that long.

The rancher thought for a moment, then said. "No, he didn't."

"Did he retain visual motor control?" The answer to this question, Holliford assumed, would be the same as the answer to the last one. All the conscious brain functions went at once.

"I'm not sure what you mean." Logan said.

"Did his eyes wander? Did they look glazed, far away?"

Logan thought about this, trying to remember if Chris

had opened his eyes, and what they had looked like. Finally, he said, "Yes, I think so."

Holliford made another note in his notebook. He was about to continue with the questioning when Dr. Thompson came back into the room, carrying a bottle of glucose solution and a catheter.

"Do you want this I.V. right away?" he asked Holliford.

"Yes," Holliford answered. "Good. And then put him in isolation." The sooner he's out of sight, the better, he added to himself. He turned back to the boy's father.

"You said he was camped out last night. Were you with him?"

"Well, I was in the tent. The boy was sleeping right outside."

Ah, Holliford thought, that's why he can still stand up. I wonder if he was exposed at all. We should have thought to do some tests on the permeability of tent cloth to MX3.

"Where were you camping?" Holliford asked.

"On my ranch. About twenty miles north, up by the basin."

"I see. That's near Medicine Creek, isn't it?"

"That's right. We were maybe a half a mile away."

Right in the middle of the drift pattern, Holliford thought. He turned away and walked over to the admitting desk, motioning for the man to follow him.

"Would you come over here and sit down," he said. He watched carefully as the rancher approached and sat down, then noted in his pad that there was a slight hesitation in Logan's gait and an almost imperceptible sign of imbalance when he sat down. Imperceptible unless you knew what to look for, or, like Holliford, could guess. He'd never seen it in a human being, but he expected there would be a strong similarity in the symptoms shown by animals and humans.

Holliford finished his notes and said, "I'm going to take your blood pressure. Would you take off your jacket and roll up your sleeve, please."

Logan didn't understand this. He had brought Chris in to be taken care of; it was the boy who was sick, not him.

"I feel all right," he said.

"It's just a precaution," Holliford said. "There's nothing to worry about." The soothing falsehoods came out easily. In a sense, Holliford found he could almost believe them himself.

Logan shrugged. He thought that, after all, the man probably knew what he was doing. There was no reason not to cooperate. He took off his jacket and rolled up his sleeve, the one Holliford had indicated. By the time Logan had finished, Holliford had gotten a blood pressure cuff from a cabinet against the wall and returned with it.

Logan held out his arm for the cuff, but he was watching the back of the room, where Chris was being wheeled out from behind the curtain. The boy's face was chalky white and covered with sweat, and a thin line of blood ran from his nose down across his chin. He had been covered with a sheet and strapped to the stretcher with a wide gray belt, like an automobile seat belt, that ran across his chest. Another belt held his right arm fixed in place on the stretcher's frame; from the inside of his elbow a tube ran up to a big, mouth-down bottle of clear fluid that hung above the bed on a silvery, tubular stand. Logan found it hard to watch as Chris was wheeled by, willing himself not to turn away from his son's distorted face as the stretcher passed close to him.

9

The briefing that Colonel Nickerson had arranged for Colonel Franklin still hadn't gotten under way at nine o'clock, a half hour after the time Nickerson had scheduled it. While they were waiting for the commanding officer and his unknown visitor to arrive, there was nothing for the others to do but stay in the spartan conference room and drink the weak coffee that was being dispensed by an enlisted man from a large metal urn at the back of the room.

Walter Steenrod and Tom Janeway stood together at one side of the broad oak conference table that dominated the center of the room. Steenrod, tall, spare, with steel-gray hair, looked slowly around the room, noting with some surprise the evidence that someone had taken great care preparing this briefing. There was a pad and several pencils and a small map of the Fort at each place around the table, and a large Coast-and-Geodetic-Survey map of the area taped to the middle of the table. On a raised platform at the front of the room there was another map, this one done on a large sheet of plexiglass, and next to it a wooden easel held a stack of large presentation cards. Steenrod had only a general idea of why the meeting had been called, but he guessed from the elaborate staging that there was more involved than finding ways to cope with an accidental overspray.

Tom Janeway, standing next to Steenrod, could see from the expression on his boss's face that the two of them were having the same reaction to the preparations for the morning's briefing. Janeway, a head shorter and twenty years younger than Steenrod, nonetheless thought a lot like the older man. They had discovered this early in their association, and it had immeasurably enhanced their working relationship. In addition, it had paved the way for fast advancement for Janeway, who, now, only five years after getting his doctorate in biochemistry, was chief of Advanced Projects at the research facility of which Steenrod was director.

Janeway took a sip of coffee and wondered who would be at the briefing. There were seven places set around the table. He counted them off: one for him, one for Steenrod, one for Nickerson, and one for Jack Reintz, who was at the moment threading film into the sixteen-millimeter projector that had been set up at the back end of the conference table. That left three unaccounted for.

In the midst of Janeway's calculations, the door to the conference room opened and a civilian—a man of about sixty, balding and sporting a slight paunch, but carefully dressed and groomed—came in and looked around. Janeway was a bit startled. He had expected that he and Steenrod would be the only civilians at the briefing. He looked questioningly at Steenrod, who shook his head, indicating that he, too, was mystified.

The newcomer smiled vaguely in their direction and then went over to get himself a cup of coffee.

10

The briefing in Conference Room A was late in starting because Bill Franklin made it a habit to get right to the center of a problem before he became involved with the peripheral aspects. He had found that otherwise it was nearly impossible to get the important sorted out from the trivial. Everyone always had his own point of view, his own interests to protect, and his own approach to any problem. It was necessary to have some sense of the structure of the situation, or valuable time and energy would be lost in trying to get everyone working toward the same goals. Franklin didn't kid himself that he could avoid this problem entirely, but at least, if he had a good sense of what was at the root of the situation, he could let the others waste their time and energy without being distracted or fooled by extraneous matters.

As a first step in getting to know the problem, he had done several hours of research in Washington. Then, when he arrived at Fort Howard, he had declined Major Reintz's offer of a tour of the VIP suite at the Bachelor Officers' Quarters and insisted instead on seeing Colonel Nickerson immediately. Since Franklin made the demand while they were all in the jeep, there was no way

Reintz could notify Nickerson of the change of plans. This had the effect of allowing Franklin to catch Nickerson off guard and unprepared, which was the way Franklin wanted him to be in their first meeting.

Nickerson turned out to be more or less what Franklin had expected. An adequate officer, perhaps once even a good officer, with a few more years in uniform than he was really up to—a man beyond any but the most habit-conditioned responses, which would carry him very well through the routine administrative chores of running Fort Howard. But he would be lax as a commanding officer, content as long as everything was going smoothly and by the book and whatever schedules he set up himself. He would tolerate Reintz as second-in-command because Reintz probably saved him a lot of trouble. It would be in Reintz's self-interest to keep things running the way Nickerson liked them.

After Nickerson adjusted to the fact that Franklin had walked unannounced and unexpected into his office, he suggested that they go right over to the conference room.

"No, I'd rather stay here," Franklin said. "I'd like to get a few things straightened out with you before I hear a formal presentation."

"Of course. Whatever you want." Nickerson managed a nervous chuckle. "Is there anything special you want to know?"

Franklin nodded. "First of all, you'd better tell me if there is anything new since last night."

"No, nothing concrete. Just the normal decay in the contamination readings, more or less what we expected. We'll be covering all that at the briefing."

"Yes, I'm sure you will, Colonel, but I don't want to be sitting in a long formal briefing while the situation is getting worse around us."

Nickerson recognized the rebuke and stiffened, trying to think of a suitable reply. Before he could get one out, Franklin was going on.

"The Joint Chiefs view this situation with the utmost concern. I'm sure I don't have to explain to you how delicate a matter this could be. The chairman, in particular, wanted me to convey the extent of his unhappiness. Everyone hopes that we can resolve this here, among ourselves. This is an army matter, and it would be extremely unfortunate if we were forced to air this particular load of dirty laundry in public. Do I make myself clear?"

Oh yes, thought Nickerson. Perfectly, absolutely clear.

"Under the circumstances, the chairman thinks that it would be best if I supervised the handling of the matter from here on," Franklin continued. "I want you to understand that our only concern in this is to see it to a satisfactory conclusion. No one is worried about your next promotion, or your pension. All we're concerned with is the protection of the CBW program."

There was a silence, and Nickerson said, softly, "Yes, sir, I understand."

11

Holliford had about finished with Logan's blood pressure when he was interrupted by the arrival of Roy Cardwell, a man of about seventy, in a rumpled suit, carrying an ancient medical bag.

The arrival of Cardwell, who had been Logan's family doctor since he was born, took some of the pressure from the rancher. Cardwell was a man he could trust, who was at home with all the medical talk and the forbidding hospital atmosphere. Logan's relief was evident in his voice as he greeted Cardwell.

"Hello, Roy," Logan said. "How are you?"

"I'm fine, Dan." Cardwell smiled at Logan with a confidence he didn't quite feel. He had been passed on his way in by the attendant wheeling Chris down the hall, and he had gotten a brief glimpse of the boy. What he had seen had disquieted him, but he knew the importance of keeping his prognosis out of his tone of voice, especially when it was based on only a quick glance in passing. He turned to the doctor who was taking Logan's blood pressure.

"I don't believe I've met you," he said good-naturedly. "I'm Roy Cardwell, Mr. Logan's physician." He offered his hand.

"I'm Doctor Holliford," the younger man said, shaking hands.

Cardwell had never seen Holliford before, or heard his name, but he wasn't in the hospital that often, so it didn't trouble him that Holliford was a stranger to him.

"Have you looked at Chris Logan?" Cardwell asked.

At first, Holliford didn't know what Cardwell was talking about. Guessing, he asked, "Is that Mr. Logan's son?"

"That's right," Cardwell said.

Got by that one, Holliford thought. It wouldn't do to admit to the old man that I didn't have any idea who it was that I was treating. "Yes, I saw him," he said. "We're putting him in isolation. Dr. Thompson is with him now."

Cardwell nodded at this information, but he was obviously waiting to hear more. Holliford decided that he'd better assert himself in a hurry, before Cardwell decided to involve himself further.

"Nurse," Holliford called. When she came over, he said, "Would you check Mr. Logan's pulse and temperature? And take two blood samples. Send one over to pathology and hold the other one for me."

When the nurse took over for him, Holliford turned and said, "Dr. Cardwell, would you come with me for a second?" He applied a little pressure to Cardwell's arm, hoping to indicate that he had something urgent to say. Cardwell grasped his intended meaning at once and followed him from the room and into the corridor.

12

TO: MAJOR J. A. WHEELER
FROM: MAJGEN RONALD PHILLIPS
RE: FORT HOWARD

Joe—

Please inform your people that we may need a team to go out to Fort Howard and deal with press interest in a developing situation. Standard cover and high-level pressure, and figure we'll need at least three reporters we can trust to do it our way. For now, think in terms of Dugway; I'll fill you in later. Also, I think we may want to involve the Chief of Information, so you had better warn them to be expecting us.

13

Exactly forty minutes after the briefing had been scheduled to begin, Colonel Nickerson entered the conference room, accompanied by Colonel Franklin and Major Kagle.

Nickerson dismissed the sergeant still on duty at the coffee machine and walked to the head of the conference table while the others began to take seats around the table. Nickerson felt a little shaky after what had proved to be a difficult hour with Colonel Franklin. He wanted what was left to go quickly and smoothly so he could have time to assess the damage that had been done in that meeting. All he was sure of was that, for the moment, in any case, the situation was solidly in Franklin's hands.

Janeway and Steenrod sat together at one side of the table, and the other civilian sat opposite them, next to Jack Reintz. Franklin took the chair at the very end of the table where he could see everyone else without turning his head. Major Kagle put his hat on the note pad at Franklin's right and went to get some coffee.

At the head of the table, Nickerson cleared his throat to get everyone's attention, then began his introductions.

"Gentlemen, this is Colonel Franklin, from Washington. He's here as a representative of the Joint Chiefs of Staff."

Franklin nodded slightly. Now Janeway understood why the preparations for the briefing had been so elaborate. He looked significantly at Steenrod, who responded with a raised eyebrow.

Nickerson continued, "Major Kagle, his medical officer." Kagle looked up from the coffee urn and nodded to the others in the room.

"And this is Dr. Walter Steenrod, from Chivington Laboratories, and Dr. Tom Janeway, also from Chivington." He turned to the other side of the table. "Major Reintz, my executive officer."

Reintz shifted in his chair under the hard gaze of Franklin, and, to avoid it, smiled thinly at Janeway and

Steenrod, across the table from him.

"And this is Dr. Spencer, from the Public Health Service."

The mystery civilian, Janeway thought. He looked at Spencer again and noticed how relaxed the man seemed. As if he was interested, but as if what was about to happen didn't really matter to him. It took Janeway a few seconds to realize that in fact it probably didn't matter to Spencer, as a PHS official, at least not nearly as much as it mattered to all the rest of them. Janeway's thoughts were interrupted by Nickerson, who had finished the introductions and was going on into the substance of the meeting.

"Dr. Spencer has worked with us before," he was saying, "and he has all the necessary clearance. I've asked him to join us because we'll be working very closely with the Public Health Service from now on."

Nickerson looked around the table and said, "I'd like to remind all of you at the outset that this meeting is subject to strict security and should not be discussed with anyone who is not in this room."

He leaned forward, putting his hands on the edge of the table. "As you all know," he said gravely, "there has been an accident on the post which may well have serious consequences. Major Reintz has been monitoring the situation, so I'll let him give you the details." He looked at Reintz, who was taking a small stack of index cards from the pocket of his uniform blouse, and said, "Jack."

Reintz got up slowly from his chair and walked to the front of the room, smoothing the front of his uniform as he went. At the head of the conference table, he turned to face the others, nervously squaring his file cards into a neat pile. He glanced down at the top card, moistened his lips, and took a deep breath.

"Gentlemen," he began, speaking briskly. "At 1530 hours yesterday, our Chemical Evaluation Unit was conducting a test of MX3, a new agent which we received from Chivington for preliminary testing. The test involved aerosol distribution from an airborne sprayer. For this test, we used a 318 sprayer mounted on an F-100 spray plane. The plane was flying over the northwest quadrant of the test zone."

At the other end of the conference table, Colonel Franklin began to make a few sparse notes on the pad in front of him.

"At twenty-four minutes into the test, at 1554 hours, the valve on the three-eighteen failed to close, causing an undetermined amount of the agent to be released outside the perimeter of the Fort. Now, this was the third test in our initial drift evaluation series for this agent. I have a film here of the first test on 23 August."

Reintz pulled a projection screen down in front of the plexiglass map and walked to the other end of the table. The darkness that enveloped the heavily curtained room when Reintz flipped the room-light switch gave him a small amount of relief from his feeling that he was being continually and minutely scrutinized.

He turned on the projector, and the screen was filled with the usual series of reverse-order numbers, interspersed with focusing patterns. It was obvious when the film began that it had been taken by a camera mounted under the fuselage or wing of a jet fighter. A big silver tank dominated one side of the frame in the foreground and beyond it stretched the plane's far wing. The rest of the picture showed the Fort Howard runway streaming by at high speed. Then the plane took off and the images of the runway gave way to a panoramic view of the Fort as the plane flew toward the test area.

The film was silent; the only sounds in the room were the whir of the projector and the occasional scraping of chairs as everyone settled into a comfortable viewing position. When the others had gotten themselves adjusted, Reintz began to narrate.

"You can see the three-eighteen sprayer there very clearly. This test, the one you are looking at, is similar to the one that was conducted yesterday, except that the size of the particles released in yesterday's test was greater and each spraying pass was shorter. As you can see, the spraying begins as soon as the plane has achieved a level course."

On the screen, the spray valve on the silver tank opened and a mist of reddish droplets streamed from the tank. Reintz continued his explanation.

"The spray cuts off at a predetermined point. In the test we are watching it was forty-five seconds on each pass. Yesterday, the cutoff time was thirty seconds. We've got more footage of this same pass, this time on the high-speed camera."

The screen turned dull yellow for a few seconds as the leader connecting the two sections of film passed through the film gate, and then the film from the high-speed camera began to run. At first, it looked the same as the earlier footage, although the placement of the silver tank in the frame showed that it had been taken from a slightly different angle. Then it became apparent that the cloud of red droplets was swirling with voluptuous slowness from the spray valve, rather than streaming out at high speed as it had been. In the background, too, the ground was passing by much more slowly.

"As you can see," Reintz said, "this is in extreme slow motion. We don't have the whole pass here, but we thought it would be instructive to watch the valve close."

On screen, the swirling red cloud was abruptly cut off and the last wisps of the nerve agent drifted out of the picture. Then the screen went yellow again. The picture that came on next was in regular speed. "We'll finish up with the end of that pass," Reintz said. "As you can see, at the end of the spraying pass, the plane climbs sharply and makes a wide turn. That brings it over the test area for another pass." Reintz watched with the others as the film showed the plane sweeping through its turn and back into position. Then the screen went bright and empty, and Reintz turned the room lights on.

The men shifted in their seats and accustomed themselves to the renewed brightness of the room. Franklin almost at once began to make notes on his pad.

Reintz, trying to ignore this, raised the projection screen, revealing once more the plexiglass map. He picked up a blue grease-pencil from the tray at the bottom of the map stand and stepped behind the map, where he could look out at his audience through the map and draw on it without turning his back. Reminding himself to relax, he started to mark in blue an area on the map. Then, still using the blue grease-pencil, he said, "The test area covers the north end of the Fort. This is the flight path, through the northwest quadrant, and this is the cutoff point, where the valve should have closed. You'll find all this marked on your own maps as well." Nickerson held up one of the small maps of the Fort to show the others what Reintz meant.

"The pilot first realized something was wrong when he swung back for the next pass," Reintz continued, marking another place on the map. "When he got back to here, a warning light went on on the instrument panel, indicating that the tank was empty. At that point, as a matter of standard procedure, the plane was called in and inspected."

Franklin noted something on his pad and then tapped his pencil impatiently, scowling. Dr. Spencer, leaning back in his chair and still looking relaxed, took out his pipe and began to fill it.

Reintz said, "We calculate that at the point where the valve failed to close, the tank was about three-quarters full. With the spray setting we were using, the plane would have traveled about five miles before the tank emptied, bringing it about to here, just short of the northeast corner of the Fort."

From the rear of the room, Franklin's voice broke in sharply. "Major."

The heads of the other listeners turned immediately toward Franklin. Reintz came out from behind the map and said, apprehensively, "Yes, sir?"

Franklin, leaning forward in his seat and looking intently at Reintz, asked, "Isn't the plane equipped with an indicator that would tell the pilot whether the valve had closed? It seems like an elementary precaution."

Reintz squirmed visibly. Watching him, Nickerson thought, Oh, shit, here we go: merrily to hell.

Reintz said, "Well sir, actually most of our planes

have that feature, but we're still flying a few that don't."

"And this one didn't."

"Yes, sir. That's correct."

Franklin said, "I see," and made some notes on his pad.

14

When Roy Cardwell came back into the Emergency Room of Carbon County Hospital, he was very troubled. For all Holliford's assurances that it was too early to make a firm diagnosis, Cardwell had been shaken by the younger doctor's description of Chris's symptoms.

Logan looked up at Cardwell as he approached, obviously anxious for some information about his son. Cardwell took a deep breath.

"Dan," he said, "Dr. Holliford has been telling me about what he found when he examined Chris. Now, we're not exactly sure what it is, but Doctor Holliford is a specialist, and I'm going to let him supervise Chris's care. He knows a lot more about this than I do." Cardwell smiled reassuringly. "You know, I always say a man isn't a good doctor unless he knows when to call in help."

"Will he be all right?"

Cardwell could see that Logan was confused and apprehensive. He put a hand on the rancher's shoulder. "He'll be fine. It's just a question of finding out what it is and taking the right steps."

Cardwell let that sink in for a few moments; then, when he thought Logan was beginning to adjust to the idea of Chris's needing further care, he went on. "We really ought to run a few tests on you, too. Doctor Holliford wants you to check into the hospital. It's just for a day or two, in case you've got some of the same thing."

"Do you really think I should?"

"Yes, I do, Dan. It'll give you a chance to be near Chris, and this way we can take a look at you."

Logan was still uncertain as to what to do, but he trusted Cardwell not to insist unless it was really necessary. He said, "Well, all right. If you think it's the best thing."

Cardwell smiled again and said, "Good. Let's go on down and get you checked in."

15

Reintz, having weathered his first confrontation with Colonel Franklin, was hoping to make back a few points in describing his efficient handling of the details that were his direct responsibility. His delivery became clipped and precise.

"The first thing we did," he said, "was to have the State Police close off a twenty-five-mile stretch of Route 287, from here to here." He made the appropriate marks on the map. "Then we sent out helicopters and ground observers to measure the spread of the gas. We found that the heaviest concentration outside the Fort was just across Route 287, near Medicine Creek. Fortunately, the winds were very light, and by 0600 hours this morning, all our readings were near zero. Of course, we ordered all personnel cleared from the Fort, so we had no immediate health hazard there. At this point, we're concerned mostly about this Medicine Creek area.

"Fortunately, the problem doesn't seem to be too critical. Our maximum reading over that area was only twenty micrograms per cubic meter, and this is only about half the lethal concentration."

Tom Janeway, who had been listening carefully to this part of Reintz's presentation, interrupted him. "Just a minute, Major," he said sharply. "If you're suggesting that any people who might have been down there are safe, you're being very misleading. Even a very small concentration of MX3 will kill you, if you breathe it long enough. There's just no such thing as a 'safe' concentration."

"I'm sorry if I was a little bit vague," Reintz said, defending himself. "What I meant was that we measured twenty micrograms per cubic meter, and we've established thirty-five as the effective military concentration."

Janeway broke in again, with growing impatience. "Yes, but that doesn't make any difference. We're not talking about a military situation here. We're concerned with possible civilian casualties. Just a couple of hours' exposure to the concentration you mentioned would kill over fifty per cent of the exposed population."

Reintz was out of his depth, and he knew it. He certainly was in no position to argue successfully with Janeway. The best he could do was make his mistake seem unimportant. He said, "Well, I suppose you're right. But I don't think there's any point arguing about it. After all, these measurements were taken from a helicopter at five hundred feet, so we don't really know what the conditions were at ground level."

Janeway exploded. "That's ridiculous, Major. Whatever the measurements were at five hundred feet, the conditions at ground level must have been worse." He turned away from Reintz and directed his explanation to the others.

"What matters here isn't the reading at any one moment, it's the total accumulation. You start out with a large cloud of the agent, but remember, it's all settling to the ground." His hands made settling gestures. "As time passes, the readings at ground level are just going to get higher and higher until the whole cloud has settled, even after the air is perfectly clean at five hundred feet."

He turned to Franklin and said very deliberately, "I think we have a very dangerous situation here, and I don't see any point in trying to paper over it."

A tense silence followed Janeway's remark. Looking around the table, Walter Steenrod realized that his bright young protégé had set up a situation that might easily become a bitter battle between the civilian scientists and the people from Fort Howard. Hoping to forestall further unpleasantness, the laboratory director broke into the conversation. "Now, Tom," he said, "Nobody's proposing that this isn't a dangerous situation. That's why we're all here."

Janeway nodded and sat back in his chair. Around the table the others looked grim and worried.

16

While Cardwell and Logan were in the administrative office going through the normal process of checking Logan and his son into the hospital, Bert Holliford went down the hall to the waiting room, where he called Fort Howard from the public phone booth. It was the only phone in the hospital that didn't go through the main switchboard, and he wasn't eager to have this particular call monitored.

The corporal on duty at the post PBX told him that Colonel Nickerson was in a meeting and couldn't be disturbed. It took some talking, but Holliford finally convinced the corporal that this call was important enough to be exempted from the order. A very worried private was dispatched to tell the CO that Major Holliford was on the phone.

Holliford's victory was only partial, however. Instead of Colonel Nickerson, it was Dr. Janeway who came on the line and asked what news he had. Holliford had worked with Janeway from time to time, and although he didn't like the cocky, supercilious civilian, he respected him. As quickly as he could Holliford told Janeway what he had observed at the hospital.

Janeway's reaction was more neutral than Holliford had expected it would be. He questioned Holliford about some of the details of Chris Logan's condition, and was especially curious to know exactly what Logan had said about his sheep, but he was completely cold and unemotional about it, a scientist gathering data. There was no hint in his tone that he was also a scientist whose whole research program was in danger of being destroyed.

17

Bill Parker was working in the open shed at the side of his house, loading a coil of fence wire into the back of his pickup, when Spike Boynton drove into the yard. Wiping his hands on his overalls, Parker walked over to the veterinarian's truck.

"Mornin' Spike," Parker said with his customary cheeriness.

The veterinarian was somewhat more subdued. He said, "Mornin'," in response, but he seemed to be distracted, thinking about something else.

"Come on in," Parker suggested. "Sarah's got some coffee."

"Can't do it. Thanks just the same. I just dropped by to tell you that I'd been to Dan Logan's place. Things look pretty bad over there. I'd say he's got more than two hundred sheep dead, and a lot more sick."

Parker shook his head. First Dan's boy got sick, and now his sheep. People's luck just seemed to run bad sometimes. Boynton said, "You'd better keep your stock as far away as you can."

"I sure will. Do you know what it is? You think it might be bluetongue or something like that?"

"I don't think so. It looks mighty peculiar. I'm going back later to take another look." Boynton paused. "You know, maybe I'll come in after all. I'd like to use your phone."

"Sure, Spike. Come on in."

Inside, Parker showed Boynton to the phone on the hall stand, then went into the kitchen to talk to Sarah, so as not to be eavesdropping on Boynton's conversation.

The veterinarian wouldn't have minded if Parker had stayed, but he appreciated Parker's gesture. He waited for a dial tone, then dialed the number of another veterinarian who worked in the same area he did. The two of them had a kind of casual partnership. When either of them got jammed up with work, he called the other to take over his routine calls. Luckily enough, the other vet was in and he agreed to cover for Boynton for the rest of the day.

"What's up?" he asked Boynton after they had made the basic arrangements.

"To tell you the truth," Boynton said, "I'm not sure what it is. I've got a couple hundred dead sheep, and I can't for the life of me figure out what they died from. I've got one blood sample and I'm going to go back and get a couple more. Maybe they'll tell me something. The symptoms sure are strange, though."

"Well, just you let me know what you find. I don't want to have to guess at it if it comes my way."

"You bet," Boynton said, and they hung up. Boynton

said good-bye to the Parkers and got into his truck.

In the dog run at the side of the house, Dan Logan's sheepdog, Emily, sat watching the veterinarian's truck drive away. She was panting heavily, and her eyes, behind half-closed lids, looked glazed. Pink flecks of foam dotted the edges of her mouth.

18

While Janeway was out of the room talking to Major Holliford at Carbon County Hospital, Colonel Nickerson sent for Stoney Cooper so the security chief could be in on any discussion they might have of security precautions. It was an afterthought, but Nickerson felt that security was going to become very important, if he had guessed correctly the reason for Holliford's call. In the meantime, while they waited for Janeway to come back, Nickerson discussed some basic questions of procedure and priorities.

"First of all, and Colonel Franklin and I are in agreement on this," Nickerson said, "we don't want to have a panic reaction in the community. For that reason, we feel that all public statements should be avoided. Of course, that doesn't affect Chivington, because there is no reason for anyone to connect you with this." He looked at Dr. Steenrod, then went on.

"We're concerned that if the public finds out the exact nature of the incident, there will be misunderstanding and panic. As you know, 'chemical warfare' has become something of a scare phrase these days.

"Of course, it goes without saying that we have to take the strongest possible safety precautions, but everything we do must be designed to avoid adverse publicity. We don't want to give some headline-hungry reporter the ammunition to shoot us down. I'm sure you all remember the trouble we went through after the Dugway incident. I can't stress strongly enough how important this is. There are elements in this country that would just be overjoyed at something like this."

Nickerson was interrupted by a knock at the door. He said, "Come in," and Janeway entered the room. "I see that Dr. Janeway has finished his conversation with Major Holliford," Nickerson said. "Before he tells us what he's learned, I should explain that we have sent our own personnel to monitor the only four hospitals within a hundred miles of the affected area, in the hope that we'd be able to intercept any cases of human exposure. Major Holliford has done some work at Carbon County Hospital in the past, so he's in an especially good position there." Nickerson paused, dreading what he knew would come next. "All right, Tom," he said. "You'd better tell us what he had to say."

Janeway, who hadn't sat down when he came into the room, began to pace around the table, talking as he went. "I don't see any point in trying to sugar-coat this," he said. "From what Major Holliford told me, we've definitely got two cases of exposure, a rancher named Daniel Logan and his twelve-year-old son. They were camped out all night on Logan's ranch near Medicine Creek, so we can be sure they were heavily exposed. The boy's symptoms are about the same as the one's we've observed in our laboratory animals: convulsions, bleeding, and so on. The father's symptoms are very mild so far, but since the action of the agent is progressive, we can expect that as time passes they will become more pronounced.

"In addition to the two humans, some of the animals on the Logan ranch seemed to have been affected, and the description we have from Logan corresponds exactly with our laboratory results." Janeway paced for a moment in silence, thinking, then went on with carefully bridled enthusiasm. "Of course, this agent is of a new type, and we've never had any human subjects. It's very important to study both these cases carefully so that we can understand exactly how the agent operates."

At the head of the table, Janeway stopped pacing. He put both hands on the table and leaned forward earnestly. "I realize that this is an unfortunate incident," he said, "but we would be foolish to overlook the opportunity it gives us to observe an agent of this type acting on human subjects."

For a short while, there was no comment. Then, from the other end of the table, Colonel Franklin said, "Dr. Janeway, from your conversation with Major Holliford, can you estimate the chances that either of these people will survive?"

Janeway was confused. "I'm sorry," he said. "I thought I made that clear. With the information we have, I see no reason to expect either of them to survive."

"I see," said Franklin.

19

The small private hospital room that they had given Dan Logan was virtually indistinguishable from any other such room. It had the same institutional-beige walls, mechanized hospital bed, bed tray, night table, and washstand that might have graced a hospital room in New York City or in Yakima, Washington. And it had the same smell of antiseptic and the same general atmosphere of isolation and despair as any other hospital room anywhere, as if the room were a repository of the sufferings of all its previous occupants.

Logan, dressed in hospital pajamas and a robe, was sitting on the edge of his bed when Roy Cardwell knocked on the half-opened door of the room and came in.

"Hello, Roy," Logan said eagerly. "Did you see Chris?"

"I just came from his room," Cardwell said. "He's resting now, pretty peacefully. I think the worst is probably over."

Logan smiled, pleased at the news. "Will they let me see him?" he asked.

"Well, there's not much you can see, really. He's still unconscious, and they've got the room closed off. All you'd be able to do is look through a small window. I think you ought to wait a while, and take it easy. We want to be sure there's nothing wrong with you."

"I'm all right. I don't know why the hell they want to keep me in here."

Cardwell smiled. This was something he could deal with. A good part of his practice consisted of dispensing reassurance, and it was something he had gotten to be very good at. "Well, now," he said, "take it easy. It's just for a day. They have to make some tests, and they can't very well do that if you're not here."

"I'd sooner go home. If they need any more tests, I can come back tomorrow."

Cardwell patted Logan on the shoulder in a fatherly way. "The tests aren't that simple, Dan. I really think you ought to stay here for a while."

Logan was unsatisfied. "I have to get back to the ranch and check my stock," he protested. "I told you about those sheep."

"Well, look, suppose I call Bill Parker. He can keep an eye on things for you. And if there's anything serious, I'm sure Spike Boynton will let you know."

"Well, I suppose you might as well. I'll just be glad when they're through and I can get out of here." Logan fell silent for a long moment, staring out the window. He began to twist the wedding ring on his finger.

"You know, Roy," he said, "this is the first time I've been inside a hospital since JoAnn died."

Logan's words brought back Cardwell's memory of how hard the rancher had found the final weeks of his wife's illness, how furious he had been at being unable to help her. Cardwell, too, had been helpless, as were even the specialists at the hospital in Salt Lake City. There was nothing Cardwell could do now to ease Logan's memories, so he sat down on the bed next to him and waited for him to say something. After a time, Logan looked around at Cardwell again.

"I was just thinking about Chris," he said. "I got pretty nervous this morning seeing him like that."

"Well, now, there's nothing to worry about. He'll be all right," Cardwell said. He wasn't sure about that, but he knew how rare it was that you could ever be sure, and he couldn't see any sense in worrying Logan any more than was necessary. Besides, he thought, Dr. Holliford seems to know what he's doing.

"You know," Cardwell said, "when a boy's that age, you can't keep him in bed very long."

"He's never been sick before. I'm worried about him. Do you know what's wrong with him?"

"It's hard to say exactly. Dr. Holliford thinks it might be a reaction to an insecticide. He'll run some allergy tests and he'll probably have the answer in the morning."

"I hope so," Logan said. "I hope so."

Cardwell patted him on the shoulder again. "Dan, don't worry about it," he said. "I'll tell you something. These young doctors today know more than I ever will. He'll be all right."

There was a light knock on the door and a nurse came into the room pushing a cart that held cups of fruit juice. "Good morning," she said. "My name is Doris. What kind of juice would you like this morning, Mr. Logan?"

Cardwell saw the interruption as an opportunity to break away from what was becoming an uncomfortable situation for him. There was nothing he could do for Logan at this point that he hadn't done already, and he had other patients to see.

"I've got to be going," he said. "You just quit worrying so much and relax for a while. It'll be good for you. I'll be back to see you soon. Tomorrow morning at the latest."

"All right, Roy. Thanks." Logan turned and looked at the tray of juice. He realized suddenly that he was thirsty and very tired.

20

Matthew Spencer took a long, slow pull at his pipe and said, "I don't really think there should be any trouble. We've had a contingency plan for something like this for years, ever since the Fort began this program. Of course, I never really knew what contingency we were planning for, just the broad outlines. But I think we're prepared to handle this, just by implementing the procedures we have already set up.

"According to your map here, it looks like there are only eight or ten ranches in the Medicine Creek area. It should be fairly simple to bring these people in and test them. There's no need to tell them exactly what we're looking for. I can have some people come down from Casper with extra equipment, and we should be able to get it all done this afternoon."

"That's excellent, Dr. Spencer," said Colonel Franklin. "We appreciate your cooperation."

"Well, we all work for the same government," Spencer

said casually. "And we all want to see this thing do as little harm as possible. There's no point in getting the whole countryside in an uproar if we can avoid it."

"And there's no point in endangering this program any further than it has been already," Franklin said, looking pointedly around the room.

21

From her chair next to the oxygen-tent-draped bed, the special-duty nurse watched Chris Logan carefully. He was unconscious, but his breathing was quite labored. Intermittently, he was shaken by tremors that the nurse attributed to the mild spasms she had observed earlier in the boy's extremities. Satisfied that his condition hadn't changed in the past half hour, the nurse returned her attention to the magazine in her lap.

22

Spike Boynton put down the magazine he was reading and got up slowly from his paper-strewn roll-top desk. Slowly, he walked around the back bedroom he had fixed up as an office and study, stretching his back and shoulders and trying to sift through the information he had gleaned from his two hours of reading, hunting for the elusive something that had passed through his mind while he was looking at the sheep at Dan Logan's ranch.

He crossed the room to the telephone and dialed Roy Cardwell. The phone was answered by Gloria Knowles, Cardwell's housekeeper.

"I'm sorry, Dr. Boynton," she said, "but Dr. Cardwell is out making calls. He said not to expect him until dinner. Is there anything you want me to tell him?"

"No, that's all right, Gloria. Just say I called and ask him to call me when he gets a chance."

Boynton hung up and walked back to his desk. He rummaged through the papers on the desk top and came up with a slightly dog-eared pad. He tore off the top sheet and started to make a list of what he knew and what he supposed.

The first thing he wrote down was a summary of the symptoms he had observed in the sheep: convulsions, stiffening of the muscles, hemmorrhage from the nose and mouth, involuntary voiding. In some of the sheep that were still standing he had noticed what seemed to be loss of motor control, a general lack of coordination, so he wrote that down as well.

Boynton figured that it didn't take a genius to know that those symptoms didn't add up to any livestock disease that was common in Wyoming. In fact, Boynton had ruled out infectious disease almost from the beginning. What troubled him was that there wasn't any kind of poisoning he could think of that would look like what he had seen. He hoped that when the lab got done with the blood samples he'd given them he might know some more. He wrote "blood" on his list, and followed it with a string of question marks.

Next, he put down the heading "quarantine." By the time he had gone back to Logan's ranch to get a second blood sample, the ranch had been placed under quarantine by the Public Health Service. There were several things about the quarantine that bothered Boynton and he added them to his list. First, there was the fact that the PHS had acted so quickly. Boynton supposed that they must have learned of the situation from someone at the hospital when Logan went there with his son, but still, they had acted very quickly, apparently without even investigating on their own before setting up the quarantine.

Boynton got up and went to the telephone again. The people to ask about that were the Public Health Service people responsible. He had a little trouble getting past the man who answered the phone. He was someone whom Boynton had never spoken to before, apparently from the Casper office, but Boynton finally convinced the stranger to put Fred Powell on the line.

Powell, who was an old friend of Boynton's, seemed unusually preoccupied, so Boynton skipped the preliminaries and got right down to business.

"You people have a quarantine on Dan Logan's place. Is there anything I should know?"

"Logan?"

"Come on, Fred. You know where I mean. Up by Medicine Creek. How many quarantines did you put on today, anyway?"

Powell didn't seem amused. If anything, his tone hardened. "Oh. Logan. No, there's nothing you have to worry about there, Spike. It's just a precautionary measure. If we find anything that you need to know about, I'll let you know."

Listening more to Powell's tone than his words, Boynton had the sense that something was up, that Powell was trying to cover up somehow, so he let the matter drop, said thank you, and hung up.

Now he was really worried. At first, when he had been stopped at the gate to Logan's ranch by an MP, he had taken at face value the explanation that Fort Howard was just cooperating with the Public Health Service in establishing the quarantine. Now, though, everything was taking on a different meaning. The Public Health Service usually was anxious to share information about quarantines with the local veterinarian. It was good policy and good practice. And the quarantines were usually mostly a matter of posting signs and relying on everyone's sense of self-preservation. Boynton had certainly never heard of the PHS employing a cordon of armed soldiers. The only conclusion that remained was that the army was involved somehow. The army, the Public Health Service, and several hundred dead and dying sheep. All of a sudden it all fit together. The idea seemed crazy at first, but it explained a lot that was very mysterious otherwise. Boynton walked over to the glass-front bookcase next to his desk. Now he knew what to look for.

23

TO: MAJOR S. J. COOPER

FROM: COL. A. A. NICKERSON, CO

SUBJECT: OPERATION EAGLE

SUPPLEMENTARY ORDERS:

1. Replace security detail Site A with regular company, rotate four full shifts per day. No contact except as necessary. Hidden cordon along entire road perimeter plus double garrison at gate.

2. Assign security detail to detox crew ordered Site A 1500 hours.

3. Establish priority one monitoring of PubAffairs Office.

4. Condition Red applies to communications facility. Until ordered otherwise, all copying equipment to be sealed. Full access all times to communications facility to be available Colonel Franklin, Major Kagle.

5. Prepare suggested security precautions for low-profile isolation of subjects Site B.

24

Logan was awakened from a troubled sleep by Dr. Holliford. The short, intense physician had another man with him, a tall man in hospital whites with a bland face that looked neutrally out at the world from behind round steel-rimmed glasses.

Holliford said, "I'm sorry to disturb you, Mr. Logan, but there are some tests we have to do."

Logan sat up slowly in bed, rubbing his face. Holliford said, "This is Dr. Bowen. He's a neurologist. He just wants to check your reactions to some things."

Holliford stepped out of the way, and Bowen took his place standing next to the bed. "Now, Mr. Logan," Dr. Bowen said, "If you'll just swing around and sit on the edge of the bed, we can get this over with before you know it."

Obediently, still not fully awake, Logan swung his legs around so that he was sitting on the edge of the bed facing Bowen, who said, "Good. Now I want you to hold your arms out straight in front of you, with the palms facing the ceiling."

Logan did as he was told, wondering what Bowen expected to see. His hands were steady as he held them in front of him, and they remained steady when Bowen told him to turn them over so the palms faced the floor.

Next, Bowen had him close his eyes, hold his arms

out at his sides, and, one at a time, touch his index fingers to his nose. As far as Logan could tell he did all right. It seemed a silly thing for a grown man to be doing, but it was Bowen's job to give tests like these, so Logan just did what Bowen told him to do.

Logan's faith was shaken a bit when Bowen next drew from his pocket a thin white feather and said, "Now, Mr. Logan, I'm going to tickle your nose. I want you to pay attention to how it feels."

After he tickled Logan's nostrils, Bowen had the rancher hold his arms in front of him again, and this time Bowen ran the feather back and forth along the inside of each of Logan's arms. After this and a few other tests, Bowen paused to make some notes on Logan's reactions. Throughout the tests, Holliford sat unobtrusively in a corner of the room, watching closely everything that Bowen and Logan did. As soon as the neurologist indicated that he was finished, Holliford got up and darkened the room. Then he took an ophthalmoscope from his pocket and switched it on and off to see that it was working properly.

As Holliford approached, Logan wondered what it was that the two doctors were looking for. When the tests were over, he asked them. Holliford's answer didn't prove very enlightening.

"We're not looking for anything in particular, Mr. Logan," he said. "We're just afraid that you may have been exposed to whatever it is that's bothering your son, and we want to watch you for a while to make sure that you're all right. It's nothing to worry about." Holliford smiled slightly, and he and Bowen left the room.

25

UNITED STATES PUBLIC HEALTH SERVICE
NORTHWEST CENTRAL DIVISION
13314 WESTERN AVENUE
CASPER, WYOMING

SURVEY NUMBER: 4Y-339
AUTHORIZATION: contract 3A6487
LOCATION: Grid 4-E, southwest quadrant

THIS REPORT IS CONFIDENTIAL

SUMMARY:

A four-man testing team was dispatched to the subject area (see map, p. 4) and a standard Waverly Sampling Program was carried out at each of eight ranches and seventeen selected intermediate points (Appendix B). Soil sample cores and flora specimens were tested at the Casper facility for toxic residue, bacterial activity, surface contamination, and trace mineral content. In addition, *in situ* examination of fauna was carried out at all eight ranches and six intermediate points. Residents of the eight ranches were removed to the Rawlins facility for physical examination and testing by technicians supplied by authorizing agency.

Findings were negative as to contamination of human subjects. Soil and flora testing indicated residual contamination within projected acceptable limits (but see Chart 3, p. 7). Tests of domestic livestock *in situ* indicated significant first-order contamination over wider area than initially projected. Affected animals were removed to authorizing agency.

26

The hill the Logans had camped on the night before was still and deserted. A vagrant wind made little plumes in the fine white powder that covered the hilltop and the sagging tent and the long-dead campfire like a kind of deadly snow.

At the bottom of the hill, dozens of sheep lay dead, dirty white lumps on a white-powdered field. Among them stalked grotesque figures in drab, baggy protective suits that gave them heavy, clumsy feet and hands, and swollen, awkward limbs. Their heads were huge, square, featureless, the only face a blank rectangle of glass that glinted in the afternoon sun.

In unearthly silence, they went about their grim tasks: taking blood from the dead sheep, pulling soil samples from the ground, clipping pieces of trees and tearing up clumps of grass. One of them bore, strapped to his back, a bulk of metal tanks, pumps, and dials from which came a transparent plastic hose ending in a pistol-like nozzle. From the nozzle there issued a stream of white decontaminant powder that the clumsy-suited figure played over the ground in front of him.

27

Logan lay in bed, fighting the nausea that had gripped him after he had choked down the tall glassful of chalky white liquid the nurse had insisted that he drink. She had told him that it was necessary for a test they were going to do soon, that it would help to see how his insides were working. He hadn't minded the other tests; this was the first one that was unpleasant. Even so, he wanted to be whatever help he could. The sooner the tests were over, the sooner he could get back to the ranch.

He wondered about the sheep, about what had made the few he had seen so sick. After a moment, he turned his mind from the image of the twitching animals. There was no way it would help him to worry about them. He knew already that the sickness was something he had never seen, so that part of it would have to be up to Spike Boynton. Spike was good at his work, and that was important. If there was something you couldn't do yourself, Logan thought, it was good to have somebody else you could rely on. Not that he often needed to rely on anyone; between himself and the boy, there wasn't much they couldn't do themselves.

He thought about Chris, about how good it felt to see him grow and join in the work on the ranch. It wasn't a big ranch, but it was too much for him to handle alone, and there really wasn't enough work to hire a full-time hand, so he and Chris made a good team, just able to keep the sheep healthy and strong and the ranch running. And when Chris was older, they could take on a couple of hundred head more than he had now, and maybe buy that piece of land he had been dickering with Bill Parker about for the past few years. Parker was stubborn about breaking up his place, but Logan thought he'd give in before too long. It was getting to be too much for him to handle what he had, and he didn't have anyone to pass it on to, anyway.

For Logan it was different. There was Chris to take over the ranch when he was gone. Not, Logan thought, that you could really own that land. He looked at it more like a kind of stewardship. You oversaw the land, worked on it, loved it, even, but you could never really own it, any more than anyone else had ever owned it: not his father, or his father's father, who had bought the first piece, which had grown now by almost three times and would keep growing in the future because it was in the Logan blood to do better and bigger than had been done before. When you came down to it, Logan thought, it wasn't the owning that mattered. What he really wanted wasn't to own it, but just to live on it and have a right to the life, not to the land. That was what he hoped he was teaching Chris: to want the life and the work and the satisfaction, the closeness to the land and the sheep and the people, the comfort of knowing you were worth something to yourself.

28

The phone rang five times before Tom Arnold answered, and in the half minute or so it took Arnold to get to the phone, Spike Boynton almost hung up twice. He was worried because when he put his deductions together to explain them to someone else, they suddenly seemed very flimsy. In spite of his misgivings, though, Boynton managed to hold on until he heard Arnold's voice on the other end of the line, and then there was nothing he could do but go ahead with it.

"Hello, Tom," he said, "This is Spike Boynton, the vet, from over in Lamont. You had me on for an interview last year."

"Sure, Spike, I remember. How have you been? And to what do I owe the honor of hearing from you?"

"I'm fine, Tom. I called because I think maybe I've got a piece of news you could use."

"Really?" Arnold sounded interested.

"I think so. Have you heard anything about a Public Health Service quarantine out in Medicine Creek?"

"As a matter of fact, Spike, I seem to recall we had a call about that this afternoon. From a Dr. Spencer, as I recall. The one who runs the Casper office."

"Oh," Boynton said and thought, I was probably wrong after all. "What did he tell you?"

"Nothing, really. Just that there were some dead sheep

up there and that they wanted to keep the area closed until they were sure what it was. He said something about insecticide poisoning, I think."

"Insecticide poisoning? That's very interesting. Did he say anything about the army?"

"No. Why should he? Does the army have anything to do with this?"

"That's what I've been wondering. I looked at those sheep before they put the quarantine on. Then when I went back, there was an army patrol at the front gate of the ranch. They were armed, and they looked like they meant business. They wouldn't let me near the place."

"That is strange," Arnold said, his interest picking up. "Maybe you do have something I can use. What else can you tell me?"

"Well, the first thing I can tell you is that the sheep I saw didn't look like they were suffering from any kind of insecticide poisoning."

"Really? What do you think it was?"

Boynton took a deep breath. "You'd better brace yourself. I've been doing research all afternoon, and the only thing I can come up with that makes any sense at all is nerve gas."

"Now wait a minute. Let's not get carried away. That sounds pretty farfetched."

"I know it sounds farfetched. I keep having trouble believing it myself. But there's nothing else that fits. You had to see those sheep. I've never encountered anything like it. But the symptoms did seem similar in some ways to descriptions I've read of the sheep that died at Skull Valley when they had that accident at Dugway Proving Grounds a few years ago."

"Still, Spike, that's a long way to go on that kind of

evidence." It seemed to Boynton that Arnold was backing off.

"For God's sake, Tom," Boynton said, feeling unaccountably desperate. "What else could it be? Look at it all at once: sheep dead and dying with unheard-of symptoms, an unexplained quarantine being enforced by armed soldiers, and suspicious silence at the PHS when you try to get a straight answer from them. Just what do they do at super-secret Fort Howard, anyway? Don't tell me you've never heard any rumors about that."

"No, of course I have. But that's the whole trouble. All of this is just rumors and guesswork." Arnold sounded tired. "I can't stake my job on rumors and guesses, even if they're pretty well founded."

"No, I suppose you can't," Boynton said. "But can't you say something? There must be some way to get this out in the open."

"I wish I could. The truth is, you've almost got me convinced you're right. But the news director and the station owner would both crucify me if I started shooting my mouth off. You know, it's not exactly a secret that Ray Adams isn't what you'd call a crusading journalist. And if he doesn't like an item, we don't run it."

"I wish I could be more help," Boynton said. "But all I can tell you is that those sheep died in a very ugly, unpleasant way, and somebody is trying to cover it up."

Tom Arnold was silent for a short while. Then he said, "Look, can we get together and talk about this some more? If I'm going to say anything about this on the show tomorrow, I'll need to have all the details."

Boynton was tremendously relieved. "Anytime you say, Tom. You just name the place, and I'll be there."

29

A4DX693-P107-E
TOPSECRETCLASSQSCRAMBLE
CODEDESIGCOWBOYSEVENSEVENFIVE
CODESQUAREDBUTTERFLYORANGE
GENERAL SAMUEL HILL
JOINTCHIEFS PENTAGON
PRIORITY BLUEBLUERED

BEGINS. REPORT DAYONE EAGLE. SITUATION: MECHANICAL FAILURE SPRAYING APPARATUS RELEASED THREE HUNDRED POUNDS EXPERIMENTAL AGENT MX3 OVER CIVILIAN AREA NEAR LAMONT BAIROIL WYOMING. TESTING REVEALS ONLY ONE RANCH HEAVILY AFFECTED. PRESENT ESTIMATE TWO HUNDRED SHEEP DEAD. TWO IDENTIFIED HUMAN CASUALTIES DANIEL C. LOGAN FORTYTWO RANCHER CHRISTOPHER LOGAN TWELVE SON OF DANIEL. BOTH CURRENTLY CONFINED CARBON COUNTY HOSPITAL RAWLINS. PROGNOSIS NEGATIVE. REQUIRE SOONEST SECURITY CHECK FOLLOWING DR. ROY CARDWELL PHYSICIAN RAWLINS WYO ARTHUR FAIRMAN DIRECTOR CARBON COUNTY HOSPITAL DR. MATTHEW SPENCER DIRECTOR PHS NORTHWEST CENTRAL. PROJECTED DANGER AREAS ALL IN AREA OF PUBLIC AFFAIRS COMPLICATED SEVERELY BY HOLDING CASUALTIES IN PUBLIC HOSPITAL. HOWEVER ADVISE STRONGEST AGAINST MOVING CIVILIANS DENVER OR OTHER CONTROLLED HOSPITAL DUE PUBLIC INFORMATION PROBLEMS THIS WOULD CREATE.

RELY INSTEAD ON SECUREST HANDLING PRESENT DISPOSITION. CURRENT EVALUATION POSITIVE DEGREE TWO. SENSITIVE PERIOD DATE PLUS FORTYEIGHT HOURS. SIGNED FRANKLIN COL.

THREE

1

At three-ten in the morning there was only a skeleton staff on duty at Carbon County Hospital. As usual, there was an R.N. in the Emergency Room and a night floor-supervisor at the main nurses' station, along with one night-duty nurse. In addition, because there was a critical patient in isolation, there was a night-shift special-duty nurse with him, and Dr. Thompson was sleeping on the couch in the staff room.

In the isolation room, the special-duty nurse was sitting in a comfortable chair next to Chris Logan's bed, reading a Gothic novel, the latest by her favorite author. She was so engrossed in the mystery of what the unsuspecting heroine would find in the locked room under the stairs of the forbidding old mansion that at first she didn't notice the change in Chris Logan's breathing.

Gradually, she became aware that something had changed in the room. She closed her book and looked up at her patient. Through the clear plastic of the oxygen tent she could see the boy struggling for breath, his face twisted and his body heaving with effort. She ran to the door and threw it open.

"Grace!" she shouted to the night floor-supervisor. "Call Dr. Thompson, right away." She whirled and ran back into the room, unzipped the oxygen tent, and checked to see that the boy's mouth and throat were clear. His color was bad, and he was still struggling for breath, making a constant wailing noise that sometimes sounded as if he were calling "Mama, Mama," over and over again.

The nurse felt Chris's neck, checking for his pulse. It was weak and ragged: slow, then rapid, then none at all. She hit him forcefully over the heart and jumped on the bed, straddling him, her hands together and her arms stiff, and began to give him external heart massage, pressing repeatedly on his chest with sharp, percussive motions.

Dr. Thompson rushed into the room, pulling a white gown around him, and pushed the nurse aside, saying, out of breath, "All right. I'll take over." The nurse got out of Thompson's way and off the bed as he took up the heart massage, pressing with the same rhythm the nurse had used, but with greater force. As he worked, the regular night-duty nurse wheeled a cart of emergency medications in from the hall.

"Give me the board," Thompson said without pausing in his massage. The special-duty nurse took a padded board from against the wall of the room and held it ready. Thompson lifted the boy slightly, and she slipped the board under his upper body. It helped the massage, providing more resistance to Thompson's forceful downward strokes than the soft mattress of the bed.

Thompson continued to push against Chris's chest while the two nurses watched. The special-duty nurse, whose training had included descriptions of similar situations, but who had never actually seen a terminal emergency, was so spellbound by the scene that she was completely unprepared when Thompson snapped,

"Adrenaline—half a cc."

She turned quickly to the tray of medications and found a bottle of adrenaline, broke a disposable syringe and needle out of their paper-and-plastic packages, and prepared the adrenaline injection. She slipped the syringe into Thompson's waiting hand, and he carefully pressed the needle into Chris's chest, stopping when he judged the needle's point was properly placed in the cardiac muscle. Then he injected the adrenaline, withdrew the needle, and resumed the heart massage.

"See if you can get a pulse," he said. The special-duty nurse took Chris's wrist and felt for his pulse. Failing to find any pulse at all in his wrist, she went quickly around the bed to where she could reach his neck and pressed her fingers to the hollow under his jaw.

"Do you get anything?" Thompson asked.

"No. Nothing at all."

"Keep trying."

Thompson went on with the massage, the muscles in his forearms knotting with the effort, a sheen of sweat forming on his face. Now there was no sound from the boy, and the room took on a desperate silence, broken only by Thompson's occasional grunts of effort and the rattling of the bedsprings under the force of the massage.

"Give me another half a cc.," Thompson said.

The nurse prepared another syringe and Thompson paused just long enough to give the injection, much more quickly and urgently than the first. Then he resumed the massage, the sweat dripping from his forehead making round wet marks on the bed and stinging his eyes.

"Any pulse?"

"Still no pulse."

In spite of the now apparent futility of his efforts, Thompson went on with the massage for another minute.

"Still no pulse."

Thompson straightened up, looking down at the limp, still figure on the bed. His hands fell wearily to his sides and he sighed heavily. "Well, that's it," he said without expression. He backed away from the bed and wiped the sweat from his forehead. Across the bed from him the special-duty nurse clamped the tube leading from the intravenous feeding bottle on the stand next to her and removed the tube from Chris's arm.

Thompson turned to leave the room. He said, "I'm going to call Dr. Holliford. See that the boy is put in the freezer right away."

2

Colonel Nickerson, Colonel Franklin, and Major Holliford were gathered in Nickerson's living room. In the faint predawn light, they sat with steaming mugs of coffee, fighting back the fatigue that came from having been awakened in the middle of the night with the news of Chris Logan's death.

"Well," Nickerson was saying, "I guess we've covered the high points. Unless there's anything else you want to add, Colonel."

"No." Franklin said. "I think that's all." He glanced

at his watch, which showed five-forty. "Why don't you call Dr. Spencer?"

"Right. I guess there's no sense in waiting any longer." Nickerson went quickly to the phone and dialed Spencer's number. The phone rang several times and then Spencer's sleepy voice came on the line.

"Hello. Who is this?"

"It's Colonel Nickerson. I'm sorry to disturb you this early."

"Oh, yes, Colonel. That's all right. What is it?"

"We have word that Chris Logan died about two hours ago."

"Oh. I see. That's too bad."

"Yes. We thought you should know about it as soon as possible. As we discussed yesterday, we're going to have to rely on you rather heavily about this."

"Of course. Of course." There was the sound of a stifled yawn. "Just what do you want me to do?"

"We're concerned primarily about the hospital staff. We can't have this news circulating in the community, and we don't want to involve the army in it at all if we can help it. Major Holliford is going over to the hospital now to talk to the doctor and the nurses who are involved, but we thought the actual instructions ought to come from you."

"Yes, that's a good idea."

"And there is the problem of Dr. Cardwell. You'll have to see that the news is broken to him properly."

"All right, Colonel. I'll go right over to the hospital, then."

"Excellent. Major Holliford will meet you in Mr. Fairman's office. And one more thing. We've discussed it at some length, and we're in agreement here that Mr. Logan must not know about his son's death. If he does, that introduces variables that we may find very hard to deal with."

"I understand perfectly, Colonel."

"Good. Thank you very much, Dr. Spencer."

"Not at all, Colonel. Good-bye."

Nickerson hung up the phone and turned to Franklin. "He'll handle it all right," Nickerson said. "He knows what to do."

"I hope so," said Franklin.

3

When Matthew Spencer got to the hospital, he went straight to the administrator's office. Bert Holliford was waiting for him there, sitting in the plastic-covered couch that stood against one wall of the office. Arthur Fairman was at his desk, looking as though his day had begun badly. Holliford stood up to greet Spencer as he came into the office.

"Good morning, Dr. Spencer," he said. "I've been talking to Mr. Fairman, and I think he understands the situation well enough."

Spencer looked at Fairman, who shifted uneasily in his seat. "I want to say that I don't understand the situation at all," Fairman said. "All I understand is that I'm to mind my own business and not pay attention to what goes on in my own hospital. I don't know what the trustees would say if they knew I was doing this."

"There's nothing to worry about, Mr Fairman," Spencer said. "In the first place, the trustees won't know anything about this. No one will know except a few people in the Public Health Service, and Dr. Holliford, who has been helping us. And the alternative, as I am sure Dr. Holliford explained, would be very unfortunate."

Fairman waved his hands helplessly. "It's all right, Dr. Spencer, I assure you. I won't be any trouble at all. I just wish these things didn't have to happen to me."

"Of course, Mr. Fairman," said Spencer. He turned to Holliford. "Do you have the others together?"

"Yes, they're waiting in the staff lounge."

"Let's go and see them," Spencer said.

The two men walked in silence down the hospital corridor. Holliford stopped at a door marked "Staff" and held it open for Spencer. There were five people in the room: Dr. Thompson, the night special-duty nurse, and the three nurses who had been on the hospital's regular night shift. Holliford introduced them to Spencer, who acknowledged the introductions and then took a seat next to Dr. Thompson.

"I know you're curious why I asked you all to meet me here," Spencer said, keeping his tone warm and friendly. "The reason is very simple, really. I want to ask your cooperation with the Public Health Service on something that's important to all of us."

4

KCPH–TV 13

CASPER, WYOMING

PROGRAM TRANSCRIPT

Program	Ranch News	Time	6:00 A.M.
Director	Ralph Johnston	Segment	28A
Producer	Harve Whitney	Running Time	23 min.

Cast
Regular: Shelby Miller, Tom Arnold (Gale Slauson), Herb Jones
Guest: Warren Brooks, Ethel Harvey

* * *

Note: This is a transcript of an actual broadcast, made from complete videotapes of that broadcast. This is not a script or a broadcast outline. Filing of this transcript complies with applicable Regulations of the Federal Communications Commission under the Communications Act of 1934 as amended (47 U.S.C.A. Section 151 et seq.).

* * *

– 1 –

RANCH NEWS THEME AND LOGO (0:30)
MILLER: Good morning, everybody. Rise and shine. This

is Shelby Miller, bringing you your rancher's morning report. We have something this morning that ought to be interesting to all you ranchers. A little later on, we'll be having a talk with Warren Brooks, the new county agent over in Platte County, and I know he's got a lot of practical new ideas for you. And of course we'll have our weather and crop reports, same as usual. But first, naturally, here's Tom Arnold with this morning's news. (0:36)

ARNOLD: Thank you, Shelby. The big news this morning comes from Carbon County. We have a report that several hundred sheep died yesterday about thirty miles north of Rawlins, right in the center of Carbon County. The Public Health Service, which reported the deaths, told me they are investigating this matter thoroughly. I have this morning's *Capper Post-Sentinel* here, and they have a quote from a Public Health Service official who says that the deaths may be the result of insecticide

– 2 –

ARNOLD (continued): poisoning. Of course, we have a lot of respect for the Public Health Service here in Wyoming, but I spoke to a local veterinarian last night who saw the dead sheep himself, and he told me that he thinks a more powerful chemical might be involved, a chemical like the ones the army tests for use in combat, something they call nerve gas. If this is true, it is a matter of great concern to everyone in our listening area. There have been rumors for a long time that tests of something like that are conducted at Fort Howard.

I'm sure that all of you remember what happened at Dugway Proving Grounds in Utah just a few years ago, when six thousand sheep in nearby Skull Valley were killed by deadly war gas. The Ranch News hopes that Fort Howard is not involved in yesterday's deaths, but we feel that the army should clear up this whole question if it wants to keep up its good relations with its Wyoming neighbors. (Pause.) In the national news this morning, the Department of Agriculture announced that the question of subsidy for corn and wheat growers would be reopened when a department-sponsored bill was introduced in the House of Representatives . . .

– 3 –

5

The morning started well for Roy Cardwell. He had gotten out early, driving quickly through the clear, crisp dawn to Chad Buckman's place, where he had delivered Ellen Buckman of a fine, strong baby boy. Then he had driven back home and eaten one of Mrs. Knowles's old-fashioned country breakfasts, the kind she made for him when she knew he had started the day early and would be out on calls until late at night.

The first thing he did after breakfast was to drive into Rawlins to check in at the hospital and see how the

Logans were doing. After that, he was planning to start making his rounds of the homes that were affected by what seemed to be a regular epidemic of chicken pox among the elementary school children. With any luck, he figured he'd be home by eight or nine at night.

He parked his dusty superannuated sedan in the hospital lot and decided to leave his bag in the car, since he wasn't going to be doing anything but visiting Dan and Chris Logan. He locked all the car doors and double-checked them, then went into the hospital. He said hello to the receptionist, remembering on his way by that she was Art Callan's daughter, and that, like little Allie Buckman this morning, he had brought her, squalling and yelling, into the world. There was one thing Cardwell always found about delivering a child: it made him nostalgic. And he had a lot of births to remember. Like Chris Logan's, and now that he thought of it, Dan Logan's, too. The way Cardwell remembered it, he had been on vacation from medical school, helping old Dr. Whitney, when Martha Logan had her first and, as it had turned out, only child. Cardwell chuckled to himself. I must be getting old, he thought; they say being able to remember forty years ago better than forty days ago is a sure sign of age.

Cardwell stopped at the nurses' station. "Good morning," he said cheerfully to the nurse on duty. "How are you this morning?"

The nurse looked up from her work. She was the regular night-duty nurse, and she didn't feel very well at all, having been on now for twelve hours, and having had a hard night and morning, between the boy's death and that long, confusing meeting with the man from the

Public Health Service. She tried to sound cheerful, though, when she said "Good morning, doctor." They had told her specifically to sound cheerful.

Cardwell didn't recognize the nurse, who was an attractive young redhead, but he did notice that she looked very tired. He couldn't imagine why, since it was only a few hours since the hospital normally changed shifts, but it didn't seem too important. He decided that she probably didn't recognize him, either, so he introduced himself. "I'm Dr. Cardwell," he said. "Do you have Chris Logan's chart?"

Recognition came into the nurse's face, and then a touch of sadness. "I'm sorry, Dr. Cardwell," she said. "Chris Logan died during the night. Dr. Holliford would like to speak to you about it. I think he's in the cafeteria right now."

Cardwell was taken completely by surprise by the news of Chris's death. He stood at the nurses' station numbed and uncomprehending. In his almost forty years as a doctor, he had developed a more than occasional acquaintance with death, but this one took him very hard. He didn't know why, but he couldn't remember being this shaken by a patient's death since his first years in practice. When he thought he could control his voice, he asked, "Where did you say Dr. Holliford was?"

"I think he's in the cafeteria, Dr. Cardwell."

"Thank you, nurse," he mumbled automatically and walked slowly and wearily down the corridor toward the cafeteria.

The cafeteria was deserted except for Dr. Holliford and a man Cardwell didn't recognize, a neatly dressed, balding, gray-haired man of about sixty, who was sitting at a corner table with Holliford, drinking coffee.

"Excuse me, Dr. Holliford," Cardwell said as he approached the two men. "I just heard about Chris Logan."

Holliford and the other man stood up. "Oh, yes," Holliford said somewhat uncomfortably. He indicated the man with him. "Dr. Cardwell, this is Dr. Spencer, from the Public Health Service in Casper."

Cardwell recognized the name, remembered that Spencer was well thought of in Wyoming medical circles, and found that in spite of his reaction to Chris Logan's death, he was pleased to be meeting Spencer. He shook hands with the PHS official and said he was glad to meet him. Then he turned back to Holliford.

"I'm sorry to interrupt you, but I have to know what happened last night. I didn't think Chris Logan was in any danger."

To Cardwell's surprise, Holliford's reply was cut off by Dr. Spencer, who said, "Bert, why don't you let me answer that?" Holliford, glad to relinquish the floor to Spencer, sat down and sipped at his coffee.

"Why don't you sit down, Dr. Cardwell?" Spencer said. "This is a little complicated."

Cardwell sat down at the table with Spencer and Holliford, wondering what was going on.

Spencer took a pipe and a pouch of tobacco from his inside jacket pocket and began filling the pipe as he spoke, choosing his words carefully. "This whole matter is rather delicate," he said slowly. "We're not exactly sure what killed Chris Logan, but we think it was a toxic chemical that we found traces of in the Medicine Creek area."

Spencer finished filling his pipe and put the pouch

back into his jacket pocket. "We haven't been able to identify the toxin yet," he said, "but we're doing our best to find out what it is and keep it under control. Naturally, we've been very concerned. As far as we can tell so far, the Logans are the only ones to have been affected by it."

Spencer looked briefly at Holliford. "Dr. Holliford has worked a lot with chemical toxication, and he's been a great help to us. Of course, he did all he could for Chris." Spencer let his voice trail off, and Holliford nodded reassuringly at Cardwell.

When Spencer resumed speaking, his voice had taken on a tone of earnest entreaty. "Right now, the thing we're most afraid of is panic in the community," he explained. "For that reason, I have to ask you not to tell anyone about Chris Logan's death. Until we have the situation well in hand, we don't want to cause any unnecessary alarm."

Cardwell understood Spencer's desire to avoid panic, but he was confused by the approach Spencer seemed to be taking. "What about the other people in the area?" he asked.

"There's no danger to them," Spencer answered firmly. "We've tested them and we've tested their ranches. What we have to do now is find out what this is and where it came from and see that it doesn't happen again."

"Why didn't you tell me this yesterday?" Cardwell asked.

"Well, I'll be honest with you," Spencer said, speaking slowly and carefully. "We didn't really think the boy's condition was serious, and as long as we thought he would be all right, I didn't see any point in bothering you about it. We wanted to keep this as quiet as possible." Spencer paused a moment. "That's why it's so important that you not tell anyone."

Cardwell found himself eager to accept Spencer's explanation. With only slight difficulty, he put his misgivings aside. "Well," he said, "I suppose you've had more experience with this sort of thing than I have."

Spencer smiled. "You'd be surprised how easily rumors get started and how much unnecessary worry they cause."

Cardwell thought about it. It made sense to him.

"Believe me, it's the best way," Spencer said.

Suddenly, Cardwell was anxious to get out of the hospital and into the clear, open day. He stood up. "Well, I'll leave it up to you. If you don't want me to tell anybody, I won't."

"I'd appreciate it. I really would." And then, when Cardwell was almost to the door, Spencer said, "There's one other thing I have to ask you."

Cardwell turned.

"Dr. Holliford is running a series of tests," Spencer continued. "He's trying to determine just how badly the boy's father was affected, and we're afraid that if Mr. Logan hears about his son's death, his reaction will interfere with the tests. So we'd like you not to tell him about it, either."

"Would it really make that much difference?"

This time it was Holliford who answered. "Absolutely. It's vital to our tests."

Spencer, seeing that Cardwell was hesitant to accept this new request, said as soothingly as he could, "I don't really see how it can hurt if he doesn't hear about this for a day or two."

Cardwell shook his head in confusion. "I suppose you're right," he said wearily, then turned and left the room.

6

Logan was restless. He had already been up for more than four hours; the habits of years on the ranch were hard to break. He had been visited five times by nurses and twice by doctors, and he knew that there were still more tests to be done. With nothing to do in the meantime but stay in the small hospital room, Logan was worrying more and more about Chris, and feeling more and more useless and trapped.

He looked around the room for the hundredth time, this time trying to find something to figure out. Logan had always found that mechanical things helped him force out of his mind whatever was bothering him. In the old days, it had been a kind of joke between him and JoAnn. He hadn't realized how much they kidded about it until one day he found out that Chris was doing it, too.

It was when Chris was in the second grade. The boy had had a teacher who he thought didn't like him, and one afternoon she had sent him home with a note. Logan still remembered it, and it still made him laugh. The confused teacher had complained that although Chris was well-behaved and always seemed to be working hard, he wasn't keeping up with the others in the class. And when she had investigated, the teacher went on, she had found in Chris's desk-top drawer a completely dismantled alarm clock and three dissected fountain pens. She had no idea where he had gotten them, she said, but it seemed to her that the Logans should come in one day after school so they could all have a long talk about it.

So they had gone in and had the talk and gotten it all straightened out without much trouble. But Logan still cherished the memory, because it had been the first indication for them that Chris was going to grow up to be just like his father.

7

UNITED STATES PUBLIC HEALTH SERVICE
NORTHWEST CENTRAL DIVISION
13314 WESTERN AVENUE
CASPER, WYOMING

To whom it may concern:
Because of a potential public health emergency, this office has determined that the body of one Christopher Logan, age twelve, resident of Lamont, Wyoming, currently in the temporary morgue facility at Carbon County Hospital, should be held for autopsy under the direction of this office. Under the public health laws of the United States and the state of Wyoming, proper certification has been obtained, and the relevant documents, bearing

the State Board of Health #A34982, may be examined at this office. The subject autopsy will be conducted by or under the supervision of Dr. B. Holliford and Dr. R. Kagle, who are temporarily attached to this office. Thank you for your cooperation.

Sincerely,
Matthew Spencer, M.D.
Director

8

Sarah Parker came into the lobby of the hospital carrying Dan Logan's big leather suitcase, which she found bulky and awkward to carry, even though she had only packed some underwear and a couple of changes of clothes for Dan. Besides the suitcase, she had a big box of candy for Chris. She stopped just inside the door to let her eyes get accustomed to the light in the lobby, which was very dim after the brightness of the day, then crossed to the reception desk and put the suitcase down, with the box of candy on top of it.

"Good afternoon, Sue," she said to the chubby-faced young girl behind the desk.

The girl looked up at her. "Oh, good afternoon, Mrs. Parker. How are you?"

"I'm fine, thank you. And how's your daddy?" From time to time, Sarah wondered if things would have been any better for her if she'd married Sue's daddy, Art Callan, instead of Bill Parker. She didn't really think so, not judging by his children, who were always in some kind of trouble, except for Sue, who was usually polite and well-mannered.

"He's just fine, Mrs. Parker," Sue Callan said. "Is there something I can do for you?"

"Yes, there is. Can you tell me what room Mr. Logan is in? I came over to visit him."

Sue consulted a small box of file cards on her desk. "I'm sorry, Mrs. Parker. It says here Mr. Logan can't have any visitors."

"Oh. That's too bad." Sarah wondered for a moment what she should do with Dan's clothes, then said, "Could you do me a favor? I brought some of his things over for him. Can I leave them here with you?"

"Yes, ma'am. I'll see that he gets them all right."

"Thank you, Sue. That's very nice of you. I wonder, would it be all right to see Chris Logan?"

"I'll check for you, if you like," Sue said, and looked again in the file. "I'm sorry Mrs. Parker. It says he can't have any visitors, either."

Sarah shook her head. What a shame, she thought, to come all this way for nothing. But at least I can leave the things I brought and that should be some comfort to them anyway. "How is Chris?" she asked. "Is he getting better?"

Sue looked at Chris's card. "Yes, I guess he is, Mrs. Parker. Anyway, his card says his progress is satisfactory."

"Oh, that's good. Thank you."

"You're welcome, Mrs. Parker. Have a good day now."

"Good-bye, Sue," Sarah said and walked back out into the bright day.

Sue Callan came around her desk and picked up the suitcase and candy box and carried them to the nurses' station.

9

In the basement of Carbon County Hospital, Dan Logan was lying motionless on an examining table. His eyes were covered with a wet compress, and from electrodes taped to his head thin wires led to the console of an electroencephalograph.

Bert Holliford stood behind the technician who was sitting at the console and watched as the machine's fine, delicate pens traced out the many-peaked lines that represented Logan's brain waves. After a while, the technician, a thin, dark-haired young SP/1 dressed in civilian clothes under his lab coat, said, "Looks all right to me."

"Fine," Holliford said. "You can disconnect him, then."

The technician got up from the console and went over to remove the electrodes from Logan's head. There was a light knock on the door and a tall middle-aged nurse came into the room.

"Did you send for me, Dr. Holliford?" she asked.

"Yes, Rita, I did," Holliford said. "We're almost through here. You can get Mr. Logan's medication ready."

Rita said, "All right," and left the room.

The technician took the last of the electrodes from Logan's forehead and wiped off the remains of the special cream that helped make the electrical connection secure. Aware that the test was over, Logan said, "How's my boy?"

Holliford continued to examine Logan's electroencephalogram. "He's doing all right," he said.

The technician uncovered Logan's eyes. Logan blinked against the light and said, "I'd like to go up and see him."

Holliford made some notes about the electroencephalogram. He gave no indication of having heard Logan's request.

Logan said, a little more sharply, "I said I'd like to go up and see him."

Holliford turned toward the rancher. "It would be better if you didn't right now," he said. "It's very important that he not be disturbed."

"I just want to look in on him."

"I can't allow it right now. Maybe tomorrow."

Logan sat part way up on the examining table. "Look, he's my son. What's the matter?"

"I'm just thinking of him," Holliford said.

"What do you mean? Is something wrong?"

"No. It's just that we had to move him to another part of the hospital, and I don't want him to be disturbed."

"But all I want to do is look in on him."

Out of patience and out of excuses, Holliford said, "All right, Mr. Logan, I'll see what I can do," and walked quickly out of the room.

He went straight to the nurses' station, where he found

Rita preparing the afternoon medication.

"Rita," he said, "I want to change Mr. Logan's medication. You can discontinue the Valium for now, but I want him to get three grains of phenobarbital sodium right away."

Rita said, "All right, Doctor," and as Holliford walked away she wondered what had made him change Logan's medication from a common tranquilizer to a large dose of a fast-acting sedative.

10

KCPH-TV 13
CASPER, WYOMING
INTERNAL CORRESPONDENCE

TO:	Tom Arnold	FROM:	R. K. Adams
RE:	This morning's Ranch News	COPIES:	none

Tom—

In the three years you've been with us, we've been very happy with the job you do here. The viewers like you, and I can't remember a time when a producer or a director complained about your work. Of course, there have been a couple of times when you've been what I'd call a little too "enthusiastic" on the air. In fact, I was very pleased at how long it had been since I've had to talk to you about the difference between reporting the news in a way that's useful to our viewers on the one hand, and on the other hand adding your own editorializing or even snooping point of view. Now, all that may be perfectly good back at some of those big city stations, but it doesn't serve our needs here in Casper. What I mean to say is that we have plenty of public service and editorial programing to satisfy the FCC at renewal time, and we don't need you to be adding any such on your own hook on the morning news. You probably know very well that if you had submitted your piece about the dead sheep and all that nonsense about Fort Howard BEFORE you went on the air, it never would have been approved. So I'm going to have to insist this time that from now on you get EVERYTHING you use approved BEFORE AIR TIME. Or else, I'm afraid we're going to have to take another hard look at your record up here. I hope I made myself clear.

Sincerely,
Ray

11

Colonel Franklin looked around the table at the other officers who were having a late lunch with him in the Fort Howard Officers' Mess. In the day and a half he had been in Wyoming, he had already formulated a list of suggested projects for the Joint Staff which might help cure the kind of laxity that seemed to be SOP out here. The question of isolated single-purpose posts like this one had been in his head since his unpleasant visit to the helicopter-training post in Texas, but conditions at Fort Howard had brought his misgivings into much stronger focus. The irony of it was, it seemed to Franklin, that they were probably going to muddle through this particular ugly situation in pretty good shape.

Across the table from him, Major Cooper was summarizing the security situation. "From what Dr. Spencer told me," Cooper said, "the people at the hospital will be cooperative, at least for now, and so will Dr. Cardwell."

"That's right," said Spencer, the only civilian at the table.

"That was our biggest area of difficulty," Cooper went on, "and we've covered just about everything else. There's only one thing left, really. I had a report from Major Dannenmann. He's our information officer," Cooper explained to Franklin. "He said there was an item on the KCPH Ranch News this morning to the effect that a local veterinarian thinks the sheep died of nerve-gas poisoning. He claims to have seen the sheep, and Major Dannenmann said the newsman linked it directly to us."

"That could be serious," Major Reintz said from his corner of the table.

"Yes, it could, Major," said Franklin dryly. "Does anyone know who this veterinarian might be?"

At first there was no response from the others. Then Nickerson said, "I don't suppose it would be too hard to find out who it was."

Reintz said, almost to himself, "Still, it's a shame we haven't established any kind of contact with the community. It could be a tremendous help now."

Jesus, Franklin thought, he's sniping at his commanding officer in public now.

Spencer, lighting his pipe, puffed forth an aromatic white cloud of smoke and said, "I can take care of that. There's sure to be a list of veterinarians at our local office."

"Good," said Franklin. "And we should spend some time talking about what approach to take with him."

"I'll tell you what," said Spencer between puffs. "Let me see if I can find out who it is and what kind of man he is. Then we'll know better how to talk to him."

Franklin nodded with satisfaction, but noted that once again it was a civilian who was dealing with the problem most efficiently.

12

Major Kagle watched from the side of the stark, tiled autopsy room as the staff pathologist prepared his instruments for the autopsy. At the other end of the room, Major Holliford, dressed like Kagle and the pathologist in a wrinkled green operating gown, leaned against a bank of steel-fronted morgue drawers.

The pathologist, with the help of the morgue assistant, lifted a small, shroud-covered body from a wheeled stretcher to the steel-and-porcelain top of the autopsy table. Then the morgue assistant wheeled the stretcher out of the way.

"All ready?" the pathologist asked.

Holliford and Kagle approached the autopsy table and stood next to the pathologist. The morgue assistant checked the position of a microphone hanging from the ceiling over the autopsy table. "All ready," he said and switched on the microphone.

The pathologist reached down to uncover Chris Logan's body. As he pulled the cloth back, he said, "This is number six-three-nine-four, Christopher Logan."

Kagle reached under his gown and took out a small notebook and a pen. Next to him, Holliford watched the pathologist intently, radiating professional curiosity, almost enthusiasm.

The pathologist examined Chris's cold, waxy-looking corpse briefly, then began speaking again. "The body is that of a well-developed Caucasian male youth appearing to be the stated age of twelve years old. Length is . . ." He paused while the morgue assistant measured the body, then resumed, "Sixty-one and a half inches. The nutritional status is well maintained. There is no external evidence of injury. The pupils are three millimeters and regular. Thorax and abdomen are symmetrical. The extremities are not remarkable."

The pathologist stopped speaking again, this time to pick up an oversize scalpel. "The body is opened with a standard Y-shaped incision," he said, and began to cut.

13

A4DX693–P124–E
CONFIDENTIALSCRAMBLE
UNCODED
MAJOR GENERAL RONALD PHILLIPS
PENTAGON 6E2962
PRIORITY BLUEBLUEYELLOW
BEGINS: REQUIRE FROM JOE WHEELER FULL COVER AND PRESSURE TEAM ALL THREE MEDIA. PLEASE BRIEF JOE AND PROVIDE SCHEDULE HERE SOONEST. SIGNED FRANKLIN COL.

14

When Matthew Spencer pushed open the glass door and walked into the one-room PHS office above the Rawlins Federal Bank, Fred Powell was already clearing off his desk in preparation for closing up for the day. After ten hours of grueling testing the day before and a full day of reorganizing and cross-filing the results and the duty reports and tying up all the loose ends that had been created by the testings, Powell was eager to get home, have a drink, and take it easy for the night.

Powell looked up from his desk and, seeing his boss, ran a hand over his smooth, bald head in an unconscious gesture of displeasure. Powell's unhappiness was not lost on Spencer, who chose to ignore it.

"Fred," Spencer began as he sat down in the one comfortable chair in the office. "Do you have a list of the local veterinarians?"

"Yes, I think I do," Powell answered. "Something up?"

Spencer made a steeple of his fingers. "Do you know anything about a veterinarian who claims to have seen the dead sheep over at the Logan place?"

Powell considered this. "No, I don't recall hearing anything about it."

"Well, there's a vet who says he was at the Logan ranch and he examined the sheep. He's talking to reporters about nerve gas."

"Jesus," Powell said. "That's awful."

"That's an understatement," Spencer said. He took out his pipe and tobacco pouch and began to fill the pipe.

"Well, what are we going to do?" Powell demanded.

"The first thing we've got to do is find out who this vet is. Why don't you go and get your list?"

His drink and his quiet evening forgotten for the moment, Powell went to the old wooden file cabinet in the corner of the room and rummaged through the top drawer. While Powell looked for the list of veterinarians, Spencer struck a long wooden match and puffed his pipe to life.

After looking without success in the file cabinet, Powell went back to his desk and pawed through its drawers.

Not finding the list there, either, he started on a pile of random papers on the top of his desk. Spencer didn't know whether to be amused or horrified by Powell's display of inefficiency, but before he could make up his mind to get angry, Powell gave a small cry of triumph and pulled a slightly grimy piece of typing paper from the pile.

"Here it is," Powell said. "I must have had it out when we were setting up the tests yesterday." He handed the list to Spencer, who looked it over quickly. Of the ten veterinarians on the list, only four lived close enough to Logan's ranch to be considered. Beyond that, there was no apparent way to single out the right one, except by calling them one at a time and asking the right questions. For several minutes Spencer sat puffing on his pipe and thinking about what questions he could safely ask. Then he got up and walked over to the telephone.

15

The phone rang insistently and repeatedly and finally woke Roy Cardwell from the sleep he had unexpectedly fallen into, sitting in the big easy chair in front of the fireplace. He walked across the room and picked up the receiver, shaking his head to help clear the fuzziness. "Yes?" he said, still not quite awake.

"Roy, is that you?" said the voice on the other end.

"Yes, it's me. Who is this?"

"It's Spike Boynton, Roy. You all right?"

Boynton's name woke Cardwell up fully. "I'm fine, Spike. I just drifted off for a while. Something the matter?" Cardwell held his breath, hoping that Boynton wasn't going to ask him about the Logans.

"Well, yes and no. The truth is, Roy, I don't know whether anything's wrong or not. That's why I'm calling you."

"I'll do whatever I can, Spike. Just what are you confused about?"

"It's about Dan Logan," Boynton said.

I was afraid of that, Cardwell thought. He sat down on the chair next to the phone stand.

"Have you seen Dan?" he asked.

"No, I figured that was more your department than mine. But I saw his sheep, and I didn't like what I saw. Have you been out to the ranch lately?"

"No, I haven't. I understand it's been quarantined."

"That's part of what has me worried," Boynton said. "The quarantine is being enforced by a company of mean-looking army boys in full battle dress. And they handle their weapons like they're loaded and cocked."

"Well, I suppose they're helping the PHS some way. I certainly never heard of the army imposing a quarantine on its own."

"Neither have I. And there's something else. I'm willing to swear that those sheep didn't die of any kind of insecticide poisoning."

"What do you mean?"

"Well, you know that the PHS is suggesting insecticide poisoning as the cause of the sheep's death. And they called in all the ranchers around here to test them.

Gave them some vague story about undiluted malathion."

"I don't understand," Cardwell said. "What's wrong with that?"

"It's wrong because I saw those sheep, and they didn't die from any overdose of malathion. Besides, it doesn't make any sense for them to be making such a fuss about a bad batch of insecticide."

"Now, hold on a minute, Spike. You have to remember they're in business to protect the public. You have to figure they know what they're doing."

"I think they know what they're doing." Boynton said, annoyed. "I think they're pulling the wool over our eyes." He paused for a minute, then started again from a new angle. "You looked at Dan and Chris, didn't you?"

"Yes, I did," Cardwell said.

"Well, did they look to you like they were suffering from insecticide poisoning?"

Cardwell thought for a moment, weighing his response carefully, partly because of his promise to Dr. Spencer and partly because he was beginning to be confused himself. "Well, let me put it this way, Spike. It's not that I've never had a patient poisoned by breathing insecticide or swallowing it or having it on his skin too long. But that doesn't mean I'm an expert. I didn't spend too much time with Chris, but what I saw could have been insecticide poisoning."

"What do you mean, you didn't spend much time with Chris? He's your patient, isn't he?"

"Well, yes, he was." What do I say now, Cardwell wondered, then plunged ahead. "He was my patient, but I've turned the case over to someone else. Someone I thought could do a better job than I could."

"Who is that?"

"A young doctor named Holliford. He's had considerable experience with chemical toxication, and he certainly seemed to know what he was doing."

"I don't recognize the name. Has he been around long?"

"To tell you the truth, I don't know him very well. I asked around a little, and I understand he's worked at Carbon County a lot, lately. He seems to be from Fort Howard."

"Isn't that interesting. The army again."

"What are you getting at?"

"Roy, I think there's something very fishy going on here. I won't really be sure until some blood tests I took come back from the lab, but right now I'd bet six quarter-horse foals to an empty saltpeter box that those sheep were killed by nerve gas."

"I don't understand. What do you mean?" Cardwell stood up and began to pace back and forth as far as the phone cord would stretch.

"It's very simple. I've been doing some research, and while I haven't found anything that fits exactly, the symptoms I saw in those sheep look more like the effects of some kind of poison gas than anything else."

"I don't know, Spike. That's a long way to go on a little evidence."

"I'm not so sure," Boynton said. "It's happened before, you know. Unless you've forgotten what happened over in Skull Valley a couple of years ago."

"No, I remember about Skull Valley," Cardwell said,

although he hadn't actually thought of it until Spike mentioned it to him. Now that he did think of it, it made him nervous. He was beginning to see what Spike was getting at. There were a lot of similarities here to the accident at Dugway Proving Grounds. And the army did seem to be popping up all over the place. Still, it didn't make any sense. If Spike was right, then everybody else had to be lying. Cardwell couldn't believe it.

Boynton's voice interrupted Cardwell's thoughts. "Well, what do you think? Could Chris and Dan be suffering from exposure to poison gas?"

"No, I don't see how," Cardwell said. "From what I know, those gases kill you right away. I can't believe that's what made Chris ill. And Dan doesn't have any symptoms at all that I saw." As soon as he said it, Cardwell wondered if he shouldn't have kept his mouth shut. "I had a long talk with Dr. Spencer," he said quickly, "and I think the PHS has this pretty well in hand. I don't see any reason for you to worry about it at all."

"Well, I do. I think you're wrong, and as soon as I get those blood tests back from the lab, I'll prove it to you."

"Well, for everyone's sake, I hope this whole thing gets straightened out soon, whatever it is," Cardwell said.

After he hung up, Cardwell walked slowly back to the easy chair and sat down. He hadn't wanted to let Spike know it, but the conversation had shaken him up considerably. No matter how he looked at it, there were a lot of peculiar things going on. And now the way Chris's death had been handled was bothering him, too. Spencer's explanations had all seemed plausible enough, but

Cardwell still felt that he should have been told sooner, that he, as the boy's physician, should have been in on whatever was happening. If they could trust him now, why couldn't they have trusted him earlier?

The line of thought he was following led him to wonder about Dan Logan. There was no reason to suppose, in spite of Dan's apparent lack of symptoms, that there wasn't something about Dan's condition they might be hiding. Cardwell resolved that he would find out what was going on when he went to the hospital the next day. This time, he wouldn't let them put him off so easily.

16

A4DX693–P123–E
TOPSECRETCLASSQSCRAMBLE
CODEDESIGCOWBOYSIXTHREEFIVE
COLONEL HERBERT MORTON
JOINTCHIEFS PENTAGON
PRIORITY REDYELLOWYELLOW
BEGINS. REQUIRE SOONEST FULL SECURITY CHECK FOLLOWING J T SPIKE BOYNTON VETERINARIAN LAMONT WYOMING. TWX SAME CODING FORT HOWARD PRIORITY REDRED. SIGNED FRANKLIN COL.

17

As far as Tom Arnold was concerned, he was doing penance. It had been almost two years since he had been given a straight reporting assignment, ever since the day he had gone from substitute to full-time newscaster and commentator for KCPH, so this assignment was a kind of demotion, another slap on the wrist for Arnold's "snooping" into Spike Boynton's nerve-gas theory. The fact that the assignment was to get the army's response to those very allegations was just more salt on his wounds.

Arnold pushed open the door marked "Major R. Dannenmann, Information Office" and found himself in a stark, militarily efficient office. To the corporal sitting behind the gray metal desk, Arnold said, "I'm from KCPH."

"Oh, yes," the corporal said. "We're expecting you. Here's a copy of our statement." He took a mimeographed sheet from a pile of them on his desk and held it out to Arnold, who took it and glanced at it long enough to get an idea of its contents.

"I'd like to see Major Dannenmann," he said.

"Just a minute," the corporal said. He picked up his telephone and pushed the intercom buzzer. "Sir, KCPH is here," he said.

Behind Arnold, the outer door of the office opened and his cameraman and grip came in. At the same time, a florid, fortyish major came into the room from a door marked "Private." The major walked straight to Arnold, the only one of the television crew who didn't have his hands full of equipment, and shook hands.

"I'm Major Dannenmann," he said. "What can I do for you?"

"Tom Arnold, KCPH. We'd like to get your comments on those dead sheep."

Dannenmann turned to the corporal. "Didn't you give him one of those statements?"

"Yes, sir. But he asked to see you anyway."

Dannenmann turned back to face Tom Arnold. "Well, Mr. Arnold, you have our statement."

"We can't very well broadcast this," Arnold said, waving the sheet of paper. "All we want to do is get some footage of you answering a few questions."

"I'm sorry, Mr. Arnold, but all I can give you is that statement."

Arnold couldn't believe he was hearing correctly. He knew he couldn't go back to Ray Adams empty-handed. "There must be something," he said. "Couldn't we at least get a shot of you reading the statement?"

Dannenmann considered this. "Yes, I suppose that's all right," he said grudgingly. He said to the corporal, "We'll be in Conference Room B for a little while," and to Arnold, "Just follow me."

Dannenmann led them down the hall a short distance from his office to a small room, more like a classroom than a conference room. Arnold sat on one of the thirty or so folding chairs with wooden armrests and reread the army's statement while the cameraman and grip set up their equipment. Since Dannenmann was just going to stand on the raised platform at the front of the room and read the statement, they only put up two small lights and then put the camera on the tripod a little to the rear of the middle of the room.

As soon as everything was ready, Arnold got the suddenly stage-struck major in place and told him what to do. It was simple enough, just a few instructions about where to look and how loud to speak, then he tested the microphone and called, "Ready."

In response, the cameraman said, "Rolling," and Arnold gave the major the high sign.

Dannenmann cleared his throat, looked down at the single mimeographed page he was holding in his slightly shaking hands, and began to read. "Recently," he intoned, "questions have been raised in connection with the apparent insecticide poisoning of several hundred sheep on ranches near Fort Howard. The army wishes to clarify its position on this matter. The army has conducted no tests of any toxic material in the vicinity of the affected ranches in the Medicine Creek area. However, Colonel Alan A. Nickerson, commanding officer of Fort Howard, has placed the Fort's facilities at the disposal of the Public Health Service to aid in its investigation. The army intends to continue its full cooperation with the Public Health Service, out of concern for the safety of everyone in the area."

Dannenmann stopped and cleared his throat again. He looked at Arnold, sitting in the first row of folding chairs. "Was that O.K.?" he asked.

Arnold nodded. From the back of the room, the cameraman said, "It looked good to me."

18

The last faint light of day filtered through the window curtains of Dan Logan's hospital room. In the closed, almost dark room, there was no sound except the steady rhythm of Logan's breathing.

He lay still, on his back, asleep, then gradually began to stir. His eyes opened, closed again, opened. He blinked and found that his eyelids felt heavy and coarse, scraping dryly and grainily over his eyes. His mouth, too, was dry, and furry, like he remembered it being that time he had the hangover, after he had gotten so drunk the night before over some woman he met in Purdy's. It had been his first attempt at having a good time after JoAnn died, and somewhere along the line something had soured him so badly on what he was doing, or thought he was doing, that he had started to drink very heavily, until he got so wild with alcohol and grief that someone had to haul him out of there. He had never found out who it was that had taken him home that night, but from the little he had heard about it afterward, he gathered that it had taken perhaps as many as three strong men to keep him from breaking up Purdy's place completely. But all he could remember was the hangover, and after that he'd just settled into the ranch work and raising Chris, and that was enough to keep him busy and content.

Gradually, as Logan became more awake, the past

merged back into the present. Logan looked around the room, as much as he could see with his head facing the door. Then, with some effort, he turned his head to the other side. He was stiff, and he wanted to turn over and get off his back. When he had his head turned, though, he noticed something odd. There was something taped to his arm, inside the elbow. He looked down at it and saw that there was a clear plastic tube coming out from under the tape. He traced the tube with his eyes, first back up toward his shoulder, and then up over the bed, along a shiny, thin tubular stand, to some sort of valve attached to a big bottle that was hanging mouth-down from the stand.

What the hell is going on? he thought and reached over with his free hand to find the bell-push that was clipped to his sheet. He groped for it, unable to move much or see what he was doing, found it, and pushed the button. He hoped there was a nurse outside who would notice that he was calling.

While he was waiting for the nurse, Logan began to drift off into sleep. He realized what was happening and fought against it, blinking his eyes rapidly and clenching his teeth, unwilling to let himself fall asleep until he could ask someone what was going on and find out something about Chris. He couldn't remember exactly what was wrong with Chris, but he knew that he was worried about him, that Chris was sick, and that he hadn't seen him in what seemed like a very long time.

As Logan was fighting to keep his thoughts in focus, his door opened and a nurse came in. "Is something the matter?" she asked in a distant, professional tone.

Logan started to speak and found that it wasn't easy

to make the words come out. He managed a barely intelligible but clearly annoyed, "What the hell is this?"

The nurse didn't have to hear all the words; she was more or less certain she knew what was bothering Logan. "That's just an intravenous," she said soothingly. "It's nothing to worry about. They do it all the time."

Logan took a deep, tired breath and tried to wet his parched lips with his tongue. He spoke again, slowly, but more distinctly. "Where is my son?" He tried to push himself up toward a sitting position.

The nurse put a hand on his shoulder and pushed him gently but firmly back down. "Now, Mr. Logan," she said, "you just rest and don't worry about a thing."

Logan, resisting her as much as he could, said, "I want to see Chris. Where's Dr. Holliford?" Exhausted by his efforts, he let his head fall back on the pillow.

The nurse patted him on the shoulder. "Now, now, Mr. Logan, everything is all right. You just need some sleep."

Logan lay staring up at the ceiling. The nurse disappeared from his field of view, and he could hear her going around the bed to the intravenous stand and fiddling with it. Then she left the room, closing the door quietly behind her. From the bottle suspended next to the bed, the sedative solution ran down the tube and into Logan's veins, flowing at a rate doubled by the nurse's adjustment of the valve. In less than a minute, Logan was sound asleep.

19

Sitting in his back-bedroom study, Spike Boynton wondered what Dr. Spencer had to say to him. There was no question in his mind of what he had to say to Dr. Spencer. He was more certain than ever that the Public Health Service was part of a cover-up being engineered by someone, probably the army, and he was going to confront Spencer with his suspicions and see what he said.

At about eight-fifteen the front doorbell rang. Boynton had told his wife hc needed the house to himself, so she had taken the children with her over to her mother's for the night. He knew he'd have to give her a better explanation tomorrow, when she came back, but for now she had just accepted the fact that there was something happening that was important enough for him to ask her to leave him alone.

Boynton let Spencer in, and after they had introduced themselves they went into the parlor. Boynton turned on both lamps, so he could see Spencer's face clearly, and offered the PHS official the best chair. "Can I get you a bourbon, Dr. Spencer?" Boynton asked, eager to keep Spencer feeling comfortable and unsuspecting.

"Yes, thanks. If you'll join me," Spencer said, for much the same reasons.

They sat and sipped at their drinks for a few minutes,

each taking the other's measure, waiting for the strain of first meeting to wear off. It was Boynton who broke the ice.

"Well, Dr. Spencer," he said. "What is it that brings you here tonight?"

Spencer shifted in the big, overstuffed chair, sitting forward to add weight to his words. "I understand you've been making some accusations about the Public Health Service. I thought you might find it more direct if you made them to me instead of to news reporters. You're much more likely to get answers to your questions that way, and less likely to cause trouble in things you don't know anything about."

Got to hand it to him for laying it on the line, Boynton thought. He said, "Well, now, I think you're being a little strong in what you say. I don't go around making accusations about things I don't know anything about."

Spencer was annoyed, but he kept it under control. "I'm sorry. Of course you don't." He smiled. "There's no sense in our fighting over a bad turn of phrase. Why don't you tell me what you think is happening, and I'll see if I can't put your mind at rest."

Boynton smiled thinly. "All right. That will save us some time, anyway. I won't bother you with a long list of research I've done, either. I'll just tell you my conclusions. My well-thought-out, carefully documented conclusions." Boynton stopped to light a cigarette, taking his time about it and enjoying the knowledge that he had Spencer hanging, waiting to hear what he had to say.

Boynton took a deep drag on the cigarette and said, "About two hundred sheep, or more likely, three hundred by now, have died on Dan Logan's ranch. Another twenty-five or so were removed from other ranches by the Public Health Service. The official reason given for the deaths is insecticide poisoning, probably from an overdose of malathion. Unfortunately for that story, I spent an hour examining some of the sheep on Dan Logan's ranch, and I can state without any question that the sheep I saw were not suffering from malathion poisoning. Besides, something like that is no reason for a quarantine, certainly not a quarantine enforced by a company of armed soldiers.

"I also understand that you have Dan and Chris Logan under quarantine in the hospital, being tended by a doctor from Fort Howard. That doesn't make much sense, if they have malathion poisoning. A quarantine is pointless. Nobody's about to catch malathion poisoning from them. So I decided, to be frank about it, that the whole thing was a crock of shit. I did some research, and I've come to the conclusion that what must really be involved is nerve gas."

Spencer didn't react visibly to Boynton's charges. After a moment's hesitation, he began to speak. "I understand how you feel about all this. It must seem very strange to you, and even somewhat inconsistent, as you said. But I think I can explain it all to your satisfaction."

Boynton interrupted him. "Before you do that," he said, "I'd better tell you that I took some blood from those sheep and sent it to the university for analysis. I even told them some things to look for. And I've been talking to a veterinarian who was recommended to me, a very good veterinarian, I'm told. He practices over in Utah, somewhere near Skull Valley, I think." Boynton took another deep drag on his cigarette. "Sorry to interrupt," he said mildly. "Why don't you go on now and tell me your story."

Spencer didn't say anything, but pulled his pipe and pouch from his jacket pocket. Filling the pipe, he thought that Boynton was a good deal more clever than any of them had guessed. As a result, Spencer found himself in a bad bind. He had to get Boynton cooled off, or the whole thing would blow sky-high, but if he involved himself too deeply, it would surely drag the Public Health Service through the mud with the army if the story came out in spite of all their efforts. And at this point, Spencer wasn't at all sure that it wouldn't. Too many people knew too much already.

As he lit his pipe, Spencer was aware that Boynton was watching him closely, waiting to see what he would do, with a growing air of superiority, like a man waiting for a good shot at a treed coon. And he does have me treed, Spencer thought. It won't do me any good to try to sell him the other story. But maybe there's another way. He drained his glass and looked intently at Boynton.

"You've been very thorough, Dr. Boynton, and I find it hard to argue with your logic. But let me ask you one question. In coming up with this theory, did you ever wonder why everyone was being so careful to keep what you suspect covered up, if it is true?"

Boynton's eyes widened slightly. Spencer gauged that he had interested the veterinarian enough to get him to listen for a while.

"After all," Spencer said, "there have been accidents with nerve gas before. Far worse accidents. At Skull Valley, which you just mentioned, there were more than six thousand sheep killed. Even if what you suspect is true, it would be minor compared to that, and what happened there is general knowledge these days."

"Maybe so," Boynton said, "if that's all there is to it. But it seems important enough for a lot of people to be going to a lot of effort telling a lot of lies around here. And there are two people in the hospital. That's not what I call minor."

"When I came here tonight," Spencer said, "it was so you could present your suspicions to me directly, instead of to the press. Now, it seems to me that I'm not the only one you suspect." He paused. "If I assured you of the serious nature of this matter, could I get your word that you wouldn't speak to anyone about it until I had a chance to satisfy you further?"

"I don't know about that. I don't want to shut myself up for no good reason. If there's something going on, why shouldn't I be able to talk about it?"

"I'm not asking you to agree to keep quiet forever, not unless you're convinced that you should. All I want is to be sure you won't run off to some reporter before you know the whole story."

Boynton thought about it. "All right," he said. "I'll keep whatever you say to myself until you've had a chance to let me know your side of it."

"Good," Spencer said. "Now, since you seem to feel that the army is involved in this somehow, I think it might be a good idea for you to talk to someone at Fort Howard. As it happens, I've been working with Colonel Nickerson on this quarantine, and I think if I ask him to, he'll be willing to talk to you about this. You understand, I'm not saying the army is involved, but if you have questions about what the army has been doing, I think you ought to get the answers from them."

Again, Boynton was taken by surprise. He hadn't expected things to come this far this fast. He lit another cigarette. "Sure," he said. "That sounds right. When do you think I can see him?"

"I'll call him in the morning. If you're free tomorrow, I'm sure he'll be able to see you then." Spencer stood up.

"All right. Fine," Boynton said.

As Spencer went out the door, he said, "Remember, not a word to anyone about this."

Shaking his head, Boynton closed the door and walked back into the parlor. Jesus, he thought as he sat down to consider what had just happened. Jesus H. Christ.

20

A4DX693-P159-E
TOPSECRETCLASSQSCRAMBLE
CODEDESIGCOWBOYSEVENSIXZERO
CODESQAREDBUTTERFLYGREEN
GENERAL SAMUEL HILL
JOINTCHIEFS PENTAGON
PRIORITY BLUEBLUERED
BEGINS: REPORT DAYTWO EAGLE. SITUATION
SUBSTANTIALLY UNCHANGED EXCEPT FOR DEATH OF
CHRISTOPHER LOGAN EARLY MORNING. AUTOPSY
PERFORMED BY HOLLIFORD MAJ AND KAGLE MAJ

WITH HOSPITAL PATHOLOGIST. RELEVANT ORGANS
SHIPPED DENVER FOR EXAMINATION. PUBLIC HEALTH
COOPERATION LEVEL ONE FULLY ACCEPTED BUT ONE
DANGER AREA LOCAL TVNEWS NAMING NERVE GAS.
STANDARD BLANKET DENIAL ISSUED INFOFFICER FORT
HOWARD. RUMOR SOURCE VETERINARIAN J T SPIKE
BOYNTON LOCAL BEING ISOLATED. FULL PRESS TEAM
DISPATCHED YOURHOUSE BY WHEELER MAJ
ZERONINEHUNDRED MYHOUSE. EVALUATION UNCHANGED
POSITIVE DEGREE TWO. SENSITIVE PERIOD DATE PLUS
TWENTYFOUR HOURS. OPTIMAL STRATEGY REMAINS
SECUREST HANDLING PRESENT DISPOSITION.
SIGNED FRANKLIN COL.

FOUR

1

Even by Wyoming standards, it was a beautiful dawn. The sky was clear, except for a patch of high, thin cirrus that reflected the pale pink light fringing the horizon. A faint, cool breeze ruffled the grass and the treetops and provided a counterpoint to the early morning song of humming insects and awakening birds.

In the wire-enclosed dog run at the side of the dark, quiet Parker ranch house, Dan Logan's sheepdog, Emily, lay stiff and motionless, her muzzle matted with blood. The Parker dog sniffed curiously at the body, disturbing only slightly the flies that had gathered around the dead dog.

2

The hospital was still quiet when Matthew Spencer pushed open the staff entrance door and walked quickly past the closed doors of the semiprivate rooms and the glass-fronted entrance to the nursery. On his way by the nurses' station, he heard someone calling his name and turned to find Bert Holliford hurrying up an intersecting corridor followed by a tall, thin man in an orderly's uniform.

"What is it?" Spencer asked impatiently as the younger doctor reached him.

Holliford said, "I'm glad I saw you. I wanted you to meet Corporal Simpson." The tall "orderly," standing now at Holliford's side, nodded to Spencer, who looked briefly at him, then back to Holliford for clarification.

"Colonel Franklin thought we should bring someone in from security to keep an eye on Logan," Holliford explained.

"That's an excellent idea." Spencer looked at Simpson again, with new interest. Even in the anonymous white orderly's uniform, Simpson looked hard and competent.

Holliford said, "Corporal, this is Dr. Spencer. You are to do whatever he tells you, unless you have specific orders to the contrary."

"Yes, sir."

Spencer said, "Good." He looked at his watch. "Excuse me," he said, "but I have to get going. I'm meeting Fred Powell in Mr. Fairman's office. There's been a slight mixup over the coroner's report. I'll see you later."

"All right," Holliford said to Spencer's already retreating back. "If I'm not in pathology, I'll be in the lounge."

3

On his way into Rawlins, Roy Cardwell tried to go over the Logan situation in his mind, but he found that he was making very little progress. He couldn't reconcile Boynton's theory with what Holliford and Spencer had told him; he couldn't believe that he had simply and maliciously been lied to; and yet he couldn't just dismiss what Spike had said. And there was still that nagging feeling that Spencer had not been completely forthright with him. He could see only one way to resolve his confusion, and that was to try to get some more information.

He parked his car in one of the spaces marked "Visiting Physician," and went into the hospital through the staff entrance. Before going to see what he could find out, he walked to Dan Logan's room to look in on his friend. It wasn't something he wanted particularly to do; his freight of guilty knowledge burdened him tremendously, and he knew it would be a strain talking to the rancher without disclosing that Chris was dead. But he felt that Logan deserved at least a friendly visit. He was probably going out of his mind with concern and frustration.

The door to Logan's room was closed. Cardwell knocked lightly so he wouldn't disturb Logan if he was sleeping. When there was no response, Cardwell turned the knob quietly and pushed the door open so he could look into the room. In the faint morning light, he could just make out the outline of Logan, lying on his back asleep. Then, as he was closing the door, Cardwell saw something that made him change direction and walk into the room for a better look.

As he stood next to the bed looking at the soundly sleeping rancher and the intravenous feeding apparatus, Cardwell thought, here's something else I have to find out about. He turned and walked quickly from the room.

At the nurses' station, he asked the nurse on duty, "Who ordered the intravenous for Mr. Logan?"

The nurse, who knew Dr. Cardwell as one of the kinder and more gentle of the doctors who used the hospital, was surprised at the brusqueness of his tone.

"I think it must have been Dr. Holliford," she said. "It was before I came on."

"Do you know what he's getting?"

"Just glucose," the nurse said mildly. "And I think he's getting a sedative every third bottle."

Cardwell was troubled. He drummed his fingers on the black plastic counter of the nurses' station. "Do you have Mr. Logan's chart?" he asked.

"I'll get it for you."

The nurse turned to the chart rack. The slot marked "Logan" was empty, so she lifted out a few of the other charts in adjacent slots to see if someone had misplaced the Logan chart. The other charts were in the correct places.

"It doesn't seem to be here," she said. Then, "I'm pretty sure Dr. Holliford had it. He's been working in Room 113. You might check in there."

Cardwell said, "Thank you," and went down the corridor to Room 113. The door was slightly ajar, but he knocked anyway, then went in. There was no one in the room, which was used by the staff and visiting doctors for research, report writing, and occasionally for private consultations with the family of a patient. Cardwell noticed that the "In Use" sign was on the door, adorned with a tag that said "Holliford/Private." The desk was strewn with papers and there was a stack of books and journals on the couch. Holliford had apparently been doing a lot of work in Room 113. Cardwell turned to leave, then hesitated. Why not look for the chart here, he thought. Maybe in the process I'll learn something.

4

Notes and Impressions/Fort Howard
Day Three—Boynton meeting
J. T. Boynton, called "Spike," apparently is a better than average veterinarian, and a hard man to argue with. He's known D. L. about ten years, tended his livestock for eight. Initial conversations last night between B. and S. made clear the impossibility of doing anything to convince B. his nerve-gas theory was wrong. Only available strategy was complete conversion. This worked, with reservations. B. briefed two hours at provisional topsec level, clearance now applied for, retroactively. He buys basic concept, admits necessity of preparedness, etc.,

etc., also sees relative value of retaining economic advantages of army presence locally. (Chivington not mentioned here at any time.) But a recurring mention of "dishonesty" by B. is negative indication.
Prognosis: fair. B. will hold, in relative absence of outside pressure.
Strategy: keep B. inside, as "consultant" or in some similar capacity to reinforce his feelings of complicity.
Note: absence of S. from meeting with B. interesting. Publicly, S. is keeping completely clear of us. Query: Is he preparing to cut loose if there is trouble?

5

At the beginning, Cardwell had felt guilty at rummaging through a colleague's files and notes, but he was driven to continue by a growing feeling that important information was being kept from him. Even though he had turned the direct handling of the case over to Holliford, he still felt that he was owed some kind of honest reports on Logan's condition. As the referring physician and the man who knew the patient's history, as well as the man who would be responsible for Logan's care after he left the hospital, Cardwell needed to know what was going on.

As he sorted through the mass of material Holliford had scattered through the room, Cardwell's sense that something was wrong grew stronger. He began to feel like a detective, or a man putting together a jigsaw puzzle out of uncounted papers and reports, with no pattern to follow in guessing which pieces fit together. He became so lost in what he was doing that he even stopped worrying about what he would say if Holliford walked in on him.

Gradually, Cardwell began to understand what kind of research Holliford had been doing, and what kind of records he had been keeping. The first few times he had any indications of it, he had ignored them, but as he went on, the conclusion became inescapable. Holliford was gathering data as if for an experiment of some kind. It had been too long since Cardwell had been in medical school or even one of the university's medical refresher courses for him to be sure what the experiment was about, but the quantity of data Holliford was amassing, and the way he was writing it down were unlike anything Cardwell had ever seen used for diagnosis. The thing that was most infuriating was that the essential information, the things Cardwell could use to tell what it all meant, was nowhere in sight. Unless he could find something in the steel box on the shelf over the desk, which meant finding some way to unlock it, or to break it open.

6

Holliford stood next to the long white counter in the pathology laboratory waiting for the hospital pathologist to set up the microscope for him to use. After almost two full days working with the pathologist, Holliford still couldn't get over how protective the man was of his laboratory and morgue. Like a woman in her kitchen, Holliford thought. Behind the thought was the realization that he himself was that way with his own laboratory, at the Fort, even to the extent of being angry if someone else fed the experimental animals, at least after a test had begun. Before they became his subjects, Holliford didn't care who fed them.

The pathologist finished what he was doing and indicated to Holliford that he could start working. Holliford took the pathologist's place on the small stool next to the microscope, reached for a box of slide glass, and began to prepare a slide from the latest sample of Dan Logan's blood. Working slowly and carefully, he made up three slides, one without stain and two stained to show more clearly the things he was looking for. He put the first slide on the stage of the microscope and adjusted the fine focus.

Roy Cardwell burst into the laboratory and saw Holliford bent over the microscope, with the pathologist watching from over his shoulder. Cardwell started toward the two men, calling Holliford's name as he hurried across the gleaming, antiseptic laboratory.

Holliford, annoyed, looked up from the microscope.

"Can I talk to you for a minute?" Cardwell said in a tone that was more demand than request.

"Is it important?" Holliford said. "I'm busy right now." Cardwell's tone and his drawn, intense expression had changed Holliford's annoyance to apprehension.

"Yes, it's very important," Cardwell said, unyielding.

The pathologist, uncomfortable in the middle of what was clearly a serious confrontation, said, "I'm going to get some coffee," and left the two men alone in the laboratory.

Holliford's impulse was to run and hide, to call the Fort for advice, anything to avoid what he knew was coming. For want of an alternative, he tried to brazen it out. He put what he hoped was a note of impatience in his voice and said, "Well, what is it?"

Cardwell took a breath and said very slowly and distinctly, "I just saw your file on Dan Logan."

This time, the impatience in Holliford's voice was real. He knew he had locked that file in the steel box marked "Confidential." Icily, he said, "Oh. Really?"

"I thought maybe you could explain a few things."

"That depends. What is it you want to know?" Stop playing cute with me, old man, Holliford thought.

Again slowly, almost painfully, Cardwell said, "I saw your electroencephalograms, and I tried to compare them with the one you marked in Bruni and Kramer." He had to look at some notes he had made to remind himself of the names.

"Now, maybe I'm not the one to be making a diagnosis," Cardwell went on, "but it looked to me like Dan has what they called Briggs-Myhrberg syndrome." Again, he had to refer to his hastily scrawled notes.

As quickly as it had come, Holliford's anger evaporated. He was in a very tight situation, one that could turn everything the wrong way if he wasn't careful. He began choosing his words more circumspectly. "Yes," he said. "That's more or less correct."

"But if I understood the book right, that syndrome is

almost always fatal."

"That's right." No avoiding that one, Holliford thought.

After a short silence, it became apparent to Cardwell that Holliford wasn't going to volunteer anything. "Well," he prodded, "do you have a prognosis?"

Holliford was stuck. He wasn't authorized to talk about this to anyone, but it was clear to him that he couldn't afford to let Cardwell go away angry and unanswered. The only thing he could think to do was to answer the question and do his best to calm Cardwell so the damage could be undone later. He said, "Well, I might as well be perfectly frank with you. I don't expect him to live more than another week."

"Are you sure of that?"

"Yes, I am."

Cardwell had been holding his own anger in check, hoping desperately that he had drawn the wrong conclusions from the file in Holliford's surprisingly easy-to-open steel box. Now that his worst fears were confirmed, his anger at the way he and Logan had been treated began to come to the surface. "Does Dr. Spencer know about this?" he asked.

"Yes," Holliford said. "He does."

"Well, why didn't you tell me? Dan Logan is my patient," Cardwell snapped. He did not expect Holliford to have an answer to his question, so when the younger man remained silent, looking at the floor, Cardwell went on.

"Why do you have him under sedation?" he asked.

Holliford said, "I thought it would help him rest."

"He surely doesn't need constant sedation."

"Well . . ." Holliford started to protest.

"I think he should be taken off the I.V."

Holliford suddenly wanted to be outside. He walked the length of the white counter to the back door of the laboratory and out into the parking lot that was behind the hospital at the basement level. The sun was bright and warm on his chest and shoulders, and a noon breeze cooled his face. He turned to face Cardwell, who had come out of the hospital behind him.

"Does he know about his condition?" Cardwell was saying.

"No, and frankly, I'd rather you didn't tell him."

"Why not? He has the right to know."

"Under the circumstances, I don't see that there's any point in getting him upset. It can't help him."

The faint sarcasm in Holliford's tone didn't mask an underlying note of plaintiveness. Cardwell realized that Holliford was uncertain, afraid of something. "I don't agree with you," Cardwell said strongly. "I've known Dan Logan for forty years, and I know he'd want me to tell him."

"I really don't think you should." Without willing it, Holliford was shaking his finger at Cardwell, shouting at him. "I have to insist!"

Cardwell didn't flinch. "I'm sorry, but I'm going to tell him," he said, and then, like a teacher to a smugly wayward pupil, "You know, I don't think you've handled this very well at all. I'm going up to see Dan, and then I'm going to have a long talk with Dr. Spencer." He turned and strode purposefully back into the hospital.

Holliford, close behind him, snatched up the receiver

of the pathology lab phone and quickly dialed the administrator's office extension. Thank God Spencer is in the hospital, he thought. He'll know what to do.

7

In fact, Spencer was just leaving the administrator's office when Holliford's call came. He had straightened out the difficulties about the coroner's report on Christopher Logan and was on his way to lunch with Fred Powell when Fairman's secretary intercepted him with the telephone.

Holliford was very quick and to the point. He sounded to Spencer like a man with special knowledge of the imminent end of the world, he put so much panic into his few words: "Cardwell knows. He's on his way to tell Logan."

Spencer said merely, "Right," hung up, and snapped at the receptionist, "Get the orderly room. I want Mr. Logan moved. Anywhere. Just get him out of his room and out of the hall within thirty seconds." The receptionist stared at him, bewildered.

"Now!" he said, and she picked up the telephone and began dialing.

Spencer skirted the receptionist's desk, slammed open the office door and rushed down the hall to Logan's room, where Corporal Simpson was slouched in a chair opposite the door.

"Simpson. Mr. Logan is being moved. Go in and get him ready."

Simpson jerked himself out of the chair and into Logan's room. Spencer's tone was enough to tell him something important was up. Quickly, he wrapped the sheet and blankets around the drugged rancher, barely noticing the fact that he was lifting and pushing more than two hundred pounds of dead weight. He unlocked the wheels at the base of the stand that held the intravenous bottle and checked to see that everything was tightly fastened and secure. Before he was finished, two orderlies wheeled a stretcher into the room. Simpson helped them move Logan from the bed onto the stretcher and guided them as they wheeled the stretcher and the stand through the door and into the corridor. When the stretcher was well on its way to the empty room at the end of the corridor, Spencer stepped into Logan's room with Simpson and closed the door.

8

Cardwell came up from the basement, his anger making him move more quickly than he had for several years. Passing the nurses' station, he was vaguely aware of a nurse holding a telephone receiver out toward him. He said, "Take a message," assuming, correctly, that it was just Holliford trying again to dissuade him from seeing Dan. On his way down the corridor, he almost ran into a nurse coming out of one of the rooms with a tray, and he did not even notice the orderly who was pushing a stretcher into the room at the far end of the corridor.

Outside Logan's room, Cardwell stopped and took a couple of slow, deep breaths to calm himself. He had no illusions about how hard it was going to be to tell Dan the news, but he was determined to go ahead with it. He knocked on the door and opened it.

Inside, he stopped short, his hand still on the doorknob, staring at the empty but rumpled bed and the figure of Dr. Spencer, leaning against the window sill. He was vaguely aware of someone else in the room, just out of sight at his left. He let go of the doorknob and took a few uncertain steps into the room. "Where is Mr. Logan?" he asked.

Spencer came forward toward Cardwell. "He's having a few more tests," Spencer said soothingly.

Cardwell wasn't willing to let himself be put off so easily. "I want to see him," he said. He could feel his hands, unbidden, clenching into angry fists.

"There's no reason to be upset, Dr. Cardwell," Spencer said. "By the way, have you met Mr. Simpson?"

Cardwell turned to look at the other man, who had moved behind him to stand blocking the now-closed door. Cardwell's immediate impression was of someone impassively, almost dully, threatening. He turned back to Spencer, about to protest this apparent forcible detention, but the PHS man interrupted him, still speaking slowly and soothingly.

"Why don't you sit down for a minute, Dr. Cardwell? We have a lot to talk about."

Cardwell would have been glad to argue with Spencer, about anything at all, but he wanted desperately to find out what had been going on, so he swallowed his anger and sat down in the visitor's chair next to the bed.

Spencer rested one hip on the bed's footboard and looked down at Cardwell. He said, "You have to understand that we have a very difficult situation here. This is something that all of us have found hard to accept and hard to deal with. I can't say we always did the right thing. What you have to realize, though, is that our prime consideration has been to handle this with the best interests of the community always foremost in our minds."

Cardwell started to break in, but Spencer held up his hand. "Before you say anything, Dr. Cardwell, I think we should make this a completely private conversation. Simpson, I'd like you to wait outside, please. Just outside the door. And see that we aren't disturbed for any reason until I tell you that we're finished."

From the way Spencer said it, there was little doubt in Cardwell's mind that Simpson was being told not only to keep unwanted visitors out of the room, but to keep Cardwell in as well.

When Simpson had gone out into the hall and closed the door behind him, Spencer said, "Perhaps it would be easiest for both of us if you told me what was bothering you."

"It's very simple, Dr. Spencer," Cardwell said angrily. "I've just learned that Dan Logan is dying. Not only that, but I learned that Dr. Holliford has suspected it for some time. And when I confronted him with it, and asked him why it had been kept from me, he said that you knew about it as well. Now I want to know why I've been kept in the dark about my own patient. And why it's so important to Dr. Holliford that I don't tell Dan Logan he's dying. For that matter, I'd like to know why you've engineered this little conference. The whole thing seems very peculiar. I might even say unethical." Cardwell stopped. He felt like he'd just run a long race, one he hadn't had a chance to train for.

Spencer took his pipe out of his pocket and started to fill it. "Well, Dr. Cardwell," he said, "that's a lot of questions all at once. I'll do what I can to answer them. First of all, let me say that Dr. Holliford and I do, in fact, expect Mr. Logan to die in the near future. Perhaps as soon as three or four days. And it's true that we've had indications of this for a little while, say since early yesterday, just after we talked to you.

"You have to realize that we've been very busy since then. Chris Logan's death took us more or less by surprise, and when we realized that his father was going to die as well, we had to revise our original estimation of what we were dealing with. If it was so much more virulent than we had originally supposed, there was no way to judge the accuracy of our projections of the danger represented by the small concentrations we found in our initial tests. In particular, we became very concerned about runoff into Medicine Creek and possible reaccumulation downstream. We had every intention of filling you in on the latest information we had about Dan Logan, but if you think about it, this is our first opportunity. We were certainly in no position to spend time tracking you down, and we knew that you would be here at the hospital sometime today." Spencer paused to gauge Cardwell's reaction.

For the moment, the country doctor was stymied. He felt deflated, as if Spencer had found some hidden valve and let out the hot air that had puffed him up with anger. Yet, even as he chided himself for imagining a host of devils where in reality there were none, Cardwell felt somehow unsatisfied, as if something important had eluded him.

Seeing that Cardwell was accepting his story, Spencer went on. "Now, you asked why it's so important that Mr. Logan not be told about his condition, or about his son." Spencer stood up and walked to the window, where he leaned his hip on the sill. "First of all, let me say that I understand your concern for Mr. Logan, and I appreciate that all this places you in an awkward situation. I want to assure you that I'm concerned about Mr. Logan as well. But my prime concern has to be the hundreds of other people who live in the area, and their lives and their livelihoods.

"We weren't able to do anything at all for Mr. Logan's son, and I strongly doubt that we'll be able to help Mr. Logan, either, at this point. But we must learn something about what we're dealing with here. Suppose we were wrong when we decided that there was no further danger of contamination. Suppose there is a heavy rain and large amounts of this—" Spencer seemed to search for a word—"this toxin were to accumulate in Medicine Creek, and as a result we were to be faced with other cases of poisoning. We have to try to get as much information as we can if we want to avoid being this helpless the next time.

"If you tell Mr. Logan now, it will upset him tremendously. It has to. And the horrible part of it is that it can't do him any good at all. On the other hand, our being able to study the effects of the poison may save many lives in the future. I'm not suggesting that he be kept in the dark until the end, but I want to make you see how important just another day or two could be."

Cardwell said, "I don't see what difference it could make if he knew."

"Well, we're getting a little outside my field now, but I gather from Dr. Holliford that he has been finding some symptoms of a depression of certain brain functions. If he's going to be able to tell what is happening in that area, he has to be sure that there isn't any effect from, say, severe emotional disturbance."

Cardwell stood up and began to pace back and forth in the small space between the bed and the door. With one hand he rubbed his jaw and the back of his neck as he paced. "I don't know," he said. "What you say seems to make sense. But there is still so much going on that doesn't make any sense at all. What about the army? Why is the army so interested in all this? Why is the only doctor involved an army man? And why are there armed soldiers on the Logan ranch? And what about Spike Boynton? He's very sure that the sheep died from some kind of war gas. I can't make any of it fit in with what you've said. And if the dangers are so great, why haven't more experts been called in? I'd expect the place to be crawling with doctors and chemists and whatnot, but the only people I've seen are you and Dr. Holliford."

Spencer puffed at his pipe. "Of course, you're right. The truth is, you're just a little ahead of me. Until now, I've been more concerned about avoiding panic and unjustified rumors. But now we have to find out as much as we can as quickly as we can. That's clearly most important. As for the army's involvement, well, I'm not really equipped for a large-scale emergency quarantine like this, and the people at Fort Howard are naturally concerned about the safety of the residents in the area, so they've agreed to help all they can. It's just our good fortune that Dr. Holliford has the knowledge he does."

Spencer stopped for a minute. He seemed to Cardwell to be going over what he was about to say. When he did speak, it was slowly and deliberately. "That leaves this question of nerve gas. I have spoken to Dr. Boynton about what he saw, because I don't want to leave any stone unturned in my attempts to find out what this poison might be. I think it is important that you know that at this stage, we haven't ruled anything out. Personally, I doubt severely that anything like nerve gas is involved, and I might say that Dr. Boynton himself has somewhat revised his opinion, as I understand it. And, of course, I can't see any reason to question the statements made by Fort Howard in that regard."

"No, I suppose not." Cardwell sat down again. He was still confused and troubled, but he couldn't find any fault at all with Spencer's argument.

9

Once he was sure that Spencer was going to deal with Cardwell, Holliford went to Room 113 to see what damage Cardwell had done and exactly what files he had gotten into. He found the room in only moderate disarray, the most notable thing being the steel file box standing on the desk, its open lid bent out of shape around the lock. Holliford looked around for the instrument Cardwell had used to open the box and found a letter opener with a broken blade. The stub of the blade was bent and nicked, as if after it was broken it had been used to pry at something hard and unyielding. Unyielding up to a point, Holliford thought as he looked at the contents of the file box piled up haphazardly on the desk.

Holliford next checked the drawers of the desk and found that the bottom left drawer was still locked. He offered a silent prayer of thanks to a God he didn't believe in and unlocked the drawer, finding his personal leather file case intact and locked. He had known he was being lazy when he brought it from the Fort, but it had come in handy to have it with him. He shuddered, though, at the thought of how hard it would have been to salvage the situation if Cardwell had found the case and the papers it contained: a complete description of the projected and actual clinical observations in MX3 exposure of human-sized animals. As Holliford remembered the file, there were even some references to Chivington in it. Holliford put the case back in the drawer and locked it.

He was straightening up his files on Logan and replacing them in the jimmied file box when Major Kagle came into the room carrying a tape recorder.

"Got the autopsy tapes," Kagle said. "I thought we ought to listen to them before they go to Denver. Maybe we missed something the first time around."

Holliford agreed, and the two men cleared an area on the desk and set the machine up, each taking a large pad so he could make notes as he listened. Kagle turned the machine on, and after a few seconds they heard the voice of the pathologist reading the number on the body tag and Chris Logan's name. Kagle pressed the fast-forward lever to get past the initial few steps of the autopsy, since they were not really concerned with the external examination. He released the lever, and the pathologist's voice resumed, thin and mechanical-sounding. "I have exposed the internal organs, which appear normal in size, shape, and color, except for an equivocal cyanotic appearance of the heart."

The pathologist stopped speaking and there was only the noise of the tape hissing through the recorder and a metallic clatter of instruments. Then the voice again: "The pleura show petechiae not consistent with the age of the subject." There was another pause, and again the hiss and noise of instruments, this time mixed with other, less pleasant sounds.

There was a knock at the door, and Kagle quickly turned off the tape recorder. "Come in," Holliford said.

The door opened and Dr. Spencer came into the room, looking tired but pleased. He closed the door behind him, pushed some books and papers to one side of the couch, and sat down in the place he had cleared for himself.

"Well," he said, "I just got through with Dr. Cardwell."

"What did he say?" Holliford asked.

Spencer shook his head. "Well, we went back and forth with it for quite a while there, but I think it will be all right. He's agreed to take himself off the case."

Holliford brightened. "Really? That's a relief. Much better than I expected." Kagle, too, looked relieved.

Spencer held up a hand. "Don't get carried away. I don't think he'll stay out of it for good. He won't bother you for a day or two, but after that I can't say. Somebody is going to have to make a policy decision on what to do about Cardwell between now and then, because I don't think that we can get away with any more emergency measures like this one. You'd better tell Colonel Franklin he'll have to come up with something in the next couple of days."

"Still," Holliford said, "it's more than I expected. And I need it, too. It'll give me a chance to get Logan off sedation for a while so I can finish these tests."

Spencer nodded. "Yes, as long as we can keep him sealed off, there shouldn't be any trouble. By the way, how are the tests going?"

"Pretty well, as a matter of fact. I'm reasonably satisfied with the results so far. The only thing I'm unhappy about is not having a better idea of the relative doses the two of them got. The blood chemistry analyses were almost useless because the father had so much adrenaline in his blood that it threw everything off. I'd feel better if I had some information on the permeability of that tent cloth."

Kagle broke in. "Speaking of which," he said, "we ought to get those clothes to Denver. They've asked for them twice now, and there's a chance that analysis of the clothes may help with your problem about relative dosage."

"That's right," Holliford said. "It could give me

something to go on, anyway."

"Do you know where the clothes are?" Kagle asked.

"I think they're still down in pathology. Or else they're in that steel locker in the morgue room."

"Good, I'll get them as soon as we're done here."

Holliford said to Spencer, "We were just listening to the tapes of the autopsy. You want to stay?"

"Sure," Spencer said. "Why not?"

10

Logan wasn't quite sure where he was, or what was being done to him. He had a vague sense of something large and metal hanging over him as he lay on something hard, and then the something metal was moved away and he was lifted and shoved from the hard thing he was lying on to something else, not quite as hard, that moved uncertainly under him.

Somewhere near his feet, there was voice. He couldn't make out the words, but it had the feeling of an order of some kind, and then he was moving, not small uncertain motions, but a long, smooth flowing motion as if he were floating along feet first through a half-seen, shiny tube. His eyes closed fully and then, as he felt that he was changing direction, being jerked around some invisible corner, his eyes opened again. This time, he could see more clearly.

His head was turned to the side now, he realized

dimly, and he was going past a wall of glazed yellow bricks or blocks that shone with the reflected light of something he couldn't see. Gradually, he began to understand that he was in a corridor, a hospital corridor, being wheeled on a stretcher.

The realization that he was in a hospital brought a series of flashes of memory: As if he were there again, he could see JoAnn, sick, alone in the empty ward, being wheeled down the corridor to the operating room, then his own waiting in the cold, antiseptic, tile-walled corridor, sitting on the hard bench not knowing, with his mouth dry and his empty stomach tied in a horrible, aching knot, and the doctor coming out into the hall so cold and even-voiced, saying, No, Mr. Logan, I'm sorry, but we're going to have to go in again, to go in again like it was some kind of amusement park and they hadn't had enough on the first ride. And then the waiting and trying to be cheerful and encouraging to JoAnn as they wheeled the stretcher down the hall and he walked alongside watching her eyes open for the first time a little and that puzzled, lost look she gave him that made him want to cry or tear down the hospital or take her somewhere else, carry her away to where she could be happy and healthy again.

But that was long ago, he remembered finally through the haze of pain, and he hadn't been able to take her away because after the next operation she had been so exhausted, and so used up and thin and pale and totally beyond hoping any more that she had just lain there in the bed and only opened her eyes once, for a second, and looked at him as if to say, forgive me, but I'm so tired, and then closed them again forever. And now he was in the hospital again, but this time it was him being wheeled down the corridor, although he had no idea to where or from where or for what reason. He was beginning to wake up from something that had kept him sleeping, he had no idea how long, and he knew that he wasn't seeing everything clearly yet, or thinking straight. It was even a strain to stay awake, to keep from drifting into dreams or fantasies, but he struggled to keep his eyes open and to remember why he was here and what was wrong.

In spite of himself, he drifted off again, and in the few seconds his eyes were closed, he had a clear, horrible picture in his mind of driving the truck into town, with Chris lying in the seat next to him, twitching and shivering, his nose bleeding, stinking of urine and sweat and sickness, his head lolling on his neck like he was dead. The thought brought Logan awake again, sweating, dragging in huge gulps of air. As he tried to control his panic, he was vaguely aware of the corridor going by, broken by beige, black-lettered doors.

One of the doors, down the corridor a little, opened, and a man in an olive-drab uniform came out into Logan's line of vision. The man was carrying something, and Logan's attention was riveted to it, although he didn't know why, just that he was staring at what the man was carrying and that it was a bag of some kind, a plastic bag, transparent, bulging with its contents, partly obscured by reflections from the shiny plastic surface but holding something that looked, as he got closer, like red and blue, blue jeans, red-plaid something, and leather, as the stretcher went by and the man holding the bag waited for it to pass, red plaid and blue jeans and boots, maybe, but very small for boots. Logan strained to turn his head to keep looking to see what it was, because somehow it was familiar and it was important. He didn't know why, but he knew it was important, but all he could see was the arm of the orderly who was wheeling the stretcher and the other man's uniform, and the door he had come out of, which wasn't beige, it was steel gray, and then he could see the bright blue light over the gray door.

He sank back onto the stretcher exhausted, flat on his back, and all he could see were the blobs of light in the ceiling, blurry and uneven and pulsating dimmer and brighter and dimmer and dimmer and growing finally dark.

11

JS96S876–3
TOPSECRETCLASSQSCRAMBLE
CODEDESIGCOWBOYSEVENFIVEZERO
CODESQUAREDDAFFODIL
COLONEL WILLIAM FRANKLIN
CARE COMMANDING OFFICER
FORT HOWARD WYOMING
PRIORITY REDREDRED
BEGINS. EYES ONLY READ AND DESTROY. VITAL YOU KEEP LID ON YOURHOUSE. BAILEY ASSTSECDOD NEEDS MINIMUM THREEWEEKS FOR CLEARANCE APPROPRIATIONS RELATED AREA. PREDICT FAILURE PROB POINTSEVEN-THREE IF BAD NEWS. INCLUDE EVALUATION THIS SUBJECT IN DAILY REPORT. SIGNED HILL.

12

This time, Logan awoke more quickly. He lay in bed, looking up at the thin cracks in the paint on the ceiling, placing himself in time and space. He knew where he was, and that he had been asleep for a long time, but he had no idea how long. Looking toward the curtained windows, he saw that it was either dusk or dawn. The faint gray light of a sunless sky filtered through the curtains. It occurred to him that it might just be a badly overcast day, but for some reason he was convinced that it was early evening.

Slowly and tentatively, he sat up, beginning to test the strength of his drugged body and the clearness of his head. He felt weak and groggy, but he was in general control of his muscles. After sitting in bed for a short while, he swung his feet around so that he was sitting on the edge of the bed. The linoleum-covered floor felt very cold on the soles of his feet, but he pressed them down firmly, hoping that the discomfort of the cold floor would help clear his head. With the same goal in mind, he switched on the lamp by the side of the bed and rubbed his face with his hands.

The combination of light and cold and rubbing his face brought him around enough to stand up, and he began to walk uncertainly around the room. At first, he thought he was going to collapse. Everything went hot and black and he started to sway, but he steadied himself on the bed and the feeling went away. As he walked, he began to feel better, more in control of himself, less bleary. He turned on the overhead light and began to stretch, then touched his toes a couple of times, finding that when he straightened up he had another wave of dizziness. When the dizziness cleared, he walked around the room some more, then opened the door and stepped into the corridor.

He looked around in the hall, not looking for anything in particular, hoping to find someone who could answer some questions for him. He had been in the corridor only a few seconds when he became aware, through his drugged haze, that there was an orderly standing in front of him. The orderly said, "Mr. Logan. Can I get you something?"

Logan looked more carefully at the man. He couldn't recall having seen him before, but the man seemed to know him. At first, Logan was puzzled, looking at the impassive face that was, unlike most faces, slightly above his own. The orderly was tall, and thin, although Logan thought he was probably very strong. Logan stared at the orderly, bemused, then said, "I, uh, I'm looking for Dr. Cardwell." He wasn't really specifically looking for Cardwell, but if the orderly wanted to get him something, Cardwell was probably what he needed most.

The orderly said, "Why don't you stay in your room. I'll have somebody get him for you." He said it softly, almost soothingly, putting his arm on Logan's shoulder and steering him back toward the room.

Logan, sensing for some reason that he should do what this man told him, said, "All right."

Then, almost back to his room, he turned and said, "Who are you?"

"My name is Simpson," the orderly told him. "Dr. Holliford told me to stay here in case you needed anything."

Logan, still groggy and disoriented, smiled at the orderly named Simpson and went back into his room.

13

When he added it all up, Spencer was pleased with how the day had gone. It hadn't been an easy day for him, not with the panic call from Holliford and the hard, tense, straining hour he had spent with Cardwell, but at least none of it had been wasted. The confrontation with Cardwell, especially, had turned out well. He had managed to get the experienced and canny doctor to accept an explanation of what was going on that was consistent with the actual situation and yet left the Public Health Service clear of any complicity if the truth ever came out.

He noticed drops of rain on the windshield of his car and turned on the wipers. He would be glad when he could stay in Casper for a while and stop commuting to Fort Howard or to the hospital in Rawlins, and then back and forth between them, like today. He had started at the hospital and then gone to Fort Howard for a conference with Nickerson and Reintz and Janeway and

Franklin. From the beginning, it hadn't taken Spencer long to realize that Franklin was the important man in that group, and he wondered, now, what it meant that Reintz had begun to be absent from their meetings. He didn't imagine that it boded well for Reintz. Spencer shrugged and concentrated on the newly rain-wet road that reflected his headlights and the blinking neon signs of a gas station and truck stop at the side of the road.

By the time he reached the hospital, the rain had stopped, leaving only the shiny, puddle-dotted pavement to show that it had rained at all. It was past visiting hours, so Spencer just pulled up in front of the main door and left the car there; he didn't expect to be in the hospital long.

He went right in, past the night guard, who knew him and buzzed open the door to the first-floor corridor. Spencer was surprised to find that Simpson was at the nurses' station, leaning on the black plastic counter and talking to the two nurses who, Spencer supposed, were there to be doing something other than entertaining Simpson, or letting him entertain them.

He took Simpson by the arm and led the corporal down the hall a short distance from the nurses, who made no attempt to conceal their curiosity at what was going on. When he was pretty sure they were out of earshot, he asked Simpson. "Are you watching him or not?" Even whispering, his annoyance was clear.

Simpson didn't seem to notice. "No problem, sir," he said casually. "Not a peep out of him."

Spencer's annoyance increased. This was no time for everything to be fouled up by an incompetent foot soldier. "Well, you'd better keep an eye on him. He's been taken off sedation." Spencer looked at the clock. It was a few minutes past eight. He asked, "Has he had his dinner yet?"

"Yes, sir. About an hour ago." Simpson sounded as if the chastisement had made some impression.

"Good," Spencer said. "I'm going in to talk to him."

"Do you want me to come with you?"

"No, it's not necessary. Just come along and wait outside."

Spencer and Simpson walked down the corridor together, Spencer thinking that Simpson had undoubtedly been bored, but that he would probably be more alert for the rest of the night. As Spencer remembered the arrangement Holliford had made, Simpson was about due for four hours off duty anyway.

When Spencer walked into Logan's room, he found the rancher sitting on the edge of his bed, staring out the window at the darkened parking lot and the faint pinpoints of street lights in the distance. On the bedtray next to him, his food sat untouched, looking waxy and unreal, like an advertising photograph for a TV dinner.

Spencer watched Logan for a moment. He seemed unaware of Spencer's presence in the room. He sat motionless, except for his hands, which rubbed at each other tensely in his lap.

"Mr. Logan," Spencer began tentatively.

Hearing an unfamiliar voice, the big rancher turned away from the window and looked over his shoulder. He saw a stranger, a neatly dressed man of about sixty with thinning gray hair. The stranger said, "I'm Dr. Spencer."

Logan stood up and faced Spencer. "Where's Dr. Cardwell?"

Spencer couldn't help clearing his throat and glancing away from Logan for a second. He caught himself and hoped he hadn't seemed furtive. "He won't be seeing you any more. He's asked me to take over your case."

"I don't understand. He's been my doctor all my life."

Spencer tried an encouraging smile. He doubted, though, that it was convincing. For some reason, he was finding it very difficult to talk to Logan. He didn't understand it; he hadn't had that problem with Cardwell.

"Of course," Spencer said, still trying. "It's just that we ran into some problems that he thought would best be left to Dr. Holliford and myself."

"What do you mean? What kind of problems?"

"There's no need to be alarmed, Mr. Logan. It's not uncommon for a doctor to take himself off a case if he feels that it's in the patient's interest."

"I want to talk to Roy Cardwell," Logan said, making it a demand.

Unconsciously, Spencer backed up a step. "Of course. I just wanted to let you know that Dr. Holliford and I would be taking care of you from now on, so you wouldn't be alarmed."

As the two men stood tensely at the foot of the bed, something changed in Logan's face. A part of the undirected anxiety went out of it, replaced by a tightening around the eyes, as if from suspicion.

"Are you taking care of my boy, too?" Logan challenged.

"Yes, I am."

Logan advanced toward Spencer. "I want to see him,"

he said harshly. "I want to know what's wrong with him."

Again, Spencer retreated. He sensed that there was something more than anger and worry in Logan's attitude. Somehow, he felt he was being tested. He said, "Well, we're having a little difficulty with the diagnosis. We don't think it's serious, but it is something unusual, and it will take us a week or two to figure out exactly what it is." Spencer found that he was beginning to believe it himself. He smiled at Logan. "These things happen sometimes."

"Why can't I see him?"

"We don't think he should be disturbed right now. Believe me, as soon as we know it's all right, we'll let you know."

"I just want to see him. All I want to do is look in on him." Logan was frustrated and getting angry.

Spencer found suddenly that he felt in control again. It was as if someone had freed him from a dungeon. The room seemed lighter, and Logan was no longer his tormentor, but merely a frightened and bewildered sheep rancher. "It's too late for that tonight," he said firmly. "We'll talk about it in the morning."

He turned and walked quickly from the room, leaving Logan staring after him, angry and confused. In the corridor, Spencer ran his hand over his forehead and wondered what had come over him there in the room with Logan. He smiled at Simpson, who was sitting alertly in the chair opposite Logan's door, and walked back toward the main entrance.

14

A4DX693–P161-E
TOPSECRETCLASSQSCRAMBLE
CODEDESIGCOWBOYSEVENSEVENFIVE
CODESQUAREDBUTTERFLYGREEN

GENERAL SAMUEL HILL
JOINTCHIEFS PENTAGON
PRIORITY BLUEBLUERED
BEGINS: REPORT DAYTHREE EAGLE. PRIMARY.
SITUATION IMPROVED. ESTIMATE SENSITIVE PERIOD
SUCCESSFULLY CONCLUDED. DANGER AREAS NEUTRALIZED
AND PRESS TEAM ONSITE MYHOUSE FOR MANAGEMENT
FUTURE DEVELOPMENTS. J T SPIKE BOYNTON FULLY
CONVERTED WILL COOPERATE WITH PRESS TEAM
AND SCIENTIFIC PERSONNEL. MAY ALSO REQUIRE
CONVERSION ROY CARDWELL PHYSICIAN RAWLINS WYO
BUT PREVIOUS SECURITY INFORMATION INADEQUATE
PLEASE ARRANGE LEVEL TWO. SECONDARY. REFERENCE
YOUR S876–3. SITUATION FULLY CONTROLLED HERE.
EXPECT FULL RESOLUTION AND TRANSFER TO DENVER
ALL RELEVANT ELEMENTS WITHIN WEEK. WILL
LEAVE PRESS TEAM TO COVER FOR FURTHER THREE
WEEKS BUT EXPECT NO BAD NEWS. RECOMMEND
CONSOLIDATION PRESENT POSITION AND MAXIMUM
LOW PROFILE. MAY NEED COOPERATION LOCAL

AUTHORITIES IF ISSUE OF LOGAN ESTATE BECOMES PRESSING. DECAY PERIOD PROJECTED THREE WEEKS PLUSMINUS ONE. CURRENT EVALUATION POSITIVE DEGREE FIVE. SIGNED FRANKLIN COL.

FIVE

1

The night nurse's name was Grace. Simpson thought she was much better than any of the others: tall and long-waisted, the way he liked them, with big, gray eyes; her long, dark hair was tied up under her cap, but Simpson could imagine what it would look like when she let it down. The thought pleased him, because he liked long hair, and it was not very common among the women he had gotten to know in Wyoming. Not that there were many of them.

While he waited for Grace to get the coffee and sandwiches from the nurses' refrigerator at the back of the locked and darkened cafeteria, Simpson reflected on how lousy his sex life had become. Back in Brooklyn, before he was drafted, he hadn't had to worry. The nice thing about the big city was that there were so many girls, so many kinds of girls. For Simpson, the only problem had been how to get them all in. He didn't know why, but they were always ready to jump into bed with him. He didn't make any particular effort; sometimes he didn't even care one way or the other; but they were always after him. When he was waiting for his induction notice, there was a period of about four weeks when he had managed to get laid every day, twice a day, never the same girl twice in a row. It still made him tired to think about it.

The Nam hadn't been so kind to him. For the little brown girls in Saigon and Danang and Muk Tho, all the GIs were the same. As long as you had a couple of hundred piastres, it didn't matter who you were, and nobody ever got it free. Simpson had re-enlisted, though, partly because he was told he would be transferred back to the States. So here he was, on his third hitch, in the security detail of some lousy post in the middle of Wyoming. It was getting to be a drag.

He had been really pissed when they told him he was going to be guarding a sick man in a civilian hospital, dressed up as a bedpan pusher. He had figured that if he wanted to carry bedpans, he didn't have to do it on some officer's orders and in the middle of Wyoming. But he hadn't figured on the fringe benefits. Like him, the nurses were bored, and they gave him a chance to see if the old magic still worked.

So when he had gotten up from his four-off sleep and come out to relieve Corporal Creighton, he had been delighted to see what kind of nurse was on the late night shift. With only four hours to work on her, Simpson didn't figure he should waste any time sitting in the chair down the hall. The jerk was probably asleep anyway. When Simpson had seen him that afternoon, he hadn't looked like he could make it to the men's room without help.

Grace came through the swinging doors of the corridor that led to the cafeteria, carrying a tray crowded with sandwiches, mugs, and a steaming coffeepot. Simpson enjoyed the view as she came across the hall to the nurses' station. She was concentrating on her burden and unaware of the soft and sinuous way her hips moved as she walked to the station and put the tray on the counter top. Simpson lifted the top slice of bread of one of the sandwiches.

"Ham?"

Grace smiled at him. "That's right. Hospital ham." Her voice was warm, encouraging.

He laughed. "Well, let's not frustrate ourselves any more, even if all we have is hospital ham."

2

In the dark hospital room, Dan Logan stood next to his bed, buttoning his shirt. On the bed in front of him was the suitcase brought by Sarah Parker and transferred to his room by Sue Callan and one of the nurses, neither of whom knew that there was anything special about the patient in 148.

Logan tucked the shirt into the freshly pressed tan twill wash pants he had found in the suitcase along with the shirt, a pair of pajamas, some underwear and socks, and his dress boots. Then he walked quietly to the sink at one side of the room, taking care in the darkness not to run into anything. He splashed water on his face, and, by the faint light that came through the barely open door, studied his face in the mirror over the sink.

He thought he looked tired, pale, hollow-cheeked, with dark circles under his eyes. He supposed it was from being in the hospital for so long, lying in bed. One thing he was sure of: he wasn't sick. In fact, he felt fine, except for being a little groggy and having a couple of dizzy spells, but those he attributed to his having been drugged.

He turned away from the mirror and looked at the plastic bracelet around his wrist. It had his name printed on it, and his room number. It was like a slave bracelet, an emblem of his imprisonment. He grabbed it and pulled, snapping it, then hurled it across the room. He wasn't going to be a prisoner any longer.

He tested the window and found that it was locked, so he picked up the visitor's chair and lifted it over his shoulder, ready to smash the window glass. Then, slowly, he lowered the chair to the floor. He realized that he had worked himself into a frenzy of anger about the way he was being treated without stopping to think what he would do if he got out. It was time, now, before he got out, to decide what the next step would be.

The thing he wanted worst was to see his son. He sat down on the edge of the bed and tried to work out how he could do that. He had no real idea where Chris was. He had heard them talk about putting Chris in isolation, and he supposed he could find that if he had to. But hadn't Holliford said that Chris had been moved? Logan concentrated on that, remembered being in a room in the basement. He had been hooked up to some machine, with wires on his head, and Holliford had said that Chris had been moved and couldn't be disturbed. That meant there was no use looking for "isolation." Unless Holliford had been lying. But if Holliford was lying, then there was no use looking for isolation, either: he might have been lying about that, too.

Logan tried to remember something else that might

help him find Chris. He noticed that he was becoming upset, beginning to sweat, that his hands were clenched. Something was frightening him, something he couldn't quite remember. He tried to focus on it, began to remember motion: bright, blurring lights, tile walls. Then he had it. That day on the stretcher, he had seen something important. He closed his eyes and tried to see it again. Red and blue. Red plaid and blue denim. It was the same red plaid as the shirt Chris was wearing that morning on the way to the hospital. Suddenly, it all came together with a rush, and Logan felt a roaring in his ears; a dizzy redness clouded his sight. He let his head drop into his hands and tried to make sense of it: the dream or vision of Chris, dead, in the truck, and the distorted memory of the bulging bag that held what must have been Chris's clothes. He couldn't tell how much of it had been dream and how much real.

After a few minutes, he had himself under control. There was only one way to find out. He had to try to find that corridor again, and the doorway in which he had seen the man carrying the bundle, the man wearing an army uniform. He stood up, walked carefully to the door, and looked through the crack by the hinge. He had to press his face up against the door, because it was almost closed, and the crack he was trying to see through was very narrow, but he could see that there was no one opposite the open end of the door. He moved to that end and peered into the hall. The chair opposite the door, the one that had earlier held the strange orderly, was empty. Logan eased the door open further, moved his head past the door edge. There was no one in sight. The corridor was dim, lit only by a few of the overhead bulbs.

About thirty feet away was a brighter area, and Logan could hear the murmur of voices, perhaps a man and a woman.

He patted his pockets to make sure he had his wallet, which had been left for him in the drawer of the bedside table, then he opened the door further, wide enough for him to slip into the corridor. Slowly, carefully, holding his breath, he took a step forward, then another, and another, pressing himself to the wall so that he would be hard to see if the people still talking in the bright area ahead of him should look down the hall. He came to a doorway and stopped, trying to hide in the small shelter it gave him, listening to the voices. He couldn't make out what they were saying, but he was sure now there were just two, a man and a woman. The woman laughed, a warm throaty sound, and then the man joined her. They sounded to Logan like two large birds in the mating season.

He found that he was panting, and he took a few slow deep breaths to calm himself while he looked around. About ten feet from him, toward the bright area where the voices were coming from, across the hall from where he was standing, there was a door marked by a sign that said "Exit" in big red letters. Logan didn't know where it led, but at least it would get him out of the corridor and away from the two people who shared it with him.

He waited for what sounded like a long and involved part of the conversation and then made for the door, pulling it open only as far as he had to and squeezing through into what proved to be a stairwell. He held the door as it closed to keep it from slamming, but when the door was fully closed the spring latch fastened with a loud snap. Logan froze where he was, waiting.

3

Simpson was enjoying himself tremendously. Grace was not only better-looking than anything he had seen in a long time, she was a lot of fun, and besides that, she was making it pretty clear that she wasn't going to give him any trouble. He had decided that he wasn't going to be spending his four hours off duty sleeping in that bed in the back room. In bed, maybe, but not sleeping. The more he thought about it, while he and Grace were having a good time joking around about this and that and getting closer and closer to what they were both thinking about, the more he thought that he might not even wait until he was off duty. Why bother? The stiff in 148 wasn't going anywhere.

Thinking about the man he was supposed to be watching gave Simpson a small twinge of worry. Suppose he was wrong. Suppose the guy wasn't so stiff by now. Simpson guessed his ass would be in the grandaddy sling of all time if the guy got out. The thought threw him off so badly that he almost didn't laugh when Grace said something with a clear double meaning. She laughed, and he should have, too, but he was late. She wondered why, and he wanted to get the tempo up again, so there was a short, awkward silence. It was punctuated by a noise somewhere in the hall, like the click of a door closing.

Simpson was suddenly very worried. He pushed his chair back, standing up and leaning into the hall so he could see the door to 148 and the exit door. There was no motion in the hall and everything seemed to be just as it had been when he last looked. Relieved, he sat down again.

"Something wrong?" Grace asked.

"Nah, it's nothing. I just didn't want to neglect my duty," Simpson said. "Don't want to be lying down while I'm on the job."

Grace laughed.

4

When he was sure there was no one coming to investigate the noise, Logan went down the stairs to the basement. He was sure the corridor he remembered was in the basement, and his intuition was confirmed when he saw the yellow tile walls, bright and shiny even though they were lit only by the occasional dim bulb that was left on at night. He walked along the hall looking for something familiar.

There was nothing he could remember, nothing that would help him tell this corridor from any other, just yellow tile walls and beige doors with black lettering that told the function of the various rooms and laboratories.

As he walked along the corridor, Logan wondered how he would know if he was walking past the very door he wanted. He had been trying so hard to see what was in that bag, and he had been so drugged and tired and dream-ridden that he couldn't remember anything that might help him. There was just an image of the plastic bag, and the orderly's arm, and then the big blurry lights in the ceiling.

He turned a corner and began to walk down another corridor, still trying to remember something that would help him, but only the same pictures kept repeating themselves. He was getting furious, and frustrated, and frightened, when something caught his eye. He stopped walking. He turned and slowly ran his eyes over the part of the corridor he had just passed. More yellow tile. A beige door. Yellow tile. A gray door. Yellow tile.

Logan stopped. A gray door. And over it, a bright blue bulb. As he looked at them, his memory filled out. He could see himself approaching the man with the bag as the man came out of a gray door with a bright blue bulb over it. A door like the one in front of him. He had found what he was looking for.

Logan opened the door slowly. For some reason, he was frightened. The room he entered was dark, but he let the door close completely, this time taking care not to let the latch snap home, before he switched on the light. At first, he didn't understand what he was looking at. The room had tile walls like the corridor, and a tile floor as well. In the middle of the room was a large porcelain-and-steel table with grooves on either side. On the floor next to the table there was a drain, and the floor sloped gently to a low point at the drain. Above the table hung a steel scale like the one Logan remembered from the fruit-and-vegetable department of the supermarket in the new shopping center. The whole place smelled, too, but Logan couldn't place the odor. The closest he could come was a smell that he had noticed one or twice around Spike Boynton's place.

It didn't make any sense to him. This was no place for them to be keeping Chris. But he remembered the man in the uniform carrying Chris's clothes out of this room. He was confused. Maybe he had dreamt the whole thing. He walked around the table, looking around the room at the cabinets that lined three of the walls, the bottles of strange, ugly things, taken, Logan supposed, from people's insides. There was a break in the tile wall for a kind of archway. Logan could see through it and into an adjoining room faintly lit by a shaft of the cold, harsh light that made the room he was standing in seem like something from a nightmare or another world. The unearthly effect was heightened by how cold the room was and by the repeated glare of reflections from tile and porcelain and stainless steel. As he thought about the oppressiveness of the room, Logan noticed for the first time that the far wall was all steel: a steel frame that held three rows of two steel doors each, running from the floor to the ceiling, like a bank of small meat lockers.

Then, all at once, Logan knew where he was, what the strange room was for. He had never seen one, but the purpose, once realized, was unmistakable. He was in a morgue. And the steel-and-porcelain table next to him was used for cutting up corpses. The coldness of the room penetrated to the center of his being, and he stood frozen where he was, staring at the six steel doors.

It seemed to him like forever before he could move again. Slowly, driven by something he couldn't control, with the dread rising in his throat, he approached the wall of doors. In the center of each door was a place for a tag, like the identifying cards on file drawers. They were all empty except one. Logan tried to read it, but his vision was blurred. He moved closer, but still he couldn't make it out. He was feeling light-headed, faint. A red film in front of his eyes blocked out the tag so he could barely see it at all. He swayed, dizzy, about to fall, and reached out to steady himself, unwittingly grabbing for support the handle of the door that bore the tag. The letters on the tag jumped into his brain and seared themselves there, burning in an impression he knew he would never lose, even as he tried to tell himself that he was wrong, that the tag did not say "Logan, C.," that it was not his son that lay behind the steel door.

There was another interminable period as he stood there with his hand on the door handle, not moving, his hand growing tighter on the handle, the tag going in and out of focus, his breath coming faster and faster. It became intolerable for him, and he let his hand drop to his side. His mind raged, out of control, at once believing and denying, wanting to know but unwilling to see, afraid to turn away and afraid to go on.

Slowly, he reached out and again took hold of the handle. For a second, he closed his eyes, and then he opened them and pulled on the handle. The door swung open.

Later, he stumbled through the darkness and the cold at the side of a road outside Rawlins. He didn't know where he was, and he didn't know how he got there. He didn't care.

Still later, he found himself walking along the side of Interstate 80. There was no traffic, and the wind was chill and biting. He buried his hands in his pockets and kept walking.

He was sobbing, out of control. Crying for he knew not what. He hadn't cried even when JoAnn died.

An underpass. The bright cold fluorescent lights reflected harshly by the concrete walls and road. Logan wiped his eyes and his nose on the sleeve of his shirt. Trembling, aware of nothing but his agony, he let out a cry that reverberated from the walls like the death shriek of some demented giant. Three words: GOD DAMN IT.

5

By the time he had walked six miles, Logan was no longer crying, and he knew where he was. Ahead of him was a darkened motel, and beyond that a huge neon sign that advertised Marie's All-Night Truck Stop. Logan found that he was very hungry. He walked slowly past the closed-up motel and across the parking lot to Marie's.

Inside, most of the place was closed off so that the

thin, wrinkled old man who was Marie's dishwasher and janitor and sometime waiter could wash the floor. At a table in the corner, a fat, dirty truck driver was drinking a beer and studying his route sheet. There was no one else in the diner except a tired waitress leaning against the cold griddle. She pushed herself upright and looked wearily at Logan as he walked to the counter. He stood there, not saying anything, staring at the fly-specked plastic case that held two wilted pieces of apple pie.

After about a minute, the waitress gave up on out-waiting him. She was too tired to play games. "Do you want anything?" she asked.

He looked up as if he was surprised to see her standing there. "Let me have some black coffee," he said slowly. His stare dropped again to the pie. "And give me a piece of that pie."

He sat down, still staring at the pie case, oblivious to the way the waitress was looking at him. He was hungry, and he had a lot to think about.

6

At seven-thirty in the morning, just over six hours after Logan left his room, a nurse came down the hospital corridor to wake him and take his early-morning temperature. She walked briskly to his door, shaking down a thermometer. She noticed as she passed him that Simpson, slumped in the chair opposite the door to

Logan's room, seemed to be sleeping. It wasn't her concern, so she didn't bother herself about it.

She knocked on the door and went in. The room was only faintly lit by gray morning light, but it was more than bright enough for her to be able to see immediately that Logan's bed was empty. Surprised that he was already awake, she crossed the room and knocked on the bathroom door. There was no response, so she knocked again, louder, and called, "Mr. Logan?" Again there was no response. She knocked a third time, still louder, and called his name again. When he didn't answer, she pushed the bathroom door open. The bathroom was empty.

The nurse walked quickly back out into the hall. She shook Simpson's shoulders. "Have you seen Mr. Logan?"

It brought him awake immediately. "What?" he demanded.

"I asked you if you'd seen Mr. Logan."

"What do you mean? He's in there, isn't he?" Simpson waved his hand toward the room across the hall.

The nurse barely paused to say "No." She turned impatiently away from Simpson and hurried down the hall toward the nurses' station.

In a panic, Simpson sprinted across the hall into Logan's room. Just as the nurse had said, there was no one there. Simpson looked in the bathroom, found that it, too, was empty. He went to the window and tested it. It was locked. That was no good at all. If the window was locked, from the inside and the outside, then the only way Logan could have gotten out was through the door. Simpson wondered for a moment whether he could palm it off on Creighton. He doubted it. After all, it was

Simpson the nurse had found sleeping on duty. Creighton wouldn't have fallen asleep; he wasn't the type. Simpson knew he'd have to do something about the window or he could probably expect to spend the rest of his life in the guardhouse.

Quickly, holding the window curtain in his hand to avoid leaving his fingerprints, Simpson undid the lock on the inside of the window. He tried to open the window, but he couldn't. He looked around the room for something to force the window with, but there was nothing that would do the job.

He stopped to think. The big question now was whether to call Major Cooper first or to go outside and unlock the window. It didn't take long for Simpson to figure out that he had to call the Major right away. Simpson knew there wasn't supposed to be any big deal made about Logan, so the hospital people would have to be quieted down right away. And they would know exactly when the nurse had gone in and found out that Logan wasn't there, so he couldn't afford to wait any longer.

7

Logan walked slowly along a quiet street of well-kept houses. In the hours he had spent in the diner and the time he had been walking since the sun started to come up, he had decided what he had to do. Once he had thought about his situation, it had become clear to him that he had to get going right away, before anybody started looking for him. To do that, he needed to have a car.

He shifted in his mouth the tobacco he was chewing. It wasn't the brand he liked, but it was all they had at the diner, and it was better than nothing. Across the street from him, in an open carport, he saw a newly polished green sedan. Logan crossed the street and ran carefully up the driveway to the car. It was locked.

He ran back to the street and then walked quickly to the next house. In the street in front of it was a dusty panel truck. It wasn't as fast as the sedan, probably, but like the tobacco, it would be better than nothing. Unfortunately, it, too, was locked. Logan went on down the street, past the next lawns and brightly painted mailboxes, looking for a car he could get into easily and quietly. He didn't think he'd have trouble wiring up the ignition switch once he was in the car, as long as the car he found didn't have one of the new steering-wheel locks, but he didn't want to waste the time and run the risk that would be involved if he had to break into the car in the first place.

Logan was in another driveway, walking quietly toward a beat-up pickup truck, when he saw in the next yard the answer to his problem. Resting on its kickstand, unlocked and unchained, was a big, blue-and-silver motorcycle. It had the look of a fast bike: Logan guessed it at three-fifty or four hundred cc's. Even from where he was, he could see the heavy tread of the tires, the kind that would make the bike equally at home on or off the road. It was just what he needed: fast, anonymous, flexible. He ran across the lawn to the side of the house and began to inch his way back to the motorcycle.

8

Colonel William Franklin crumpled into a small ball the paper he had been using to draft a telegram to General Hill and dropped the ball into the big metal ashtray on his desk. There was plenty of time for him to notify Washington if they didn't recapture Logan, and Franklin had the sudden frightening realization that if he acted too quickly he would just be jumping into the fire with Nickerson and Cooper and the others. This was his project now, and there was no question in his mind that Sam Hill would skewer him and roast him whole if it went wrong. And it could go very wrong indeed. Franklin shuddered when he thought of General Hill's telex about the appropriations bill that was coming up. He touched a match to the ball of paper in the ashtray and watched with no particular enthusiasm as it burned.

When the paper was completely consumed, Franklin stirred the ashes and then carried the ashtray into the bathroom and flushed the ashes down the toilet. He looked briefly in the mirror and was pleased to see that the strain of the situation didn't show on his face. Not yet, anyway, he thought as he went back into the bedroom and reached into the closet for his fresh uniform.

9

It didn't take Logan more than a couple of minutes to hot-wire the motorcycle, once he had pushed it a good distance down the street, away from the house he had taken it from.

In the time he had spent in the diner, Logan had managed to make part of himself numb, and he wanted to keep it that way. He concentrated on the motorcycle, checking the gas tank and adjusting the gas-flow valves carefully, then kicking it over, pleased that it started immediately. He started slowly down the street, getting the feel of the bike, testing the brakes and the clutch and shifting up and down through the gears.

He had never been a nut about motorcycles, the way some of the kids were these days, but he enjoyed them for what they could do. A good trail bike was a lot more use around the ranch than a horse was most of the time, and Chris had really gotten a kick out of riding with him. It was something Chris had over most of his classmates, and he made the most of it. Logan caught himself as he was about to slide into memories of things he had shared with Chris, the hopes and plans they had enjoyed together. He forced himself to pay attention to the motorcycle, to the feel of it bouncing over the sloppily paved road, until the sensations took him back to another time, to a memory that didn't hurt.

Twenty years before, he remembered, he had been in Korea, not far from Inchon, just after the invasion. There was a bridge that flanked the line the brass had chosen for the UN advance, and somebody decided that it had to be destroyed just in case the Chicoms might decide to use it. So, after the orders had come far enough down the ranks, the job had been given to him. A scout patrol went out ahead of him, but he had to make most of the trip alone, on a motorcycle, on a road that might have been paved by the same men who paved the one he was riding on now. The big difference was that in Korea there had been seventy pounds of high explosives riding on the motorcycle with him.

Later, when it was all over, they had given him a medal for it, but he had never worn it. He hadn't wanted a medal. It seemed vaguely wrong to him that they gave medals for killing people and destroying things. It was just a job, a dirty job that had to be done, but it wasn't anything he wanted to celebrate.

Logan guessed that it was just before eight o'clock when he got to Roy Cardwell's place. He saw that Cardwell's car was still in front of the house, but he didn't pull into the driveway. Instead, he drove past for some distance and hid the motorcycle in a clump of high bushes at the side of the road. For some reason he didn't understand, Logan felt he shouldn't let Cardwell know how he was traveling.

He walked quickly to the house and knocked on the door. He could smell bacon and coffee. Mrs. Knowles must be cooking breakfast, he thought, and then the door opened and Roy Cardwell stood there in his shirtsleeves looking at him as if he was an illusion, or a ghost.

"Dan," he said finally. "How did you . . ." He stopped, the question unfinished.

Logan said, "Can I come in?"

"Sure. Sure. Of course you can come in." When Logan was inside, Cardwell closed the door and called into the kitchen, "Mrs. Knowles, put two plates on for breakfast, will you, and then you can go upstairs. I have to be alone for a while." He looked again at Logan. The rancher looked terrible: drawn, pale, and haunted. Cardwell wondered what he knew about himself and Chris.

"You don't have to feed me or anything, Roy. I'm all right."

"Nonsense. It'll do you good." There was the noise of plates and flatware from the kitchen. "Besides, Mrs. Knowles is putting it all on the table already."

Logan sat down on the parlor divan and put his head in his hands. Seeing Cardwell, who he was sure knew something about Chris, had brought all the horrible images of the past hours back to him. He shuddered.

Cardwell, watching him, was worried. He wondered if he should call anyone, but discarded the idea almost as quickly as he thought of it. His responsibility was to his patient first, and it wasn't going to do anyone any harm if Dan had breakfast with him before he went back to the hospital. Cardwell went into the kitchen and hurried Mrs. Knowles along. As soon as she was on her way upstairs, he went back into the parlor, where Logan was still sitting on the divan with his head in his hands.

"Dan," Cardwell said.

The rancher looked up.

"Come on, Dan, let's go inside and have some breakfast. We can talk in there."

When they were sitting down and Cardwell had served both of them big helpings of scrambled eggs and bacon and muffins and had poured two big mugs of steaming black coffee, he said, "Now you can tell me how you come to be here."

Logan looked down at his plate. The eggs and bacon were a meaningless pattern of color. The acrid smell of the coffee stung his nostrils. He rubbed his eyes, pushed himself back from the table. He was having trouble getting his breath.

Cardwell, alarmed, started to stand up, but sat back down when Logan looked at him. There was something in the rancher's eyes that warned Cardwell what he was going to say.

"Roy," Logan managed to choke out. "Roy, I saw Chris."

"My god," Cardwell breathed. "You *saw* him?"

"In that . . . room. He was in a drawer." Again, Logan was having trouble breathing. "He was all . . . cut up." The rancher dropped his head into his hands. Then he looked up again, his teeth clenched so that there were big lumps of muscle standing out at the corners of his jaws. His breath whistled in and out between his teeth.

Cardwell stared at Logan, not knowing what to do or say. If they had done an autopsy on Chris, a thorough autopsy, and Dan had seen the results . . .

After about a minute, Logan had relaxed again. He mumbled, "I'm sorry, Roy, I didn't mean to do that."

"My god, Dan, you don't have to apologize. I just don't know what to say." From his own reaction, Cardwell understood that he had been kidding himself all along, and that some part of him had known it from the beginning. He had deserted his patient and his friend and justified it by convincing himself that he was doing the right thing, the only thing he could do under the circumstances. The guilt that washed over him was so strong that he felt powerless to try to make amends. He could only stare mutely at the man he had so severely wronged.

Logan saw Cardwell's confusion, but he couldn't guess at its source. For a moment he thought that he should comfort the older man, say something to make him understand that he didn't blame him for Chris's death, but he realized that actually, he did blame Cardwell. He blamed all of them: for lying to him, for doing unspeakable things to his son, for failing to save Chris's life. But he had thought all that out in the diner. It wouldn't help to blame them; he had to find out what had happened. He had to know the truth. That was why he was here. It wouldn't do either of them any good to try to redeem what was past help.

He said, "Roy, I have to know what happened."

Cardwell, for the moment still in the thrall of his own personal demons, looked blankly at Logan.

"You have to tell me, Roy. You owe me that much." He looked intently at Cardwell. "When did Chris die?"

Cardwell thought, he's laying it right in my lap. He's right, too. I do owe him that much. I owe him a lot more. He put his fork down next to his plate and took a swallow of coffee to fortify himself.

"I'm afraid there's a lot that I have to tell you," he said. "I don't really know where to begin. The problem is that most of the time I didn't know what was happening myself.

"Chris died two days ago, Dan, the first day he was in the hospital. Sometime that night. They tried to save him, but there was nothing they could do. When I came in the next morning, they told me about it, and it was as much a surprise to me as it was to you. I had no idea he was that sick."

"But how could that happen?"

Cardwell felt a million years old. "I don't know. I know it must seem odd to you, that his doctor didn't know how sick he was, but I was taking a lot of things on faith. It seems like misplaced faith now, but I believed them then."

"Who?" Logan was angry now, angry that Cardwell wasn't making sense, was blaming some unseen force that neither of them could confront. "Who was it that you believed?"

"I'm not even sure myself. Holliford, I suppose, because he was so sure of his ground, so familiar with the modern techniques. It's hard for me to keep up, you know, working out here. I don't really have the chance to find out about the new advances in medicine." Cardwell realized that he was making excuses for himself.

"I suppose it was really Spencer, though," he said. "It seemed very clear, at the time." Cardwell found himself getting exasperated. "For god's sake, he's the head of the Public Health Service out here. You'd suppose he knew what he was talking about."

"What did he say?" Logan asked.

"He told me that there was some kind of poison in the area, that they were trying to find out what it was, and that, in the meantime, they were afraid that there would be panic if the news got out. About Chris."

"But why didn't you tell *me?*" Logan demanded.

"Spencer told me not to."

"Goddam it, Roy, I'm his father. Why the hell couldn't you tell me?"

Cardwell had to struggle to keep his voice under control. "I don't know, Dan. I wish I understood myself."

"Shit." Logan said. They weren't getting anywhere. It seemed to him that there was something important unsaid, that Cardwell was talking around the question to avoid telling him the truth. And he had to know the truth.

He said, "Look, Roy, I don't blame you for this. You didn't kill Chris, and I don't suppose you cut him up."

Cardwell shook his head in denial, and Logan went on. "You must have thought you had good reason when you turned his care over to Holliford. Then they made you lie to me, and you must have thought there was some reason for that. But there's something more. I don't know what it is, but you're afraid of something. And I've got to know the truth. You have to tell me the truth, because all this lying has only brought grief to all of us."

But you don't know what you're asking, Cardwell thought.

"Goddam it, Roy. Tell me."

Cardwell shook his head. He didn't have the strength.

Logan reached across the table and took the doctor's hand. "For god's sake, Roy," he said, his voice shaking, "I don't have anyone else to turn to."

Cardwell tried to compose himself. Logan was right. There was no one else who could help him. And the only way Cardwell could help was with the truth. He took a long, deep breath and let it out slowly, put his free hand on the hand of his friend. "I don't really know how to say this, Dan, so I'll make it as simple as I can. You're going to die. In a week perhaps, but probably less."

10

In Conference Room A at Fort Howard, six worried and unhappy men were gathered to plan a way out of their mutual dilemma.

As much as Bill Franklin hated to admit it, he was in the same mess as Nickerson and Spencer and Holliford and Janeway and Cooper. Until they found Logan, they were all in very bad trouble. He sat back in his chair, pushed well away from the conference table so he could see all the others, and listened to Cooper.

The security chief was reviewing the immediate precautions he had taken when word first came from the hospital that Logan was gone. "Under the circumstances," he was saying, "I felt that the best thing was to decide where he was most likely to go and have our men there when he showed up. I've sent a detail to his ranch, and I've got men at the airport and the bus depot. I've also got three men looking for him in Rawlins, downtown, and another one waiting at his bank. And I've asked the police to call me if they pick him up."

Franklin interrupted. "Have you thought about putting up roadblocks?"

"Yes, sir," Cooper said. "We talked about it, that is, but we ruled it out because we were afraid it would cause too much comment. Besides, he didn't have a car, and, if he got one, he'd probably drive it to his ranch, and we've got men stationed there."

Not bad, Franklin thought. I hope we can afford to be so cautious. He said, "I see," and noted on his ever-present pad that he should bring up the question again if Logan didn't turn up right away.

Janeway was not as ready to wait and see. He said, "Major Cooper, I wonder if you're not being too casual about this."

"I assure you," Cooper replied, "we're doing everything we can."

Janeway wasn't satisfied. "You have to remember how important it is that we find this man as quickly as possible. It would be inexcusable to throw this opportunity away. If we can just study him for the next week, it could save us months of research, and give us information we could never learn any other way."

Holliford shifted uncomfortably in his chair. After a few days in soft, wrinkled hospital whites, he was finding his uniform hard to get used to. It seemed to him, listening to the others, that they were overlooking something important. He said, "You know, you can't just assume he's going to act predictably. We don't know what effect the agent is going to have on his brain."

The others looked at him. He saw that he had been right: they hadn't thought of that possibility.

Not one to be left behind, Janeway joined in. "That's right," he said. "What if he goes to the press?"

Holliford didn't see the connection, but Janeway's remark obviously made Cooper nervous. The head of security was clearly irritated when he said, "Well, Doctor, there are limits to what I can do. I can't just send a man to every newspaper in the state and say, 'Disregard this man if he shows up.' "

Franklin, too, was annoyed, but for a different reason. He could see the meeting degenerating into a series of petty squabbles. He had found that men often did that when they had a problem to deal with that made them all nervous. Arguing among themselves took attention away from the thing that was really bothersome. On the other hand, this question of publicity did merit further attention. He said, "I think we can discount for the moment the question of his going to the press. But there is something along those lines that we do have to consider. Major Cooper, you said that the police would inform us if they picked him up. Let's suppose they do pick him up. He might not be able to get to a newspaper editor, but there are always reporters at police headquarters. If the police find him, how are we going to keep the story from leaking?"

Cooper thought for a moment, then said, "I think we can count on the cooperation of the police. I'm sure I made it clear to Captain Petrone that no one is to speak to Logan if he's picked up, but just to be safe I'll call him again and spell out what he's to do, so there won't be any question."

Dr. Spencer, who had been puffing silently on his pipe, took it from his mouth and pointed it at Cooper. "Excuse me," he said, "but what do you intend to do about Dr. Cardwell?"

"That's a good point," Franklin said. "There must be a lot of people at the hospital who could cause trouble about this."

"Yes, sir," Cooper said. "I was just coming to that."

Janeway was sitting back in his chair, leaning against the wall. When he sat up suddenly, the front legs of the chair slammed down against the floor. The others turned to look at him. "What about the nurses?" he said sharply. "What have they been told?"

Holliford broke in quickly. "I don't think we have to worry about them."

"I'm glad to hear it, *Doctor* Holliford," Cooper said sarcastically, stressing the civilian title. "As I recall it, you didn't think we needed more than one man to watch Logan, either."

Holliford saw that Cooper was trying to nail him with the blame for Logan's escape. He knew that just having Simpson in the guardhouse was not going to satisfy everybody, so he fought back. "If he'd done his job," he accused, "there wouldn't have been any trouble."

"If Logan had been sleeping, there wouldn't have been any trouble, either," Cooper said, trying to shift the blame back to Holliford. "I could have sent more than one man."

Nickerson interrupted them. "Gentlemen. That's enough."

"Precisely," Franklin said. "We're here to solve a problem, not assign blame. There'll be plenty of time for that if we fail here. Let's get back to the question of Dr. Cardwell." He asked Cooper, "Do you have a man there?"

"No, sir," Cooper said. "I didn't want to make any

direct contact on that level until I had your approval."

"I'm not talking about making contact, Major. All I have in mind for now is assigning a man to watch him and another to watch his house. If I were Logan that's the first place I would go."

Cooper knew from Franklin's tone that he had lost some important points. He swallowed and said, "Yes, sir. I'll get a team on it right away."

Franklin stood up and brushed imaginary lint from his uniform. "Good," he said. "I think that covers it for now. I'll want an update in two hours."

11

Logan and Cardwell stood together on the doctor's front porch. "I still think you should go back to the hospital," the older man said.

"I can't, Roy. It doesn't make any sense. If all I have is a few days, I'm not going to spend them in any hospital. I have to find out what happened. I've got to see the ranch again."

"They'll be looking for you."

"I guess so. I hope they don't bother you much."

"Don't worry about me, Dan. I'll be fine. And I won't say anything about seeing you."

Logan said, "Thanks," and the two men shook hands solemnly. Then Logan went down the steps and walked quickly away from the house. Cardwell watched him go and thought: Now he's still numb; it hasn't gotten to him yet. I wonder how long it will last.

Ten minutes later, when Cardwell came out of the house, on his way to his first call of the day, he noticed a strange car parked in front of the Carter house across the street. Cardwell only glanced at it briefly, but he had the definite impression that there were two men sitting in the car. It seemed very odd.

12

Logan turned off Route 287 and onto the sand-and-gravel road that passed the gate to his ranch. The motorcycle slid sideways when it hit the loose surface, but Logan had expected that and allowed for it; he accelerated smoothly out of the turn. On either side of the road stretched the rolling land of his ranch, the grass still green in places, dotted with stands of trees. In the distance ahead he could see the high grazing land that marked the far edge of the ranch. In the morning haze it was only a blue line of hills and low mountains. Logan twisted the throttle in his right hand, speeding up and shifting into fourth gear. He was anxious to be home.

As he approached the gate and the turn to the house, Logan slowed down again, downshifted so that the motor would slow the motorcycle, and let up on the throttle. It didn't seem right to come roaring up into the yard, even though there was no one there to disturb. He was barely going ten miles an hour when he came over the small rise that gave him a view of the house. It was still and peaceful, the eastern windows golden with the reflected morning sun. Logan stopped for a moment, looking at the house and the well-remembered yard, the toolshed, and Emily's bright green doghouse that Chris had helped build when he was barely big enough to hold a hammer. Unexpectedly, the ranch-house door opened, and a man came out of the house; a man wearing an army uniform. Logan watched, confused and uncomprehending, as the man walked to the end of the porch and peered off toward the gate, then walked back to the door and into the house again.

The rancher was suddenly dizzy and weak; the world went fuzzy and red. His grip on the motorcycle's handlebars tightened as he tried to keep himself from falling. Through the blurry red haze, he saw again the hospital corridor and the man in uniform coming out of the morgue carrying a plastic bag full of clothes. His vision cleared. Coming toward him was an army jeep carrying four soldiers. The jeep turned at the ranch gate and drove up to the house; the jeep's horn blared twice, and another man in uniform came out of the house. There was saluting, and the five soldiers went inside.

Logan decided that he had seen enough. He started the motorcycle again and drove quickly past his gate and the lane that led to his house. He had been bewildered by Roy Cardwell's stories of the Public Health Service and the hospital staff and mysterious epidemics of poison. Finding the army wherever he went just made things even more confusing.

He knew he would get onto his ranch somehow, but he wasn't ready to try just yet.

13

Notes and Impressions/Fort Howard
Day Four—Logan, Daniel Charles
It seems that we may have made a mistake about Logan from the beginning. He has been a rancher virtually since he was born. It shouldn't have taken a genius to know that he would find a long period in the hospital less tolerable than most, especially since he didn't have any symptoms that would have been apparent to him. We were probably lucky that he followed "doctor's orders" as long as he did. We got a lot of good data those first three days. The only trouble now is strictly a p.r. question. Of course, expect Janeway and company to get as much mileage as they can from the military screwing up their research. That shouldn't be too much problem if handled correctly. Most likely thing now is that Logan wants to get back to his ranch. Fort Howard can't cover an area that big, but all we really have to worry about is the peripheral roads. If he wants to go out onto his ranch and stay there, he has my blessing. Query: how much does he know?

14

While the clerk wrote down the prices of the other things he had picked out, Logan looked at the long row of rifles locked into a display stand behind the counter. It was a good selection, ranging from small-caliber varmint and target rifles to a big bolt-action match rifle. Logan noticed two rifles among them that had counterparts on his own rifle rack: a centennial copy of the old Winchester '73, and a long-barreled bolt-action twenty-two. At the very end of the row, he saw what looked like a small plastic rifle stock, with no action or barrel. It seemed strange, because it wasn't a gun shop, just a sporting goods store, and Logan didn't expect them to carry such specialized accessories. He asked the clerk about it.

The clerk laughed. "Everybody asks me that. It's not a stock, though, it's a whole rifle. Here, I'll show you." He unlocked the display rack and handed Logan what still looked to him like a plastic rifle stock. If it was really a whole rifle, Logan was surprised at its weight. It couldn't have been much more than four pounds.

"Pull off the shoulder piece," the clerk told him.

Logan tugged at the rubber guard that covered the shoulder end of the rifle stock. It took a little work, but it came free. Beneath it, there were two large holes in the plastic, one round and the other rectangular: each of the holes had something in it. Logan turned the thing over and shook it slightly. From the rectangular hole came a metal contraption that looked like a barrel-less automatic pistol. Logan put it on the counter and drew from the round hole a metal tube that could only be a rifle barrel. It took him no more than a couple of minutes of fooling with the pieces to figure how to put it all together. When he was done, he had a light, compact, semiautomatic rifle.

The clerk smiled at him. "Neat, isn't it? Floats, too. They made a whole bunch of them for the air force, and then they decided to let us poor civilians in on it, too."

Logan said, "I'll take one." It was just what he needed. He was no good at all with a handgun, and he had been wondering how he was going to carry a rifle around with him without attracting a lot of attention. This would solve both parts of the problem.

The clerk took a box from the shelf behind him and listed the price of the rifle with Logan's other purchases.

"I guess you'll want some shells."

Logan nodded, and the clerk put two boxes of cartridges on the counter next to the rifle box.

"Now, let's see," the clerk said. "That's one AR-seven rifle, one sheepskin jacket, one motorcycle helmet with full visor, pair of gloves, luggage straps, two boxes of hollow-nosed twenty-two long rifles, and . . ." He picked up a corner of the jacket to look under it, "And one pair of 8X50 binoculars. Did you want anything else?"

"No, that's all."

The clerk punched the prices on his adding machine and rang up the total.

"That'll be two forty-seven and eighty-nine cents, with the tax. How did you want to pay that?"

"I've got a credit card," Logan said, hunting through his wallet for the never-used plastic card the bank in Rawlins had sent him months ago. "Here it is."

The clerk took the card and fished a dog-eared pamphlet from under the counter. Logan watched the man check for his card number in the pamphlet. While he watched, he took the jacket from the counter and put it on, slipping the two boxes of cartridges into the pockets. He hoped that nobody at the hospital would think to trace him through the credit card.

15

Stoney Cooper knew how important it was for his men to find Logan in a hurry. If they did, he could still come out of this a hero. If not, then there would be a frantic search for someone to blame, and the most likely candidate was Stonewall Jackson Cooper, Major, United States Army.

He sat in the cab of the troop transport truck, ignoring the bouncing, dusty ride and the noise of the twenty men jammed into the back of the truck, trying to figure out how to deploy his men. He had a lot of territory to cover, mostly hilly, and a lot of it wooded. On top of that, he didn't even have enough men to cover the perimeter the way he wanted to.

He pulled the dirty, torn, much-folded USGS quarter

map from the pocket of his fatigues and unfolded it. He got it open to the section that covered Logan's ranch, only ripping it once in the process, but the truck's progress was too bumpy and uncertain for him to be able to read the small map markings. He gave up for the moment. There would be plenty of time for map reading when they got to the ranch house in a couple of minutes. Meanwhile, he imagined he was Logan and wondered where he would go.

16

Logan glanced behind him to be sure the luggage straps were holding and then he turned off the road and headed the motorcycle across an open, grassy meadow. At first, it felt about the same as the road, but before long he began to hit rabbit holes and old tractor ruts and big, loose stones. The bike jumped around a little, jolting Logan when he hit a large hole or bounced over a dead branch, but the big engine and the knobby tires kept him going without any real trouble. From time to time, he was hit by a pebble or a clump of dirt kicked up by the front wheel, and some unlucky insects were splattered into oblivion on his visor. He ignored it all, and the wind that buffeted him as well, completely engrossed in the problem of getting onto the ranch.

He knew there were soldiers at the house, so he would have to avoid that end of the place. He had seen no other soldiers when he passed by in the morning, but it seemed reasonable to him that there might be more now. On the way in from Bairoil, where he had done his shopping, Logan had tried to place himself in the position of an army officer trying to cover the ranch with a company or two of soldiers not particularly trained for that kind of work. He had figured out six different ways to cover the boundaries of the ranch well enough to make it very hard to get through.

There were some things in his favor, though. Most important, he knew that the standard maps of the area were incorrect in at least two places, and he meant to take advantage of the fact.

At the far end of the meadow, the going began to get much rougher, and Logan slowed down. He was looking for an old, dried-up stream bed that came down from the hills at the meadow's edge. When he found it, he followed it for about half a mile along the foot of the hills. Then it widened and deepened, and he carefully and precariously maneuvered the bike down into the bed itself. There was a patch of loose, gravelly pebbles where the stream-bed walls met the floor of the bed, and he hit it at a bad angle. The front wheel went out from under the bike, and Logan flew over the handlebars to land jarringly on his side and slide several feet.

Shaking, he picked himself up. He had ripped a hole about six inches long in one leg of his pants and torn out the palm of one glove, but, except for being bruised and frightened, he was all right. The motorcycle lay on its side, still running, the rear wheel spinning furiously. Logan limped over to it and hit the kill button. Immediately, the motor went dead and the rear wheel stopped spinning. With some effort, Logan got the bike upright again, straining against its three hundred pounds. He checked to see that the wires he had spliced to make it run were still firmly attached to each other and that he hadn't lost anything from the luggage rack. Then he kick-started the motor back to life.

As the stream bed progressed into the hills, it got deeper and wider. Logan had wondered, the first time he found it, why there was so much more to it in the hills, until he discovered that the main bed, which he was riding in now, broke up into a dozen or more smaller streams just before the meadow. He stayed in the bed, climbing slowly, until it became a narrow, twisting canyon. This was the part that wasn't on the map. Seen from overhead, or in an aerial photograph, the overhanging sides of the canyon merged into an apparently unbroken hillside. The stream bed was completely invisible. Even if someone were scanning the terrain above Logan as he passed, he would have no idea that Logan was there, or even that there was anywhere that Logan might be.

After another two miles, the stream bed began to grow smaller and shallower again. Logan speeded up, because he didn't want to linger where he could be seen. He was careful to avoid the large rocks that littered the floor of the stream bed, and as soon as the walls were gradual enough, he shifted down into first gear and scrambled up out of the bed, showering rocks and dirt behind him, the motorcycle going sideways and almost over but the tires holding enough to get him to the top.

He stopped there, getting his breath back and looking around for signs of anything hostile. He realized that he was taking his fears about the army's searching for him very seriously, even though he had no concrete reason to feel that way. His caution came from more than just the tension of trying to get onto the ranch undetected. He had some kind of instinct or premonition: somewhere in all this unbelievable horror, the army had an important role.

Logan's imaginings and fears were borne out more quickly and more completely than he had expected them to be. He came out of the stream bed not far from the corral that held Chris's sheep, and without even thinking where he was going, he headed immediately in the direction of the corral. As it came into view, Logan was aware that something was wrong. The fence was intact, complete with its proud sign put up by Chris when he had reason to suppose that he would be able to raise his four sheep, and the bucket still hung from the spout of the old water pump, but there was something wrong with the sheep. Three of them lay motionless on the ground, inert lumps of mutton and wool, and the fourth, Logan could see as he got closer, was staggering slowly around the corral, stiff-legged and uncoordinated.

Logan left the motorcycle next to the pump, resting it on its kickstand. Once he was inside the corral, he could see for sure that the three sheep lying motionless were dead. Each was host to a busy swarm of flies, and the smell was almost overpowering. Logan looked at them briefly, saw that their muzzles were caked with dried blood and yellow-white foam. He was reminded of the sheep he had seen on the hill that morning when he found Chris sick, the day after Chris had last tended the sheep he was looking at now.

Logan blinked tears from his eyes and walked toward the single living sheep in the corral. It tried to avoid him, but it couldn't move well enough. It stumbled, went down on its knees, then staggered up as Logan reached it. He pulled its head up so he could look into its eyes, saw that it, too, had dried blood on its muzzle, with fresh blood seeping from its nostrils. He turned away.

In turning, he caught sight of something attached to a hind leg of one of the dead sheep. Steeling himself against the smell, he bent down so he could see it better. It was a large tag, held to the sheep's leg by a piece of heavy wire that passed through the leg just above the hoof. The tag read:

U.S. ARMY

FORT HOWARD

ANIMAL:	Sheep
CAUSE OF DEATH:	Undet
AGENT:	MX3
TEST NUMBER:	None assigned
SUBJECT NUMBER:	4–301–R

Logan stared at the tag, at one time understanding everything and understanding nothing. He noticed, through his fog, that there was a red mark on one of the other sheep and he got up to see what it was.

It must have been the one that had been dead the longest, but even so, Logan would never know why it was the only one to be so marked. The red thing that had caught his eye was a gaping, rotten-edged gash in the sheep's side that must have been made by a coyote or perhaps a buzzard. Logan couldn't pull his eyes away from the raw flesh and the gleaming bone and tendon underneath. It made him think of the thing he had found in the drawer in the hospital, that thing that had only a few days before been his son.

Everything went black for a second, and he swayed and fell to his knees. He held his head in his hands and took long, deep breaths, trying to keep himself under control.

He was vaguely conscious of struggling to his feet and stumbling out of the corral. There were fleeting sensations of being on the motorcycle again, going somewhere. To find out about something.

When his head cleared, he was on a hilltop, lying prone with the binoculars in one hand and the rifle in the other. Looking around, he saw that he was on the hill that he and Chris always called the "the lookout," because it gave a view of almost the entire ranch. He put the binoculars to his eyes and scanned the vista that lay before him.

The ranch house was quiet. It looked deserted, except for the jeep and two army trucks that were parked behind the equipment shed. On the road that ran by the gate, there were a few soldiers standing at uneven intervals. Closer to the hill, there was a grazing area that was the scene of a great deal of activity. Four large, open, olive-drab trucks stood in a ragged group in a field littered with dead sheep. Among the trucks and the sheep stalked a score of grotesque figures that looked like nightmare parodies of men. They had huge, bloated limbs and bodies, and swollen, misshapen heads with blank, shiny, rectangular faces. Loose grayish skin or clothes hung from them in ugly folds. The figures were loading the dead sheep into the four trucks.

As Logan watched the men in the bizarre protective suits, he became aware of the faint, ragged buzz of a distant helicopter. He looked up from his binoculars and searched the sky for the source of the noise. He found the helicopter quickly. It was passing over the ranch at no more than a few hundred feet, a little beyond the grisly scene he had been watching. He followed the helicopter for a while and then returned to his scrutiny of the men loading dead sheep into the trucks.

One of the trucks, full now, pulled away from the unearthly group and started toward the dirt road that led to the ranch house. Almost immediately, it was replaced by another truck that appeared as if by magic from the direction of the main highway.

Logan remained absorbed in the scene until he realized that he could still hear the helicopter, long after he would have expected it to have gone well out of hearing. In fact, it was considerably louder than it had been the first time he had noticed it. He looked up again. When he found the helicopter, it was going in the same direction it had been before, crossing the ranch on a rough north-south line. But now it was much closer to the lookout hill. Logan watched it until it reached the southern edge of the ranch, where it turned around and came back on a path parallel to the one it had just been following, but even closer to where Logan lay watching. It was as if the helicopter was searching for something. Logan realized quickly that it was probably searching for him.

He got up quickly and ran to the motorcycle, carrying the rifle and the binoculars. He didn't bother to break the rifle down, but just strapped it and the binoculars to the motorcycle's luggage rack. He was reaching out for his helmet, which was on the seat of the motorcycle, when he felt suddenly faint. He grabbed for the motorcycle to steady himself and knocked the helmet to the ground.

When he thought the dizziness was past, he reached for the helmet. He had been premature: he almost fell. Steadying himself on the motorcycle, he tried again, reaching down slowly and carefully.

He retrieved the helmet and put it on. Then, straddling the motorcycle, he kicked the starter, but so weakly that the engine barely turned over. He held the grips tighter and raised himself as high as he could, using his weight to add to the force of his next kick. This time, the motor turned over and caught. He started down the hill, back toward the corral. His sudden weakness puzzled him; he wondered if it had anything to do with whatever it was that, little by little, was bringing him closer to death.

As he came into sight of the corral, Logan saw that there was a large army truck parked near the water pump. Instantly, he reached out for the motorcycle's kill button and coasted down the hill in an eerie silence broken only by the noise of the wind whipping at him and the scrabbling of the tires on the loose dirt of the hillside. He crouched down over the handlebars and headed the bike into a thick stand of trees and undergrowth. Once he was well into the trees, Logan stopped the motorcycle and slid quietly to the ground. Holding the rifle ready, he watched as two soldiers in fatigues, high rubber boots, and gas masks led the one remaining live sheep from Chris's corral up into the back of the truck.

While Logan crouched out of sight in the shelter of the trees, the searching helicopter passed overhead.

17

A4DX693–P172–E
TOPSECRETCLASSQSCRAMBLE
CODEDESIGCOWBOYEIGHTZEROZERO
CODESQUAREDBUTTERFLYORANGE
GENERAL SAMUEL HILL
JOINTCHIEFS PENTAGON
PRIORITY BLUEREDRED
BEGINS. REPORT DAYFOUR EAGLE. CANCEL ALL PREVIOUS ESTIMATES. SITUATION CHANGED NEGATIVE BY ESCAPE SUBJECT DANIEL CHARLES LOGAN ZEROFOURHUNDRED HOURS MYHOUSE PLUSMINUS TWO. MAINTAINING LOW PROFILE SECURITY NET WITH MINIMUM INF COOPERATION WYO STATE POLICE. NO CONTACT TO HOUR THIS REPORT. PRESS TEAM ALERTED AND FUNCTIONING. PROBABILITY BAD NEWS LOW BUT MEASURABLE. ASSUME SUBJECT IGNORANT OF CONDITION AND CAUSE. CURRENT EVALUATION NEUTRAL. SENSITIVE PERIOD DATE PLUS NINETYSIX HOURS PLUSMINUS FORTYEIGHT. ALL ACTIVITY MYHOUSE TO BE MONITORED AND RECORDED STARTING DATE THIS TRANSMISSION. PLEASE ADVISE OF SPECIAL HANDLING RECOMMENDATIONS IF ANY NEEDED IN LIGHT OF SITUATION YOURHOUSE. SIGNED FRANKLIN COL.

18

Matthew Spencer was in bed, reading. At the foot of the bed his Persian cat was industriously cleaning his paws. Spencer reached out for the tall glass on the bedside table and took a small sip of the highball he had mixed himself. The cool glass felt good in his hands; he pressed it momentarily to his cheek, then replaced it on the table and opened his book again.

His concentration was interrupted by the loud, insistent ringing of the doorbell. He looked at the clock on the table. It was well after ten. Annoyed by the repeated ringing of the bell, he got up and belted his dressing gown closed over his pajamas. The cat, startled, jumped from the bed. Spencer hurried to the door, stopping briefly to pull back the curtain over the window next to the door and peer out onto the porch. He couldn't see anything. Whoever it was, he was standing in the shadows beyond the illumination of the porch light.

Spencer opened the door a crack and asked, "Who is it?"

There was no answer, but Spencer sensed someone moving on the porch. He opened the door a little wider and asked again, more annoyed, "Who is it?"

He had the impression of a drawn, pale face and unkempt hair. A hoarse voice said, "Dan Logan."

Spencer was amazed. He opened the door all the way.

The rancher was standing in the doorway, dirty and disheveled, one arm pressed to his side as if in pain. Spencer said, "Come in."

He stepped aside to let Logan into the entrance hall. Looking at the rancher, he was moved immediately to say, "You know, you should be in the hospital."

While Spencer was in the middle of his sentence, Logan, inside the house now, kicked the door shut. He raised the arm he had been holding by his side: in it was the rifle. He shoved its cold, hard muzzle toward Spencer's face; the doctor gasped and back-pedaled away until he was brought up short against the living-room doorframe. Helpless and frightened, he stared down the small dark hole in the barrel of the rifle and held his breath.

"Is there anybody else here?" Logan growled.

Spencer started to raise his hand to wipe his sweating face, but as soon as he moved, Logan pressed the rifle hard against his forehead.

"What do you mean?" Spencer stammered.

"Are you alone in here?" Logan punctuated the question by putting extra pressure on the rifle.

Spencer winced as the muzzle of the rifle bit into his forehead. He said, "Yes," then added, but not quite quickly enough to be convincing, "That is, I'm alone right now."

"I want to see the rest of the house." Logan said.

Spencer hesitated and felt the rifle dig into his head again. "All right," he said quickly.

He turned and started through the living room.

"Slow down," Logan said.

Spencer stopped. Again, Logan pressed the muzzle of the rifle against Spencer's head, holding it there while he looked around the living room. He saw a small room, well furnished but neither warm nor inviting. It was somehow too neat, too carefully arranged, with small dishes and statues precisely arranged on inlaid tables, and the overstuffed cushions of the sofa and chairs meticulously plumped up, as if they had never been sat in.

Spencer looked again at Logan. With the opportunity to see him in good light, Spencer noticed how grimy he was: boots caked with mud, trousers stained and torn, even his new-looking jacket bearing scuff marks and patches of dirt. The rancher's face was tight, drawn, pale, the eyes wide, a small muscle jumping in the corner of his jaw.

When Logan was satisfied that there was no one lurking in the corners or behind the couch, he lowered the rifle and poked Spencer in the belly with it.

"All right. Go ahead."

Spencer took him through the dining area and into the kitchen. Again, Logan stopped him so that he could see into all the corners of the room. He was acting, Spencer thought, as if he expected to find someone hiding in the kitchen cabinets. Beginning to get himself back under control, Spencer wondered if there was some way he could turn the situation to his advantage.

When Logan was done surveying the kitchen, Spencer said, "Mr. Logan, just what is it you're looking for?"

Logan didn't acknowledge the question. He prodded Spencer with the rifle and said, "Keep going."

Spencer turned and led Logan out of the kitchen and into a short hallway.

"In there," Logan said, indicating a partly open door.

Spencer opened the door. The room beyond it was dark.

"Go inside and turn on the light."

Spencer shrugged and stepped through the doorway. He flipped the light switch, revealing a crowded pantry and storeroom, lined with shelves of canned food, household cleaners, and miscellaneous tools. Logan backed up so that Spencer could come back out into the hall. The next room was Spencer's bedroom. The book lay open on the pillow, where Spencer had left it, and on the bedside table the ice was melting in Spencer's highball. The two men stood in the middle of the room while Logan looked around. He saw two closed doors at the other end of the room, pointed the rifle at one of them. "Open it," he said.

Spencer started to protest. "But . . ."

"Open it."

Spencer went to the door and opened it. It was a clothes closet.

"The other one," Logan said.

Obediently, Spencer walked to the other door. It led to a bathroom. Logan came up to stand beside him.

"Go inside."

When Spencer was well into the bathroom, Logan stepped into the doorway. He saw a long, narrow tiled room, spotless and gleaming. There was no one in it but Spencer, who stood helpless at the far end, near the toilet, looking trapped and frightened despite his efforts to appear calm.

Logan backed away from the door. "All right," he said. "You can come out."

Logan made Spencer come out into the bedroom and then lead him back into the living room. On the way past the front door, Logan stopped to slam home the heavy bolt that Spencer used for nighttime security.

When they were in the living room again, Logan stopped Spencer. "All right," he said. "Sit down."

Spencer was standing next to the sofa. Slowly and carefully he sat down, watching Logan warily. Neither man noticed Spencer's cat, curled up in an easy chair at the far end of the room.

"You know, Mr. Logan," Spencer said carefully, "you don't need that gun. Nobody wants to hurt you." He spoke slowly, choosing his words with caution and enunciating them clearly, as if he were dealing with someone dangerously unbalanced.

Logan sat on the arm of a chair near the sofa and rested the rifle on his knee so that it pointed at Spencer's chest. His voice was tense, almost quivering, but controlled.

"I want to know what happened to my boy."

The demand ran through Spencer like a knife. So he does know, he thought. Then: I've got to be careful here; I don't know how much he knows and how much he's guessing.

He said, "I wish I knew that myself."

Logan's voice was harsh. "My boy is dead," he grated. "I want to know what killed him."

"I'll be honest with you, Mr. Logan. We still don't know."

Logan's intense control began to slip; Spencer's evasiveness was sharpening his anger. He said, "Damn you, don't lie to me. You told me Chris was all right."

"I didn't want to upset you just then . . ." Spencer was reaching for justification he knew was not there.

"In the morning, I was going to . . ."

Logan cut him off. "Don't give me that shit! He's been dead for two days."

Oh my god, Spencer thought. Oh my good god.

Logan spoke from between clenched teeth, his words measured and deliberate. "Something got to me and my sheep, and it killed my boy. Now the army's all over my ranch. I want to know what happened."

"I didn't have anything to do with it," Spencer said.

"You've been in this from the beginning. You and the army."

Spencer saw that it would be dangerous to try to evade Logan's questions much longer, but he thought he might see a way out. He spoke slowly and cautiously, keeping his voice low and even. "I think there must have been a misunderstanding." He tried to smile. "I'm not with the army, I'm with the Public Health Service. I didn't have anything to do with it."

"Goddam it, my son is dead! I want to know what's going on."

Spencer shrank back into the couch. Again, he tried to smile comfortingly at Logan. "You know, Mr. Logan, you really ought to be in the hospital. The disease that killed your son is killing you, too. If you don't get back to the hospital, you'll be dead within two weeks."

Logan stared at Spencer, who took the rancher's silence to mean that his words had struck home. Spencer sat forward, about to press his advantage.

Very softly, Logan said, "I know how sick I am. I talked to Roy Cardwell, and I know I'm going to die in a few days."

For a long moment, neither man spoke.

Then Logan, suddenly furious, grated, "Now I want to know what the hell is going on."

"Really, I don't know," Spencer stammered. "And what I do know . . . I can't tell you." He looked pleadingly at Logan. "This is all secret information."

Logan felt that he couldn't hold himself back much longer. "Tell me, goddam it," he shouted.

Spencer shrank back in the sofa. When he spoke, he was frankly begging Logan for relief. He said, "Look, Mr. Logan, what good could it possibly do you if I told you these things? How could it help you?"

Enraged, Logan raised the rifle over his head and smashed it down into the porcelain lamp on the table next to Spencer. The lamp shattered and crashed to the floor, taking the fragile table with it.

Spencer, his back pressed hard into the sofa, stared at the fallen, fragmented lamp with wide, straining eyes. Across from him, Logan took long, deep, shuddering breaths. His nostrils flared and bunches of muscle jumped at the corners of his jaw. In one hand, he held the rifle with the muzzle touching Spencer's throat. He reached out with his free hand and grabbed the collar of Spencer's dressing gown, lifting the terrified doctor part way off the sofa.

"Goddam you," Logan raged.

At the far end of the room, the cat, startled by the noise of the falling lamp and frightened now by Logan's fury, jumped from the seat of the easy chair to the top of the chair back.

Catching the motion out of the corner of his eye, Logan whirled and fired. The noise of the shots reverberated deafeningly in the small room. The cat, killed instantly, was slammed back against a bookcase, its body jerking with the repeated impact of several bullets before it fell to the floor, a gory heap of bright fur mottled with the brighter red of blood.

Instinctively, Spencer moved toward the cat, but his motion was stopped by the smoky muzzle of the rifle, which moved to a point about two inches from his left ear. He sank back onto the sofa.

The violent outburst left both men shaken. Spencer cradled his head in his hands, wisps of gray hair straggling out between his fingers as he rocked back and forth, sobbing. Logan watched him and fought to get himself back under control, gripping the rifle so tightly that his knuckles stood out white on the backs of his hands.

Slowly, Spencer looked up. He seemed smaller, and older. He rubbed an uncertain, shaking hand over his face and shuddered.

"All right," he said, without spirit.

"Tell me what killed my son."

Spencer rubbed his face again, then braced his hands on the seat of the sofa as if to hold himself up.

"It was a chemical called MX3," he said weakly.

"Go on."

Spencer closed his eyes. "MX3," he said again. "It was developed at Chivington Research Laboratories in Sinclair. They develop chemicals there for the army. They were conducting tests with it at Fort Howard." He stopped, exhausted. Now it was out. From now on, nothing mattered except being left in peace. Dimly, he heard Logan say, "Go on."

SIX

1

Franklin looked around the room at the others. The three officers and the civilian were blank-faced from a combination of sleeplessness and shock.

Nickerson, who was wearing his uniform slacks and an unpressed tunic open at the neck, banged his hand on the big conference table.

"All right," he said wearily. "Let's get going." Before Nickerson could say anything else, Franklin cut in.

"Gentlemen," he said. There was no trace of tiredness in his voice. "As you know, I'm here at Fort Howard as the representative of the Joint Chiefs of Staff. For that reason, I've been given special command authority here. I hoped not to have to use that authority, but I'm afraid I no longer have any choice."

Nickerson looked at Franklin with the wide eyes of the newly betrayed. He had expected Franklin at least to warn him. Cooper and Holliford were dumbstruck, as if they had just found a corpse buried in their back yard.

Franklin said, "I'm not going to take up your time right now with a long briefing, and I don't think we have to subject Dr. Spencer to an exhausting interrogation which I'm sure he isn't up to right now."

Spencer looked up from contemplating the thick white bandage that covered his right hand. Franklin was right. The last thing Spencer could stand now was to be grilled by Nickerson and Cooper and the others.

"Right now," Franklin said, "I'd like to be alone with Dr. Spencer. I'll be with the rest of you in a few minutes."

The three stunned officers filed from the room, leaving Franklin and Spencer alone. Franklin waited for a minute, then said, "You must be exhausted."

"Oh, Jesus, yes," Spencer said. He lifted his injured hand gingerly and rested it on the table. "I could use about three days' sleep."

Franklin stood up and began to walk around at the head of the table. "I think I have a suggestion that will solve my own worst problem and let you get your rest, too."

"That would be a miracle."

Franklin stopped pacing and put his hand on Spencer's shoulder. "I really think it's the best thing. My medical officer, Major Kagle, has had special training in sedation and anesthetics. He's also an expert debriefing officer. Why don't I have him get something out of his kit that will kill your pain and put you to sleep and at the same time, while you're under, let him get some details of what happened to you. You won't even know what's happening."

Spencer couldn't suppress a shudder. He guessed that Franklin was talking about Pentothal, or scopolamine. And there was nothing to do but go along with it. He couldn't stand up to interrogation in his condition, not again. He just had to figure that it didn't matter. There was no way he could help himself by keeping anything from them at this point.

Slowly, defeatedly, he nodded his agreement.

2

STATE OF WYOMING
HIGHWAY PATROL

Communications Division — DISPATCHER'S COPY
Std. Dispatch Form AD-142 — ALL UNITS TRANSMISSION

TIME: 0645
CODE: (10–16)
ADDTL: A–T–L

TEXT: All units: Attempt to locate: Daniel Charles Logan. (descr) White/male/6′2″/Hair:brn/Eyes:brn/210 lbs
Reported ARMED with rifle
Do *not* (REPEAT) apprehend—
Report location and maintain contact.
Last location: Casper, north side

REPEAT MESSAGE EVERY: hour
FILE WITH: none
SOURCE: N/A

3

The Highway Patrol cruiser pulled to the side of the road in a cloud of fine, dry dust. The trooper behind the wheel cut off the siren that Holliford had thought was going to drive him crazy as they sped down the highway. Captain Petrone got out of the cruiser, and Holliford followed him. As they walked toward the roadblock, they were flanked by the driver and the other trooper who had been riding in the front seat.

Holliford glanced at the three Highway Patrol cruisers that blocked the road and the line of cars backed up, waiting to be passed through. It seemed to him that they were being very efficient, taking so much care when they already thought they had the man they were looking for.

Petrone seemed to read his mind. "No sense calling them off until we're sure. Right, Major?"

"Absolutely." Holliford looked around. "Where are you holding him?"

Petrone pointed to the side of the road, where a late-model station wagon was parked next to two more Highway Patrol cars. There was a group of troopers gathered around the station wagon.

As they came around past the first patrol car, Holliford could see a man leaning on the station wagon with his arms outstretched, his hands on the station wagon roof, and his feet well back. Two of the troopers held their revolvers pointed unwaveringly at the middle of the man's back while a third and fourth trooper examined a sporting rifle that Holliford guessed they had found in the station wagon.

The man being guarded looked about six feet tall, although it was hard to tell because of his awkward and apparently uncomfortable position. He was wearing tan work pants and a fleece-lined sheepskin jacket. Close, Holliford thought, but not close enough.

He said, "That's not him."

"Are you sure?"

Holliford glared at the portly Highway Patrol captain. "Of course I'm sure." He turned and walked back toward the car that had brought them.

4

Crouched next to the motorcycle pretending to fiddle with the battery leads, Logan looked across the road at the long, low, modern building marked by a large, oddly angular, brown sign that said "Chivington Research Laboratories." Logan found it hard to tell the difference between the building he was looking at and any of the other new factory and office buildings that had begun to spring up inexplicably here and there off Route 80.

The one difference he knew about wasn't apparent from the outside. This building had been built with a more important motive at work than the search for profit. If Spencer was right, the government had built itself a death factory here in the scenic outskirts of Sinclair, Wyoming. Logan believed that Spencer had been telling the truth, even though it was impossible for him to imagine by looking at the outside of the building what really went on behind the clean concrete walls and the impressive expanse of glass.

Logan scanned the grounds carefully, placing in his mind the long curved driveway, the parking lot, and the carefully pruned bushes and small trees that lined the sides of the building. Logan estimated that there were about two acres of cleared and landscaped land around the building. Then, for several hundred yards on either side, the road that ran past the building was flanked by thick, untended woods.

As Logan surveyed the slight hill to the north of the building, a car came over the top of the rise and started down in his direction. Logan closed the side panel of the motorcycle and stood up, watching the car. It was a sedan, painted a uniform, dull olive-drab. Logan flipped down the visor of his helmet and started the motorcycle.

By the time the sedan turned into the long driveway leading to the laboratory building, Logan was accelerating down the road. He had a brief glimpse of four soldiers in the car and the legend "Military Police" in small white letters on its door.

5

No matter how often he worked with Arnold Lieberman, Bill Franklin couldn't get over the feeling of uneasiness he had whenever they were in the same room. Franklin had no clear idea what it was about Lieberman that made him feel that way. He knew that the tall, dark-haired lieutenant colonel was at least ten years older than he was, but he knew equally well that he looked at least five years younger. Yet, Franklin wasn't jealous of his craggy good looks, or his success with women. Franklin didn't think he was bothered by Lieberman's Jewishness, either: among other things, Lieberman was a committed atheist, and, in any case, Franklin paid less attention to such things than most of his fellow officers. Nor was it Lieberman's job. Franklin passed no judgments on the fact that Lieberman had killed at least twice in cold blood, at close range, in quiet and unheralded defense of his country, before he had been elevated to the more sedate post of deputy commander of the small, elite group that did special jobs for the Joint Staff.

Franklin guessed that what really bothered him most about Lieberman was his air of casual, uncaring aloofness. Lieberman was in every sense the man who wasn't there, the very indispensable but invisible and untouchable man who wasn't there, and he wore his invulnerability like a badge.

Right now, he was puffing serenely on a hundred-dollar briar pipe and considering the brief outline of Eagle that Franklin had just given him. After a moment he spoke, his voice carrying an odd mixture of New York and Virginia.

"All right, Bill, I can see your problem. What I can't see so well is what you want the Special Detail for."

"It's very simple, Arn. We've got to keep the lid on this as long as possible. Mostly, it's an investigative problem. To put it as simply as possible, we've got a madman loose out there. Or we have to assume that we do." Franklin stood up and walked over to the window.

"The people here are no good at this," he said, looking out across the Fort Howard parade ground. "It's got to be handled very delicately. Otherwise, we'll just defeat ourselves."

"Yeah, I can see that," Lieberman said. "Go running around in uniform asking questions and frightening people and you'll stir up a lot more curiosity than Logan would if you just left him alone."

"Exactly. What we've got to do is find him fast and at the same time try to anticipate his moves and be ready to neutralize them in case we don't find him first. I want you to take a look at the transcript of Major Kagle's interrogation of Dr. Spencer. I think there's a lot in it for you."

"I'll get on it right away. But I have a suggestion right now."

Franklin turned away from the window to face Lieberman. "What is it?"

"We know that this Dr. Cardwell told him about Holliford and Spencer. Then Logan disappeared for a whole day and turned up at Spencer's house. But he didn't do Spencer much damage, just got the story out of him. I'll bet he turns up here next. Or back with Cardwell or Spencer. I think I should put a man on the two civilians, and put my men on security here. And maybe at that laboratory, too."

"It sounds good. There's a local security man on Cardwell now, but he'd frighten Logan away, and I'm afraid he's making Cardwell uneasy. Cardwell called the PHS this morning and asked for Dr. Spencer. He was pretty angry, I gather. When he didn't get through, he left the message that he wanted them to leave him alone. Maybe your man would be less obvious."

Lieberman took his pipe out of his mouth. "Maybe," he said mockingly, and laughed.

Franklin walked back to his chair. "Let's say you put a man on Cardwell and Spencer. I think you should put a man on Janeway, too, but I don't want to disturb the regular security arrangements at Chivington right now. They have a very carefully built-up cover, and I don't think we should do anything that might hurt it. If Logan starts ranting about a nerve-gas factory, it won't help for the civilian employees in the front offices to start wondering about the strange new security people that have begun to turn up."

"That makes sense." Lieberman stood up. "I'd better get going, then. I'll arrange for the tails and read that transcript. Meet you back here in half an hour."

"Fine."

"And I think I'm going to need some maps and personnel rosters for here and the laboratory."

"Right." Franklin watched as Lieberman walked briskly from the room. Whatever uneasiness he felt at being with Lieberman, it was still a relief to have him around to rely on.

6

Logan walked back and forth next to the gas pump, stretching his legs, while a grease-smeared teenager filled the motorcycle gas tank. Logan still felt weak, even after sleeping twice, for four or five hours each time. The confrontation with Spencer had taken a lot out of him.

"That's seventy-three cents," the teenager said, putting the hose back into its slot in the gas pump.

"Here." Logan handed him the credit card.

"It's only seventy-three cents, Mister."

"Well," Logan said. "I'm a little short on cash, and I need what I have."

The attendant shrugged. "O.K.," he said. "What the hell." He went into the station's small, crowded office to make out the credit slip.

Logan leaned on the motorcycle. He was getting dizzy again. His vision was dark and blurred, and he was having trouble breathing. He wondered how much longer he had to live.

7

"The way I see it," Lieberman said, "there isn't anything else I can do. Truth is, you had the whole thing pretty well doped out. All that was left for me was to put the right men in the right slots."

Lieberman took the cover off the plate on the table in front of him and looked with no great enthusiasm at a thin slice of roast beef and some gluey mashed potatoes, both covered with thick, floury gravy. Across the small table from him, Franklin surveyed his own meal with comparable distaste.

"Good. I'm glad you feel that way," Franklin said. "No matter how sure I am of my judgment in a situation like this, I can't get completely free of the nagging feeling that I've missed something simple. It's always good to get a confirming opinion. It's always hard to believe that sitting and waiting is the best course of action."

"Yeah, I know what you mean," Lieberman said through a mouthful of mashed potatoes.

The two men ate in silence for several minutes, Franklin glad to have the opportunity to detach himself from the problems of Fort Howard and clear his mind. In the small room, usually reserved for Colonel Nickerson, there was no sound but the clink of silverware on the two officers' plates and the sound of Lieberman's heavy breathing as he shoveled down his food. He finished well ahead of Franklin and sat back with the taste of the gravy still clinging to the back of his throat. He lit a cigarette.

"You know, something just occurred to me," he said after a few slow puffs.

Franklin looked up from his plate. "Oh?"

"Yeah. We've covered every place he's likely to go, as well as we can, under the circumstances. But we haven't done anything much about where he's been."

Franklin pushed his plate away from him. "What do you have in mind?"

"Well, to begin with, according to Spencer, Logan had a rifle and a sheepskin coat. He didn't have them when he left the hospital. He had to get them somewhere. And we're talking about stuff that costs money. A hundred, a hundred fifty dollars, anyway. Do you think he had that kind of money?"

"No, I'd be very surprised if he did."

"Exactly. So where did he get it? Not a bank. According to Major Cooper, Logan's bank was covered from the moment it opened yesterday. And Cooper had three men wandering around downtown besides."

"That's fine as far as it goes. But even out here they have credit, you know." Franklin had lost interest in Lieberman's idea. He had long ago rejected as impractical the approach he assumed Lieberman was leading up to.

Lieberman wasn't willing to be cut off so easily. "All right. He had credit. Why not find out where?"

"Look, Arn, we've been over this already. We can't start polling merchants to see where Logan has credit. Think of the comment it would cause. This way, Logan is just a man who left the hospital upset and raving. Right now, the only ones outside our little family who know for sure the army is interested in Daniel Logan are Captain Petrone, Dr. Spencer, Boynton, and Fairman. And even that is far too many. In fact, I'm going to call off the roadblocks, because I think they do more harm than good. It's enough just to have Petrone's people keep looking for Logan."

Lieberman nodded and lit another cigarette.

"Speaking of which," he said, "I saw the latest stolen vehicle report."

"Anything there?"

"Just one that looked likely: a stolen motorcycle about eight miles from the hospital. There was a car, but it was too far away."

"A motorcycle? Well, maybe that will give us something."

8

Logan would have preferred to have his pickup truck. The panel truck he had rented was uncomfortable and not very responsive. Besides that, it was smaller than he would have liked. It had taken him ten minutes to get the motorcycle into the back of it. Still, it would serve, and it was more or less inconspicuous.

He pulled off to the side of the narrow country road and stopped. He wriggled around on the cramped front seat, trying to get comfortable. The dizziness had come back again, and he wanted to get some sleep, if he could. He expected that he was going to need it.

9

Sarah Parker hung up the phone slowly, perplexed. She couldn't remember when she had last heard Roy Cardwell sound so snappish. The thing that made it really strange was that he had sounded perfectly fine until she had asked him about Dan and Chris Logan.

Thinking about the odd phone conversation, she went out into the yard, where her husband was working on the engine of their pickup.

"Bill," she called, "have you been over by the Logans' lately?"

Bill Parker pulled himself out from under the truck. "What's that, Sarah?"

"I just wanted to know whether you had been by Dan Logan's in the last couple of days." She came out to where he was working.

Parker stood up, wiping his greasy hands on his pants. "No, Sarah, you know I can't go over there. I haven't even thought of it since Spike called the other day to say he had seen the sheep again and I should keep away for at least two weeks."

Sarah shook her head. "I forgot about that. But I'd sure like to know what's wrong."

Parker looked hard at his wife. "Sarah. What's bothering you?"

"Well, I just had a very funny talk with Roy Cardwell. He got all full of mystery when I asked him about Dan and Chris. He just wouldn't say anything, and when I told him I thought I had a right to know, being the nearest thing they have to a mother in the family, he just told me to mind my own business."

"That's not like Roy," Parker said.

"No. That's what I thought when it happened." Sarah paused for a moment. "You know what I'd like to do? I'd like to go into town and go by the hospital. This time I won't let them put me off so easy."

"I don't know, Sarah. I was going to use the car myself, to go over to Hinkson's." He waved an explanatory hand at the temporarily disabled pickup truck.

"Well, you can just take me with you to Hinkson's, and then we can both drive in to the hospital."

From the expression on his wife's face, Parker knew better than to argue with her.

10

Standing amid the bales of fence wire and the racks of tools in the hardware store, Logan looked down at himself and realized that his clothes were unusually grimy and torn, even for a rancher on a hard day. He hadn't shaved in two days, either, so he assumed he looked pretty ragged. He thought it might make trouble for him, cause people to ask questions he couldn't answer, or remember him where he would rather, for a day or two, that they forgot him. He decided to be careful where he let himself be seen.

Fred Hinkson came out of the small office at the back of the store.

"O.K.," he said, "I put it all on your bill. Let's go outside and see how Billy is doing."

Logan followed Hinkson through a narrow aisle between two big balers. Above them a variety of ropes and hoses hung from the low ceiling.

Outside, both men had to blink against the sudden brightness of the clear autumn afternoon. Not far from them, the hardware store stock clerk was loading crates into the rented panel truck.

As they walked over, Hinkson looked hard at Logan. "You know," he said, "Bill Parker was in about an hour ago."

Logan stopped and turned to look at Hinkson.

"He said you and your boy had been feeling poorly."

Logan hesitated. "That's right," he said, his voice tight and controlled.

"I'm sure sorry to hear it," Hinkson said. "You do look a little tired. "Don't want to work too hard, now."

Logan said nothing.

"Not that I mean to speak out of turn. Just being neighborly."

"It's all right," Logan said and turned back to walk toward the truck. He saw that Billy had already loaded most of the things he had bought. All that remained were two cardboard cases that stood on the handcart behind the panel truck.

Hinkson hurried up to walk beside Logan. "Those rock slides sure are a pain, aren't they?" he said, his inclination toward friendly chatter stimulated by his mistake in pushing the question of Logan's health. "This must be the third one you've had since spring."

He waved at the two cases, which bore the black-and-red legend:

APACHE POWDER COMPANY
EXPLOSIVES
DANGER

"You've got enough there to clear two or three big ones," he said. "That ought to hold you until next year."

Billy, the stock clerk, came out of the truck for the two cases of dynamite and saw Logan and Hinkson standing to one side, watching. He called a greeting.

"How're you doin', Mr. Logan?"

"All right, Billy," Logan said evenly. "How are you?"

Billy put the boxes in the truck and Logan, to forestall further conversation, helped him close the truck's back doors.

Logan walked to the front of the truck and opened the cab door.

"Say, Mr. Logan," Billy said before Logan could get into the truck. "I hear you lost some sheep the other day."

Logan felt a wave of dizziness coming over him. He grit his teeth and hung on to the truck door. Through his clamped jaws, he managed to say, "That's right, Billy," and then he struggled to pull himself smoothly into the driver's seat. He slammed the door, then sat there for a moment, catching his breath and waiting for the blackness to pass. Fred Hinkson's face appeared in the side window. "Good luck now, Mr. Logan," he said. "Let us know if you need anything else."

Logan put the truck in gear and drove out onto the highway.

11

Stoney Cooper was furious. "Goddam it, what else could I do?" he demanded.

"You could damn well have taken more care with the hospital people," Franklin snapped, angry himself.

"The hell you say." Cooper threw his hat onto the desk Franklin was using. It bounced and rolled off onto the floor. "What was I supposed to do? Lock them all up? Or swear them into the Fort Howard secret society?"

Franklin stood up and went across the room to close the door. The movement gave him a chance to pull his reactions back under control.

"All right," he said. "There's no sense in this." He turned on the overhead light to brighten the gloomy, dusk-webbed room.

"What were they told, exactly?" he asked Cooper.

"I don't know the exact words, of course," Cooper said, somewhat calmed by Franklin's change in attitude. "The receptionist told them no visitors, of course, and then as I understand it, this Parker woman started to go through into the hospital anyway. So the guard I put on stopped her. That got her husband mad. He claimed the man had mauled his wife, or something, and there we were, with a full-scale brawl brewing in the hospital lobby. Lieutenant Arthur, whom I left in command down there, decided that he couldn't let that happen, so he got them into Fairman's office and tried to calm them down. He told them the boy was very sick and had been moved to another hospital, and that Logan had left the hospital against doctor's orders. They were confused, but they bought it.

"I suppose we'll have to live with it," Franklin said, sitting down behind the desk again. "Was Arthur in uniform?"

"No, sir. The Parkers have no idea the army is involved at all."

"Good." He drummed his fingers on the desk top. "All right, Major, I think that will do for now."

"Yes, sir." Cooper saluted briskly and left the room.

When the door had closed behind Cooper, Franklin picked up the phone and dialed the internal number that connected him with the command post Lieutenant Colonel Lieberman had set up in the Fort Howard Security Building.

"Arn?" he said when he heard the special detail officer's voice, "Do we know where Cardwell is right now?"

"Sure thing. Maiden Avenue, near the corner of Anderson. North side of Rawlins."

"Has he been home in the last hour or two?"

"Nope. But if he runs true to pattern, this should be his last call today. In fact, he's a little overdue."

"I want you to send out a man to pick him up. Before he gets back to his house. That's important."

"Received and understood. Intercept Cardwell on his way home. What's up?"

"There was a little foul-up down at the hospital, and I want to make sure that we don't end up with too many inconsistent stories. Besides it's about time we had a talk with the good doctor. Even if it means that he finds out just how interested the U.S. Army is in his former patient Mr. Logan."

"I'll get right on it."

Franklin hung up and sat staring at the phone. He thought, I hope I can get the messy ends of this thing tied up before we all strangle on them.

12

In the back of the panel truck, Logan sat leaning against the motorcycle. A hissing Coleman lantern hanging from the roof cast a cold light that turned the inside of the truck into a stark pattern of hard shadows and glaring reflections.

Logan finished taping a dry-cell battery to a bundle of six sticks of dynamite and put the bundle down on the floor of the truck. He wiped the sweat from his forehead, then looked around for the half-eaten hamburger he had put down somewhere and lost track of. He found it and took a bite. Already, after working only a little over an hour, he was feeling the need to rest.

When he had chewed and swallowed the cold, tasteless mass of cheap, rubbery meat and stale bread, he reached into a paper shopping bag and took out a cardboard box. From the box he extracted a styrofoam package that protected a cheap wind-up alarm clock. He broke the plastic face of the clock with a small hammer, carefully picking out the shards of plastic until the hands were completely exposed.

He cut two short lengths of wire from a reel that he fished from a corner of the truck, then stripped the insulation from the ends of the pieces of wire. Again he had to stop to wipe his forehead. He worked his way toward the back door of the truck and pushed it open wide enough for the cold night air to wash into the truck. He took several long, grateful breaths, then closed the door most of the way again.

It took him a little while to figure out how to rig up the wire to the hands of the clock, but once he had worked it out, it was relatively simple to do. When he was finished with that, he looked around. Everything was done. He wound up the clock, set it, and activated the alarm, pointing the alarm indicator at some time around twelve. Then he turned off the lantern and, using a canvas duffel bag as a pillow, went to sleep.

13

A4DX693-P191-E

TOPSECRETCLASSQSCRAMBLE

CODEDESIGCOWBOYNINEZEROZERO
CODESQUAREDDAFFODILORANGE
GENERAL SAMUEL HILL
JOINTCHIEFS PENTAGON
PRIORITY BLUEREDRED
BEGINS. REPORT DAYFIVE EAGLE. SITUATION SEVERELY DETERIORATED. SUBJECT LOGAN ASSAULTED MATTHEW SPENCER PUBLIC HEALTH SERVICE CASPER WYO THISDAY ZEROONEHUNDRED HOURS. INTERROGATION CONDUCTED MAJOR KAGLE INDICATES SPENCER REVEALED INTELLIGENCE SUFFICIENT TO EXPOSE ENTIRE WYOMING INSTALLATION. NO CONTACT LOGAN SINCE THIS INCIDENT. SPECIAL DETAIL COVERING ALL PROBABLE CONTACT POINTS. PRESS TEAM PREPARING COVER STORY FOR RELEASE NEXTDAY EMPHASIS ESCAPE DISTURBED INDIVIDUAL. NO CURRENT INVOLVEMENT CIVILIAN AUTHORITIES BECAUSE THAT ACTION THOUGHT POTENTIAL SOURCE BAD NEWS YOURHOUSE. NOTE MINOR INCREASE LOCAL RESIDENT PRESSURE DUE VIRTUAL DISAPPEARANCE LOGAN AND SON. PRESENT STRATEGY CONGRUENT WITH PRESS STRATEGY. ROY CARDWELL LOGAN PHYSICIAN PARTIALLY CONVERTED BUT REMAINS POSSIBLE SOURCE BAD NEWS. WIDE EXPOSURE OF CARDWELL IN COMMUNITY PREVENTS OVERT STRONG MEASURES BUT SUGGEST CONSIDERATION OF REMOVAL IF CONVERSION INEFFECTIVE. EMPHASIZE HERE MY UNDERSTANDING OF EXTREME URGENCY AND DELICACY YOURHOUSE ON WHICH PLEASE ADVISE FURTHER. CURRENT EVALUATION NEGATIVE DEGREE THREE. SENSITIVE PERIOD DATE PLUS SEVENTYTWO HOURS PLUSMINUS THIRTYSIX. SIGNED FRANKLIN COL.

14

The alarm rang, loud and shrill, until Logan finally was awake enough to clamp his hand over the clock and feel for the wobbly brass button that cut off the bell. He sat up slowly, rubbing his face. He started to stand up and remembered barely in time that he was still in the low-roofed panel truck. There was an ache in his side where he had lain on a stick of dynamite, and his arms and legs were stiff. His bladder ached.

He pulled himself to the back door of the truck and got out. He walked around a little, waving his arms and trying to work out the stiffness. Then he walked away from the road and urinated against the base of a tree.

By the time he had walked around for another few minutes, he was feeling pretty good. He got back into the truck and turned on the lantern, leaving the flame burning just brightly enough so that he could see what he was doing. He looked at the clock. It was twelve-twenty.

Moving slowly and carefully to conserve his energy, Logan began to put the taped-together bundles of dynamite into a canvas duffel bag.

SEVEN

1

The panel truck's headlights made a swiftly moving pool of light on the ragged blacktop of the road that led out of Sinclair. When he thought he was nearing the turnoff, Logan slowed the truck and shifted it into first gear, flicking with his foot the floor switch that put on the high beams. A mile farther down the road, he saw the small street sign that marked the turn onto Pantano Road. He put the lights back on dim and made the turn.

After a carefully measured two and seven-tenths miles, Logan cut the lights entirely. He was going uphill. Carefully, he drove through the darkness until he reached the crest of the hill, where he stopped. Ahead of him, he could make out the glow that marked the glass-walled lobby of the Chivington Research Laboratories. Between the panel truck and the top of the next hill, beyond the laboratory building, the narrow country road was deserted. Logan put the truck in low gear long enough to get a good start down the hill, then moved the gear selector into neutral and turned off the engine. He coasted in a whisper of tire noise to a point opposite the laboratory building, where he pulled off the road and braked the truck to a stop.

When he had put the parking brake on, Logan discovered that he had been holding his breath for the whole ride down the hill. He let it out slowly and began to take long deep breaths to fight the dizziness he felt beginning to edge over him. While he caught his breath, he looked through the truck's side window at the building across the road.

The building was dark, except for the glass-fronted lobby, which was lighted brightly by a bank of overhead fluorescent lights. Logan could just make out a single car in the darkness of the parking lot next to the building, barely visible in the faint light that reached it from the lobby. There was a man in a guard's uniform sitting at the reception desk in the lobby. Otherwise, the building looked deserted.

Logan felt in his pocket for the cigarette lighter he had bought. He took it out and tried it, spinning the wheel and then flipping the lighter closed the instant the wick caught. He took his rifle from the seat next to him, checked to make sure the clip was full and there was a cartridge in the chamber, then rattled the two spare clips in his coat pocket.

Satisfied that he was ready, Logan got out of the cab and walked around to the side of the truck. Cradling the rifle in the crook of his arm, he carefully and quietly slid the side door open. From inside the truck, where he had propped it near the door, he lifted the larger and more fully loaded of two bulging duffel bags. Then, with the bag leaning against the truck, he carefully slid the door closed again, stopping it just before it latched.

He peered around the truck at the laboratory building. The guard had his feet up on the reception desk; he seemed to be reading a magazine. Logan picked up the heavy bag and slung its strap over his shoulder. Then, holding the rifle ready, he ran across the road toward the building.

There was a slight depression, like a gully, that ran parallel to the road about fifty feet from the road edge, off to one side of the building. Logan pushed through a line of neatly trimmed hedges and dove into the gully. He let the heavy duffel bag down onto the cool, moist earth and stopped to catch his breath.

He took from the bag the reel of wire and the clock to whose hands he had attached strands of wire. He put down the clock and the reel and next to them placed a large dry-cell battery. Working quickly, Logan wired the clock to the battery. Leaving them set up but unattached, he wrapped the end of the wire on the reel around a large rock and tested to see that it was secure. He rummaged in the duffel bag and pulled out a pair of wire cutters, slipped them into his pocket, then slung the bag over his arm again, picked up the reel of wire and his rifle, and climbed out of the gully.

Quickly, he ran in a crouch to the side of the building, letting wire off the reel as he ran. He pressed himself there, panting. With the rifle ready at his side, he took a bundle of dynamite from the bag and placed it in a small hole he scooped out in the dirt against the wall of the building. Fumbling slightly, he used the wire cutters to separate from the reel the long stretch of wire that ran back to the big rock in the gully. He stripped the insulation from the newly cut ends of wire and attached them to the blasting caps he had imbedded in one of the sticks of dynamite. When that was done, he took a few turns of wire around the bundle so he wouldn't pull the connections apart if he pulled on the wire, and then he moved a short distance down the wall toward the back of the building, letting wire off the reel as he went.

He stopped after a few yards and took another bundle

from his duffel bag. As he was cutting and stripping the ends of the wire, he felt suddenly weak and faint. He stopped working, panting for breath, and leaned forward, resting his forehead against the cool concrete wall of the building.

After a moment, Logan began to feel better. He wiped the sweat from his forehead and went back to wiring the dynamite. He noticed that his hands were shaking.

It took him five bundles to work his way to the back of the building. At the back corner he stopped, looking along the back wall to decide how frequently to place his bundles. It was even darker in the back than it had been at the side of the building, where a series of small decorative lights among the shrubbery had helped him see what he was doing. In back of the building, there was no light at all.

When he was breathing easily and his hands had stopped shaking, Logan stepped into the blackness and crouched down to place a bundle of dynamite.

2

Captain Douglas Enyard chuckled at the article he was reading, but it was more from scorn than amusement. There wasn't much that was amusing to be found in the *Agricultural Research Monthly,* which was the most interesting magazine he had been able to find in the Chivington Laboratories lobby and waiting room.

He shifted in his seat, swung his legs down to the floor, and closed the magazine. He was generally uncomfortable: nothing to do, no one to talk to, and the borrowed guard's uniform he was wearing didn't even fit right. He had seen some rotten duty as a member of the Special Detail, but nothing that compared to this for sheer boredom. He thought for a minute of going out and doing a tour of the grounds, but his orders were to stay in the building. He was there to protect the lobby, which was the only point of entrance to the building. The windows were all sealed and connected to a complicated, computerized alarm system, and none of the emergency doors could be opened from the outside. So Enyard had to stay in the lobby, except for two quick tours of the building to make sure everything was all right back there. Enyard had suggested that himself, as a precaution against someone somehow getting in during the day and hiding inside the building. He had been assured that it couldn't be done, but someone was obviously doubtful enough so that, after they had all conferred about it, Enyard was told to go back and check the whole building a couple of times during the night.

3

Logan had no idea how long it had taken him to get all the way around the building. On three separate occasions, he had been forced to sit down with his back against the building, while dizziness washed over him and he couldn't breathe and his hands shook. He wasn't even sure he had remained conscious. Once, he remembered, he had been on the verge of unconsciousness and he had thought: What if I die here, now; they'll find me here in the morning with my dynamite, and that will be all. I won't have done anything. The thought had been enough to bring him back to alertness, though he had waited for several minutes before getting up, to let the strength flow slowly back into his body.

Now, at the far side of the building from where he had started, he wired up the last bundle of dynamite in the duffel bag. When he was done, he dropped the bag and the reel of wire, and carrying only the rifle he crept to the front corner of the building. He had planned to run back to the gully around the back of the building, the way he had come, but he was afraid the long run would tire him too much.

He studied the front of the building, trying to gauge whether he had a chance of making it unseen if he went past the lobby. The driveway in front of the lobby was bright with the light that spilled through the glass walls, but by ten yards out the light fell off to nearly nothing. Just short of the dark zone, the big, angular sign provided inviting shelter. In addition, Logan assumed that the guard would have some trouble seeing out of the bright lobby into the dark night. The reflections in the glass walls would probably obscure his view completely unless he pressed his face to the glass, and Logan didn't imagine he would do that.

Logan took a deep breath and crouched over, scuttling through the dark area until he was protected from view by the sign. He lay there for a minute or two, getting his breath, then sprinted across the driveway and the lawn to the gully where he had left the clock and the battery. Crouching in the gully, he carefully and solidly spliced the clock-and-battery wires to the wire he had wrapped around the rock, the wire that now ran to the bundles of dynamite he had placed around the building. He checked to see that the clock was wound and running, then set its hands so that the wires would meet in ten minutes.

Conserving his energy, he climbed out of the gully and walked quickly across the road to the panel truck. He opened the still-unlatched side door and pulled a wooden plank from inside the truck, placing it so that it made a ramp from the inside of the truck to the ground. Moving as quickly as he could, he untied the motorcycle from the spare-tire holder, where it had been held by strong elastic straps. He pushed the bike awkwardly into position and got it going down the ramp, barely managing to keep it from falling as its weight pulled it rapidly toward the ground. When the motorcycle was resting on its kickstand next to the truck, Logan went back to the truck and took the remaining full duffel bag and put it in the cab of the truck, resting the rifle on top of it. Then he went back and closed the side door of the truck, latching it solidly this time. Still moving quickly, conscious of the ten minutes that were ticking swiftly by, he climbed into the driver's seat of the truck.

Immediately, he was struck by a wave of dizziness, the worst he had experienced. Everything went instantly black, and he slumped forward, his head glancing off the horn button of the steering wheel as he lapsed into unconsciousness.

4

In the lobby, Douglas Enyard was eating one of the sandwiches that he had been given in an authentic-looking lunch box. He stopped in mid-bite, sure that he had heard something from in front of the building. It had sounded like a very short blast on a car horn. It seemed improbable to him, but he decided to get up and check on it.

He walked toward the glass wall, but he could see only the reflections of the bright lobby. What the hell, he thought, how am I supposed to see anything out there? I can't open the damned door or I'll ring every alarm in the state.

He ended up by pressing his face against the glass. It made him feel ridiculous, like a kid gawking at a fancy cake he didn't have the money to buy. When he couldn't see anything outside the building that could have made a noise like a car horn, he decided that sitting around the lobby was making him jumpy. He looked at the big clock on the wall. It was three-fifteen. As good a time as any to walk through the building. He picked up the watchman's punch clock from the desk and slung it from his shoulder. After checking to be sure his big Magnum pistol was loose in its holster, he started back through the building.

5

Logan raised his head slowly and looked at the laboratory building across the road. Nothing seemed to have changed, and he had the clear sense that he had been out only a few seconds. He looked again at the building, his eye caught by some small motion. He saw immediately what it had been: the guard was leaving the lobby. Logan smiled. The guard's timing couldn't have been better.

Logan turned the ignition key and the truck's engine jumped to life. He put the truck in gear and started down the dark road, the headlights still off. At the laboratory driveway, he turned off the road and accelerated up the driveway toward the parking lot. He passed it, his foot still pressed firmly down on the accelerator.

As the truck drew abreast of the lobby, Logan wrenched the steering wheel over. The truck turned sharply toward the building, jumped the low curb and hurtled through the glass wall of the lobby, bringing the wall down in a shower of shattered glass and setting off a loud security alarm.

Logan, braced against the steering wheel, brought the lurching truck to a halt just inches short of the empty reception desk. He snatched up his rifle and raised it just as the guard came out of a hallway at the side of the lobby, pulling a gun from the holster at his hip, the lobby lights reflecting dully from the matte-blue finish of the big revolver.

Almost instinctively, Logan's finger squeezed the trigger of the rifle. Then, unwittingly, again. The two shots drove through the windshield of the truck and caught the guard in the body. He staggered backward, trying to raise his revolver.

Logan watched in horror as the guard slumped over, struggling to remain standing. Then he took aim and fired the rifle again. The impact of the light but high-speed bullet knocked the guard down, sitting him down hard on the polished floor. His gun skittered across the floor, and he fell over on his side, dead. The alarm went on ringing deafeningly.

Logan got out of the truck, holding the rifle in front of him. He pulled the duffel bag from the front seat and slung it from his shoulder. Then he crossed the lobby, stepping over the inert form of the guard so he could look down the hallway. It was short, not as brightly lighted as the lobby. At its end, Logan could just make out a door marked "Basement." He went quickly along the hall, through the door, and down the stairs.

In the basement, the noise of the alarm ringing on the floor above became tolerable. Logan walked down a corridor, looking at the closed doors on either side of him, getting an impression of the layout of the building. Not far from the stairway he found a door with a sign that said:

HIGH VOLTAGE

DANGER

MAINTENANCE ONLY

He opened the door and went through, finding himself in a high-ceilinged boiler and power room. He crossed quickly to the boiler and the big, grimy oil tank that stood beside it. From the bag slung from his shoulder, he pulled a large bundle of dynamite to which he had taped a battery and a clock. He bent down to place the bundle under the oil tank, attaching the last wire to the battery and setting the clock for ten minutes. Then he straightened up and ran back to the door.

Back in the basement corridor, Logan walked toward the stairway. He stopped at the first door he came to, took the cigarette lighter from his pocket and lit it, then pulled a bundle of dynamite from his bag and lit its fuse with the cigarette lighter. He threw the bundle into the room and went on to do the same thing in the next room.

When he reached the stairway, Logan glanced down the corridor in the other direction. It seemed to be about twice as long as the one he had just come out of, and a sign about fifteen feet from him warned that most of it was a restricted area. Logan stopped at the sign. Restricted. That was probably what he was looking for.

As he walked down the long hall, he lit the fuses of several bundles of dynamite and dropped them next to the walls. At the end of the corridor, he found a pair of heavy doors with large panes of translucent glass. There was lettering on the glass, an abbreviation that Logan didn't understand, but that seemed technical. He tried the doors. They were locked.

He raised the rifle and smashed its butt into one of the glass panes. When he had made a hole large enough, he reached through and unlocked the door from the inside. There was a light switch beside the door. Logan flipped it, revealing in the bright fluorescent lights that immediately flickered to life a pair of long laboratory tables littered with test-tube racks and arrays of convoluted liquid-filled bottles and tubes and retorts. He went to the back of the big but crowded room and left a bundle of dynamite there, its fuse sputtering. On his way back to the corridor, he dropped two more, one on each of the long tables.

There were two other rooms at the end of the corridor, both locked. In a hurry now, Logan placed dynamite by each of their doors and ran back toward the stairway. Opposite the door that led back up to the lobby, there was another short corridor. Logan lit the fuses of two bundles of dynamite and rolled them, like bowling balls, down the corridor, then pushed through the door and ran up the stairs.

On the main floor again, Logan had to stop, leaning against the wall, to get his breath. He shook his head against another attack of dizziness, pushed himself upright, and staggered down the hallway. The noise of the alarm was an intense, intolerable clangor that resonated with the ringing in his head, amplifying it to the point where he couldn't walk, or see, or think. He looked wildly around, saw mounted high on the wall the foot-wide brass disk of the alarm bell. In blind fury, he shot at it, again and again, until the whining, ricocheting bullets ripped it loose, bent and torn. It clattered to the floor, and the pressure in Logan's head was released, although he could still hear the noise of another alarm, somewhere else in the building, that continued to ring.

Logan went along the corridor toward the lobby. As

he stood near the wall, lighting the fuse of a bundle of dynamite, Logan heard noises from behind a door across the corridor. He put the bundle of dynamite next to the wall, and tried the door. It was open. Inside the room, the noises were louder: snufflings and scratchings and chatterings. And there was a distinct smell of animals, mixed with the acrid odor of disinfectant. Logan turned on the room's lights. All around him, the room was full of cages of animals, lining the walls from floor to ceiling, filling the room in long, high rows. Logan could see what looked like hundreds of white rats, hamsters, rabbits, even monkeys. On the wall near the door there were bright steel cages that held a dozen small dogs and cats. Logan turned to leave the room, hesitated. He thought of his ranch, of the sheep lying senseless on their sides, twitching horribly and vomiting blood. He took one of the last bundles from his duffel bag, lit its fuse, and placed it on the floor in the middle of the room.

As he crossed the lobby, Logan heard, over the noise of the still-ringing alarm, the sound of a siren, thin and distant but growing quickly louder and changing in pitch as it sped toward the building. Logan ran back to the middle of the lobby and crouched down behind the truck. He ejected the empty clip from his rifle, replacing it with a fresh one. The siren was much louder now, very close.

Logan reached into the bag and pulled out a bundle of dynamite. Headlights swept across the lobby while he struggled with his wire cutters, snipping the fuse short on the dynamite. The siren stopped as the police car screamed to a halt outside the lobby. The lobby walls were dappled with moving streaks of red and yellow light from the flashing beacon on the car's roof.

Logan lit the cigarette lighter and held the flame to the stubby fuse he had just cut. Grains of powder in the rough end of the fuse caught with a smoky flash, and the fuse started to burn. Logan lobbed the bundle out toward the police car.

Next to the car, a state trooper was watching the lobby of the building, his riot gun resting on his hip while he surveyed the building. From the corner of his eye, he caught the motion of something coming out of the lobby and turned to see what it was just as it hit the roof of the car. He had just enough time to open his mouth to warn his partner that it was dynamite before the bundle exploded, tearing the doors off the car and blowing the gas tank, throwing both troopers a hundred feet into the bushes, aflame with burning gasoline.

While the smoke was still clearing, Logan ran crouched over out of the lobby and past the ruined car, straightening up and pushing headlong through the bushes and trees, heedless of the whipping branches, running desperately for the gully and throwing himself down into it. Out of breath, barely conscious, Logan reached out for the clock. With difficulty, he focused on it, saw that it still had just over two minutes to run. After half that time had passed, he was breathing better, getting himself under control. He grasped the two hands of the clock, pushed himself deep into the gully, face down, and squeezed the hands together.

The dynamite wired together around the outside of the building went off all at once, with a deafening, earth-shaking roar. The explosion demolished the outer walls of the building and rained debris for hundreds of yards. Logan lay motionless, his arms covering his head, as fragments of the building pelted down around him.

Logan picked himself up and climbed out of the gully. There was another concussion as one of the bundles of dynamite inside the building went off. Logan stumbled across the road, his way lit by the eerie red glow of the burning building.

Logan found the motorcyle on its side, blown down by the force of the first explosion. He bent over and grabbed the handlebars, strained to right the motorcycle. Everything went black and then hot white and red, and he found himself lying beside the motorcycle. He closed his eyes and tried to summon what strength he had left. A series of explosions shook the ground under him.

Somehow, he found the will to get up again, to struggle with the motorcycle until he had it upright, to get on and feebly kick the starter. Then, when the motor didn't catch, he sat there on the motorcycle, looking across the road at the splendor of the destroyed laboratory. Somewhere in the bowels of the building, exploding dynamite found a chemical storage tank and there was a shower of brightly colored sparks like a huge Fourth-of-July rocket.

Logan kicked the starter again, and this time the motor caught. The roar of the engine as he accelerated down the road was drowned out by the blast of a new explosion.

After Logan drove off, the building continued to burn, disturbed only by an occasional small explosion. A car came up the road; its black-and-white doors bore the shield of the Carbon County Sheriff's Office.

The deputies had heard some of the explosions as they came up Pantano Road, so that, when they came into sight of the building, they had already raised the headquarters radio operator.

"Jack," the second deputy was saying, "this is Harry. We just got here." He stopped, his eyes widening at the sight of the ruined, burning laboratory.

"I can't believe it," he said into the transmitter. "The whole goddam building is gone. Looks like somebody dropped a bomb on it."

The radio crackled and sputtered with static. The deputies heard the unbelieving voice of the radio operator. "What do you mean, the whole building's gone?"

"It's just gone, that's all. Looks to be some kind of explosion. . . ."

Harry would have said more, but he was interrupted by a series of explosions as some of the last of the dynamite went off.

"You hear that?" he shouted. "Something just exploded right there. You ought to get some fire engines out here." He stopped again, his attention caught by the sound of a siren.

"Hold on," he said. "There's somebody coming. Looks like maybe the state police."

A state police car, its siren fading to a snarl, pulled up next to the sheriff's office car. Two troopers got out. One said, "What's going on?"

"I don't know," Harry said. "All I know is we got an alarm."

"We had a car over here. Did you see it?"

"Nope. We just got here ourselves."

Inside the demolished building, the clock wired to the bundle of dynamite that Logan had left under the oil tank was still working, ticking quietly amidst the raging fires and crumbling walls. Its hands met.

The explosion was tremendous, spreading a fireball of flaming oil which enveloped the ruins of the building and the nearby shrubs and trees, lighting up the sky and turning the moonless night into a fierce, unearthly red day that flickered and pulsed and slowly died into fiery dusk.

The four policemen watched in awe. After a while their concentration was broken by the faint but unmistakable beat of helicopter rotors.

6

A4DX693-P175-E

EYES ONLY

URGENT

TOPSECRETCLASSQSCRAMBLE

CODEDESIGRIVERBOAT

CODESQUAREDEGGFOUR

GENERAL SAMUEL HILL

JOINTCHIEFS PENTAGON

PRIORITY REDREDRED

HANDDELIVERSEALEDONLY

BEGINS. PROJECT ALPHA TAU MAIN FACILITY TOTALLY DESTROYED REPEAT DESTROYED EXPLOSION UNKNOWN SOURCE ZERO THREEFORTY THISDAY. NO CURRENT COUNT OF CASUALTIES. CIVILIAN FIRE AND POLICE

ON SCENE BEFORE AREA SEALED. CLEANUP NOW IN PROGRESS. CURRENT STRATEGY RETAIN COVER IF POSSIBLE IN LIGHT OF EAGLE DIFFICULTIES. FIRSTGUESS SUSPECT DANIEL LOGAN. ADVISE SOONEST ON INVOLVEMENT OF FEDBURINV AS ALPHA TAU COVER IS GOVERNMENT INSTALLATION. FURTHER REPORT DATE PLUS FOUR HOURS. SIGNED FRANKLIN COL.

7

In the first faint light of dawn, Logan drove the motorcycle off the narrow, badly paved road he had been traveling on after he left the highway. About thirty yards from the road, there was a large stand of trees. When he was among them, Logan stopped and got off the motorcycle, letting it fall unheeded as he slumped to the ground beside it and fell immediately asleep.

8

A4DX693-P181-E
EYES ONLY
URGENT
TOPSECRETCLASSQSCRAMBLE

CODEDESIGRIVERBOAT
CODESQUAREDEGGSEVEN
JOINTCHIEFS PENTAGON
PRIORITY REDREDRED
HANDDELIVERSEALEDONLY
BEGINS. REPORT DESTRUCTION ALPHA TAU MAIN FACILITY. CASUALTIES ASSUMED INCLUDE DOUGLAS ENYARD CAPTAIN SPECIAL DETAIL. ALSO TWO MEMBERS WYO HIGHWAY PATROL. TWO LOCAL VOL FIREMEN OVERCOME SYMPTOMS INDICATE EFFECTS OF DERIVATIVE STOCKPILED FOR MX SERIES RESEARCH. PRESS TEAM ENFORCING SMOKE INHALATION AGAINST PROBABLE MORTALITY BOTH MEN. PROPOSE INCLUSION FEDBURINV THIS STAGE PURPOSE AVOID FURTHER INVOLVEMENT LOCALS. NO DEFINITE EVIDENCE PERPETRATOR BUT NOW DOUBT ORIGINAL GUESS DANIEL LOGAN. DEMOLITION TOO COMPLETE TO ALLOW CONCLUSION PERFORMANCE BY SINGLE UNASSISTED INDIVIDUAL IN ABSENCE FURTHER EVIDENCE. CURRENT EVALUATION EAGLE TENTATIVE ONLY NEGATIVE SQUARED DEGREE TWO. ENTIRE SITUATION EXTREMELY UNSTABLE. WILL ADVISE SOONEST IF NEW DEVELOPMENTS. SIGNED FRANKLIN COL.

9

Lying among the trees asleep, Logan became aware on some not quite conscious level of something threatening. As part of his mind groped through the sticky mire of exhausted sleep, the threatening something congealed into a noise, a low, rumbling, coughing noise: the noise, he became aware gradually, of a vehicle motor coming close to where he lay sleeping but growing slowly more conscious.

He rolled over suddenly, grabbing the rifle at his side and moving farther into the shelter of the trees, the metal body of the motorcycle between him and the noise as he searched for its source, which he saw now, coming closer along the edge of the road. He focused on the vehicle, squinting because the morning light was too bright for him, having trouble getting a clear image, but knowing that the rifle was pointed at the moving yellow machine that as it came closer resolved finally into a tractor with a huge-toothed hay mower bent upright into traveling position at its rear, towing a trailer piled high with bales of hay.

Slowly, Logan relaxed, making his breath come at a more even rate. He rolled over on a bed of moist, rotting leaves and fell asleep.

10

After reading over the same page four times without seeing a word, Roy Cardwell slammed shut the book he had been using to try to distract himself. There was no way he could get around it any more: he was disgusted with himself. He wondered for an instant whether moral weakness was a sign of approaching senility, then banished the thought from his mind. He wasn't that far gone yet. But there was *something* wrong with him: he couldn't remember a time in his life when he had cut and run like he had in this thing with Dan Logan. He wondered if there was anything he could do at this point to make up for his mistakes.

After a while, he thought of something that he had somehow pushed to the back of his mind and forgotten. He went to the phone and dialed quickly. On the third ring, the phone was answered.

"Spike?" Cardwell said. "This is Roy Cardwell."

"Yes, Roy. How are you?"

"I'm fine, Spike." Cardwell decided to skip as many of the preliminaries as he could. "I'm calling about that conversation we had a couple of days ago."

"Oh?" Boynton sounded guarded.

"I was very interested in the things you said about nerve gas and the dead sheep on the Logan ranch. It's been on my mind ever since. I was wondering if you ever got those blood tests you were waiting for."

There was a pause on the other end of the line. "Oh, yes," Boynton said slowly. "Well, to tell you the truth, they did come, finally. They were a little disappointing, though."

"How so?"

"Well, there were some traces of the things I was looking for. A couple of things. What I was most concerned about was organophosphorous compounds. Sure enough, they turned up, but I've been doing some more research and I'm just not so sure any more that I can necessarily say that the blood tests point to nerve gas."

Cardwell had the uneasy feeling the Boynton was hedging. "But they're a good indication that it might have been nerve gas, is that it?"

"Well, I suppose so," Boynton said. "But it could be something else. Besides, just suppose for a minute that it was nerve gas. There's no point in making a crusade about it. They get along with Dugway pretty well over there in Tooele. I don't want to go around interfering with the government. You have to figure they know what they're doing."

Cardwell didn't know what to say. He was stunned by Boynton's complete change of attitude.

Boynton, taking Cardwell's silence for acquiescence, said, "Have you heard anything from Dan Logan? I hear he's out of the hospital."

"Well, yes, he is," Cardwell said.

"That's good. Now that he's up and around again, he'll get things going on the ranch so he hardly misses that couple hundred head he lost."

Cardwell had a brief impulse to argue with Boynton, to tell him the truth, if for no other reason than to shock him out of his complacency. But he decided to think about it first. The more he heard, the more he was convinced that there was more going on than any of them suspected. He wanted to act, but not rashly.

He mumbled an excuse into the phone and said goodbye.

Cardwell walked across the room to the easy chair and dropped himself into it. His mind ran back to the strange meeting he had had with a tall, thin, gray-haired man named Franklin, a colonel as he remembered it. Franklin had made it clear to him then that there was more at stake than the Public Health Service's fear of community panic. The brisk, imposing officer had been very free with phrases like "the national security" and "patriotic duty." He hadn't ever really talked about the question of nerve gas, although he did make a few references to "exotic chemicals" and "seepage." Cardwell realized when he examined the encounter carefully, that Franklin had never been specific about anything. Most infuriating, he had completely aovided dealing with the fact that two human lives had been forfeited because of whatever it was that was going on. Not only that. He had made Cardwell forget it himself, at least for the length of the meeting. He remembered feeling on his way out of Franklin's office that he didn't know what had been said or what he had agreed to, just that he was supposed to keep quiet about the Logans and that something very important was at stake.

Cardwell could remember Franklin's parting words. "We're not here to lie to anyone. That's not our function. We're here to do what's best for the country."

The aging doctor was brought back to the present by the realization that his entire body was shaking with anger and frustration.

11

JS96S896-1

TOPSECRETCLASSQSCRAMBLE

CODEDESIGRIVERBOAT

CODESQUAREDDAFFODILMAUVE
COLONEL WILLIAM FRANKLIN
CARE COMMANDING OFFICER
FORT HOWARD WYOMING
PRIORITY REDREDRED
EYES ONLY
BEGINS. READ AND DESTROY. IN VIEW SITUATION YOURHOUSE SELF AND BAILEY ASSTSECDOD CONFERRED THISDAY ZERO ELEVENHUNDRED MYHOUSE SUBJECT CAPHILL STRATEGY. FURTHER CONFERENCE CAPHILL INDICATES SOME SUPPORT AVAILABLE. NO DETAILS REVEALED OUTSIDE BUT GROUND PREPARED FOR MINIMAL BAD NEWS. NECESSARY YOU RESOLVE OUTSTANDING PROBLEM SOONEST REPEAT SOONEST. INDICATION HERE THAT DEMOLITION ALPHA TAU MAY CREATE UNFAVORABLE INTEREST IN SITUATION YOURHOUSE. ALL COSTS LOCATE SUBJECT AND SUPPRESS IMMEDIATELY. SIGNED HILL.

12

Logan took a bite of his sandwich and watched the cars going by on the highway. In the parking lot where Logan was leaning against the seat of the motorcycle, eating, rows of cars stood in the bright early-afternoon sun waiting for their drivers and passengers to emerge, well-fed and eager for the road, from the glass-and-plastic franchise restaurant that had swallowed them for the midday meal.

Logan put the sandwich down on the motorcycle seat, took a long drink of Coke, and wiped his stubble-surrounded mouth with the back of a grimy hand. On the motorcycle seat next to the sandwich was a small transistor radio, all that remained of his purchases of the day before.

The thin, tinny voice of a newscaster buzzed from the radio's miniature speaker. He was beginning a new item. "At least three men, including two police officers, died early this morning in a series of dynamite explosions at the Chivington Research Laboratories near Sinclair." Logan paused, about to take a bite of sandwich, and turned up the volume on the radio. "The dead officers are Chuck Beard, forty-two, and Thomas Dawson, thirty-five, both of Rawlins. They had gone to the research facility in answer to the laboratory's security alarm, and they were killed instantly by the explosions. Also dead is Douglas Enyard, a night watchman at the laboratory. Police report that the building housing the research laboratories was almost completely destroyed by the mysterious explosions. No motive has been suggested for the bombing, and the identity of the persons responsible remains unknown. The army, the Federal Bureau of Investigation, and the Carbon County Sheriff's Office are all investigating. More than one hundred soldiers have been sent from Fort Howard, thirty miles away, to seal off the area and search for further victims of the blast."

There was the sound of shuffling papers, and then the newscaster's voice resumed. "Chivington Research Laboratories was established during World War Two," he said in a background-information tone. "It currently employs more than one hundred and fifty people from the Rawlins area in the development of agricultural products and in related research." Hearing that, Logan smiled, a bitter grimace devoid of humor. He began to clean up the debris of his meal as the news broadcast continued. He carried the garbage to a big metal trash basket next to the vending machine from which he had gotten his sandwich and dropped in the papers and the Coke bottle. The newscaster droned on, saying something about two volunteer firemen who had been overcome fighting the fire at Chivington.

Logan hefted the tiny radio in his hand and, as the news shifted to a report on the local high-school football team, he dropped it into the trash basket.

13

Matthew Spencer turned off the radio. He was dressed in the bathrobe and slippers that had become a kind of uniform for him while he stayed at home recuperating from his encounter with Logan and his interrogations by the people at Fort Howard.

Spencer walked slowly across his living room, thinking about what he had just heard on the news and wondering why it didn't come as more of a surprise. Chivington destroyed. He tried to imagine what the building looked like now, but found that he couldn't.

In the kitchen, he took a glass from the drainboard and went to the refrigerator for some ice. He poured himself a generous shot of bourbon and sat down with it at the kitchen table. He didn't care how early in the afternoon it was; after listening to the news, he wanted a drink.

He wondered whether it had been Logan, supposed it had, although it did seem like a lot for one man to blow up a whole building. Somehow, it didn't really matter to Spencer who had done it: the whole thing seemed inevitable to him. And after all, what difference did it make if Logan had done it or someone else had? It was still a kind of abstract revenge.

For no reason that he could identify, his mind ran back to his childhood, to the verses he had been forced to memorize in Sunday school. He remembered something from Matthew: Jesus saying to the disciples, "Do not think that I have come to bring peace, but a sword. For I have come to set a man against his father and a daughter against her mother, and a man's foes will be his own household."

14

Roy Cardwell was visiting a bedridden patient with a badly infected hand. In the course of the chatter that always accompanied Cardwell's visits, he learned about the explosions at Chivington.

It seemed to him, as he left to go home, that the whole world was going crazy. First there was the horrible thing with Dan and Chris Logan, and now a bombing at an agricultural research center. Life had become a series of nightmares.

15

"If you ask me, he's dead by now," Lieberman said.

Franklin turned in the back seat of the staff car so he could get a better look at Lieberman, who was sitting next to him. "Maybe," he said. "But we'd be fools to count on it."

"I'm not arguing with you. I just think he's dead. Holliford seems to think so, too. And if he really pulled off that birthday party at Chivington, you have to admit it must have tired him out a mite."

Franklin nodded. "I'll be interested to hear what the FBI has to say." He looked at his watch. "We should be there in a couple of minutes."

After a minute, he said, "Although I don't know why we should have any doubt about what they'll say. Now that we have his service record, there isn't that much doubt, is there?"

Lieberman paused. "No. Not really. Did you tell the FBI what Boynton said?"

"Not directly. I was afraid there would be too many

things to explain. Remember, they don't know quite the whole story. And if there are going to be any long-term repercussions, the fewer pieces they have, the better off we are. I ended up calling it in myself, as an anonymous tip. Disguised my voice and everything." In a grotesque, mock-German accent, he said, "Ask Fred Hinkson who he sold dynamite to yesterday."

Lieberman laughed. "Very good."

Franklin said in a sober tone, "You know, I'm worried about Janeway. I thought he was going to have some kind of breakdown when he heard."

"He'll be all right," Lieberman said. "It'll just take a little while. He must have had a lot of work go up with the building."

"I hadn't thought of that. You're probably right. He must have kept all his research notes filed there." Franklin shook his head.

Changing the subject, Lieberman said, "Did you get a chance to look at those security suggestions I dropped off?"

"I glanced through them. In fact, I wanted to have a talk with you about them when we get done here." The car turned onto Pantano Road, headed for what had once been the Chivington Research Laboratories.

"Oh?" said Lieberman. He had detected a definite note of criticism in Franklin's comment.

"Yes. I think you've got hold of the wrong end of the bull. We certainly want to be well guarded against Logan's doing any damage at the Fort. I don't question you on that. But I'm worried about your methods."

"What do you mean?"

"Well, the more I think about it, the more strongly I

feel that we don't want to end up with a shoot-out on the perimeter of the Fort. That's public territory. We have no real control there. On the other hand, if he gets onto the Fort, we can do what we want and not have to explain it to anybody."

Lieberman thought about what Franklin was saying. It made a great deal of sense to him.

16

Logan drove the motorcycle slowly down the off-ramp and turned through the underpass. He was having some trouble keeping the front wheel steady, and he had twice almost driven off the side of the road keeping up with traffic on the highway.

At the second crossroads, Logan turned again, going still slower, heading for a destination he could visualize as he had last seen it the day before, although his vision was playing tricks on him now and he knew he might have trouble finding it.

When he got to the big, gnarled tree, though, he recognized it immediately. He turned off the road and went a short distance to a small group of shrubs and bushes growing wild and untended by the side of the road. He got off the motorcycle carefully, afraid that he might dump it and then have to pick it up again. He didn't know if he had the strength.

With the motorcycle safely on its kickstand, he

walked to the edge of the clump of bushes, his motions broad and slow, with a dazed, absent quality about them. He bent down to part the bushes, uncovering the two cases of dynamite he had hidden there after his visit to Hinkson's. Looking at them, he was glad that he had opened them then, and fastened the lids with tape. It was one less thing to do now.

He clawed one of the boxes out from under the bush that hid it and pushed it with his feet over toward the motorcycle. Then, slowly and carefully, he bent over to lift it. It was heavier than he remembered, so heavy that he doubted for a moment that he could lift it at all. He strained at it, felt the red haze dropping in front of his eyes, held his breath and pulled with his entire being, staggered upright holding the case, and hobbled to the motorcycle. He lurched the case upward to get it onto the luggage rack, missing his goal, hooking only the corner of the case on the steel tubes of the rack. Panting, his heart pounding, he pushed, leaned himself against the case to keep it from falling, trying to get it up somehow onto the luggage rack, managed only to unbalance the motorcycle. It rocked on the kickstand under the sideways pressure of rancher and dynamite and crashed over onto its side, the case of explosives sliding down the back wheel onto the ground. Logan fell in a heap beside it.

Logan, spent, breathless, seeing only in intermittent flashes, crawled toward the case of dynamite, pushed at it to get it off the wheel. He made an attempt to get up, to pull at the motorcycle and get it upright again, but he couldn't do more than rise to his knees, wavering there and then sinking back so he was sitting on his feet.

He stared blankly toward the motorcycle, seeing only a blur of green grass broken by the bright blue-and-silver of the motorcycle. He fell over on his side and his eyes closed.

Lying there, he knew he had to keep trying. There was something more he had to do. By an immense effort of will he lifted himself onto one elbow and opened his eyes. In a brief moment of clarity, he looked down at himself. His pants were soaked with urine. For another long moment, he held himself up and kept his eyes open, even when the red haze blotted everything out. Then, slowly, he sank back to the ground unconscious.

17

A4DX693-P201-E

TOPSECRETCLASSQSCRAMBLE

CODEDESIGRIVERBOAT

CODESQUAREDCOWBOYNINEFIVEZERO

GENERAL SAMUEL HILL

JOINTCHIEFS PENTAGON

PRIORITY REDREDRED

HANDDELIVERSEALED ONLY

BEGINS. REPORT DAYSIX EAGLE. FEDBURINV AND SPECIAL DETAIL INVESTIGATION LEAVES NO DOUBT ALPHA TAU INCIDENT ATTRIBUTABLE DANIEL LOGAN. CANNOT RULE OUT POSSIBILITY OF ASSISTANCE OTHER QUARTERS. NO CONTACT LOGAN BY ANY PERSON OUR

LIST SINCE PASTDAY MYHOUSE ZERO ONEHUNDRED AT HOME OF MATTHEW SPENCER AS REPORTED. LAST KNOWN CONTACT PASTDAY MYHOUSE FIFTEENHUNDRED DYNAMITE SALESMAN. PRESS TEAM EMPLOYING AGREED STRATEGY. COOPERATION OF ESSENTIAL ELEMENTS EXPECTED. INTERVIEW ROY CARDWELL PHYSICIAN SUCCESSFULLY CONCLUDED THISHOUR MYHOUSE IN SPITE OF MEASURABLE RESISTANCE. SUGGEST STRONGEST ADVISABILITY OF CONTINUING SURVEILLANCE CARDWELL. REFERENCE YOUR S896–1 NICKERSON COL. CO FORTHOW RECEIVED THISDAY COMMUNICATION FROM REP. MICHAEL PAINE MEMBER CBW SUBCOM. INQUIRY ABOUT STATUS ALPHA TAU AND RUMOR OF NERVE GAS LEAKAGE RESULTING IN LOCAL CASUALTIES. CONSIDER STRONGLY PROBABLE HIS SOURCE CARDWELL. ALL OTHERS SECURE OUR OPINION. PLEASE ADVISE SOONEST PROPER HANDLING THIS ELEMENT. CURRENT EVALUATION NEGATIVE DEGREE FIVE AND IMPROVING. RECOMMENDED STRATEGY UNCHANGED MAINTAIN SECUREST HANDLING PRESENT DISPOSITION. ONLY UNPREDICTABLE FACTOR REP PAINE AS ABOVE. CURRENT ESTIMATE PRESENT SURVIVAL DANIEL LOGAN TWENTY PERCENT PLUSMINUS FIVE. SIGNED FRANKLIN COL.

EIGHT

1

Joe Wilson picked at his teeth as he walked down the steps of the diner. The toothpick splintered almost immediately, as he expected it would, so he threw it into the darkness and pulled another from his shirt pocket. He always took a big handful of the thin, flat toothpicks, because one of them never was enough.

Wilson was glad that it was a clear night, and not too cold. He hated the late-night shift, and he looked forward to the day when he would have enough seniority not to draw it at all. Already, he had enough years in the company that he only got it maybe once in two weeks, but even that was too much. Tonight, at least, wasn't too bad a run. Just back over to Cheyenne, and without a load, at that. Not even a trailer, in fact, just the big white cab with an empty hitch. He might even have a little fun, blowing off some hotshots in cars. Nobody in a car could touch what he could do with the cab when it was empty like that.

Wilson was lost in an imaginary drag race when he opened the door of the cab, so he got almost all the way in before he saw that there was somebody in the passenger's seat. He stopped short and started to bawl the guy out for sleeping in his truck, when he saw the rifle pointed at the tip of his nose. Wilson just froze where he was, half in and half out of the truck, staring at the wild man who was holding a gun on him.

It was dark, and Wilson couldn't see very much, but he had the impression of a fierce face covered with about a week's growth of beard, dirt smeared, the cheeks and forehead scratched, with burrs and twigs and dead leaves caught in the wild, unkempt hair. He didn't have a chance to look further, because the wild man interrupted him.

"Don't make a sound or I'll kill you," he whispered in a harsh, grating voice.

Wilson didn't doubt the man for an instant. He realized that his mouth was hanging open, and he closed it.

"Get in," the man grated.

Wilson climbed all the way into the cab and gently closed the door. He looked at the man in the passenger's seat and noticed that a thick line of blood had started to well from his left nostril. Wilson started to tell him about it, but decided it would be safer if he didn't.

His hesitation didn't go unnoticed. "What is it?"

Wilson hesitated again. The rifle barrel inched closer to his face. "Your nose . . ." Wilson said.

The man wiped at his nose with one hand and looked at the blood smeared on his palm. It didn't seem to make any impression. The man wiped his hand on the shoulder of his sheepskin jacket.

"Start it," he said.

2

Once the dynamite was loaded into the cab, Logan relaxed slightly. Giving the driver directions and watching to make sure that he didn't try anything heroic had taken most of his energy. As it was, the man had almost caught him sleeping when he got into the truck. Now that he had the dynamite close at hand, Logan doubted that the driver would do anything stupid.

Sitting there in the truck, speeding through the night, Logan concentrated on getting his energy back, what there was of it. The rifle was in his lap, pointed at the driver, and when Logan felt strong enough, he worked at putting fuses into sticks of dynamite he took from the open case on the cab floor in front of him.

He stopped to wipe blood from his nose and transfer it to his sleeve. The bloody nose had bothered him at first. It had brought him back to the morning on the cliff, looking at Chris lying there shivering and sick. Chris's nose had been bleeding, too. Logan had furiously clamped the thought from his mind. There was no way it could help him now.

As the truck continued down the dark highway, Logan looked at the clock on the dashboard. It was four o'clock, just about twenty-four hours after he had left Chivington. He wondered if he could get the all-night radio station in Cheyenne and pick up the hourly news. He reached out slowly and turned on the truck's radio. In the driver's seat, Wilson looked curiously at his passenger.

The radio came on, hissing and sputtering. Logan played with the tuner in what he thought was the right part of the dial, until he got a static-filled voice. It wasn't Cheyenne, but it was the news. There were a couple of items that Logan didn't listen to, and then the newscaster said, "The Federal Bureau of Investigation has identified Daniel Charles Logan, forty-two, of Carbon County, Wyoming, as the prime suspect in the dynamite bombing of the Chivington Research Laboratories near Sinclair, in southern Wyoming, early yesterday. The FBI said that Logan's fingerprints were found on equipment used in the explosions. A widespread manhunt for Logan is under way throughout the Mountain States area."

Wilson looked at his passenger again. The wild-looking man had forgotten everything else and was listening intently to the radio. My god, Wilson thought, he must be the guy they mean. He looked down at the cases of dynamite. God, he thought, Why me?

The newscaster was saying, "Meanwhile the Pentagon has refused to comment on allegations that the research facility was engaged in top-secret defense work. Dr. Walter Steenrod, director of the Laboratories, has also refused to make any statement about the incident."

In spite of the pain that was turning him into a bundle of burning knots, Logan smiled. Then, at the newscaster's next word, the smile left his face.

"A Wyoming physician, Dr. Roy Cardwell, has told the Associated Press that the suspect, Daniel Logan, may be suffering from an incurable nervous disorder and that

Logan was upset at the recent accidental death of his son. Officials of the hospital where Logan was being treated say that they are not free to comment at this time." The newscaster paused to clear his throat, then went on.

"In Washington, Congressman Michael Paine, member of the House Subcommittee on Chemical and Biological Warfare and a long-time critic of the Pentagon, has called for a full congressional investigation."

The newscaster went on to another subject, and Logan turned off the radio.

3

For some reason he couldn't understand, Roy Cardwell woke up at three o'clock in the morning. It had happened to him before, but not for years. Once he was sure he wouldn't be able to get back to sleep, he dressed and paced around his office, trying to figure out what was bothering him.

No matter how many things he tried out, he kept coming back to the same two: Dan Logan and Colonel Franklin. And the more he thought about them, the more he became convinced that unless he did something about it, something awful was going to happen. What he found agonizing was the fact that he had no idea what to do.

At about five o'clock, he hit upon the only thing that made any sense to him. He would go to Fort Howard and confront Colonel Franklin. He had no clear idea of what he would say, and when he thought about the idea for more than a minute, it seemed crazy, but he was going to do it anyway. This time, he was not going to turn his back on his impulses. He had done that already in the sad, confusing business with the Logans and the Public Health Service and the army, and it had only brought him grief and self-recrimination. Cardwell had been around too long to back down on something he felt was important to him, and was too old to be able to afford to spend time feeling guilty.

4

Sitting in the small, uncomfortable sentry box on the west boundary of Fort Howard, Captain Billy-Joe Slocum hoped that Logan would try to get onto the Fort through the gate he was guarding. Doug Enyard had been an old friend of his, not only from the Special Detail, but going all the way back to their days at the Point together, and Slocum wanted a crack at the bastard who had burned him. He didn't care if he had to stretch his orders to do it.

Slocum looked up from the magazine he was thumbing through, a *Penthouse* left there by one of the enlisted men who had this duty on a more regular basis than he did. He had been distracted by the sound of a truck motor, and when he looked up he saw a pair of headlights coming down the road toward the gate. He put the magazine down and picked up his M-16, checked to be sure it was cocked and set at full automatic, and opened the sentry-box door. As he stepped out in front of the gate, he threw the switch on the special alarm that Lieutenant Colonel Lieberman had ordered installed that afternoon. If Slocum didn't come back and flip the switch back in three minutes, alarms would go off all over the Fort.

As the truck approached the gate, it slowed to a stop. Slocum stepped to one side of it and walked toward the driver's window. He was disappointed. This gray-haired, mustached, red-faced trucker wasn't the man he was waiting for. Slocum couldn't see the relief man too well, but he didn't look like the right one, either.

"You fellows lost?" Slocum asked.

He never even saw Logan raise his rifle and fire. The bullet caught him just above the bridge of the nose and blew away his helmet and most of the back of his head. His lifeless body flew backwards almost five feet before it hit the ground.

Wilson sat motionless behind the wheel, stunned. He was unable even to take his hands from the wheel to touch the searing powder burn across his throat. There were bright flashes in front of his eyes, and his ears rang with noise of the shot. He could barely hear Logan when he said, "Drive through it."

When the driver didn't move, Logan shouted at him, "Go on!"

Moving like an automaton, Wilson put the truck in gear. He engaged the clutch, and the truck jumped forward, bucking, and hit the striped metal barrier that blocked the road, bending it and pushing it aside. Wilson fought to keep the truck under control as it swerved from the impact.

When they were traveling straight down the road again, Logan reached across in front of Wilson and turned off the headlights. Wilson, still stunned and frightened by the murder he had just witnessed, drove on, his hands locked again on the wheel.

The dark tree-lined road they were driving along more by feel than by sight led them quickly to a crossroads. A sign illuminated by a small spotlight listed the directions to the important buildings and functions of the Fort. Logan raised the rifle and placed the muzzle against Wilson's ear.

"Stop the truck," he said harshly.

Wilson stopped the truck and looked sideways out of the corner of his eye, afraid to turn his head. From the position he was in, he couldn't see Logan at all. He turned his attention back to the road.

Beside him, Logan was trying to read the sign. The words swam and blurred and drifted and Logan found that he couldn't read them at all. All he could see were a series of yellowish blotches on a dark background. He grit his teeth and concentrated, but without success. He felt a light tug in the rifle, sensed that the truck driver had moved, and looked around at him.

Wilson froze, wide-eyed with fear.

In a soft, level voice, Logan told him, "Open the door and get out."

Wilson knew what to expect next; he was terrified. "Look Mister, I did everything you told me."

Logan didn't seem to hear him. He looked around wildly, snapped out, "Go on."

Wilson could feel a warm spot spreading through his pants. It was all he could do not to blubber and cry. He pleaded: "Come on, Mister. Please."

Logan seemed to see him clearly for the first time. "Go on," he said, his voice infinitely weary. "I won't hurt you."

Slowly, not believing he could have heard the truth, Wilson opened the door and backed out of the truck. As soon as he had both feet on the ground, he turned to run, slipped, recovered himself, and ran headlong into the night, afraid with every step that the next would bring a bullet between his shoulders.

In the truck's cab, Logan struggled over the cases of dynamite into the driver's seat. He reached out for the door that Wilson had left open, and slammed it. The motor was still running, the gears in neutral. Logan sat motionless in the driver's seat, unable to move, too weak even to drive the truck. He rested his head on the steering wheel for what seemed like forever. He was so tired. All he wanted to do was go to sleep, so he could forget the pain that had gripped him now so completely and for so long that he no longer had any sense of what it was like not to be in pain.

Deep inside his mind, something told him that he couldn't stay where he was, that he had to go . . . somewhere. He licked his parched lips with a dry tongue, tasted something wet and warm and sharply sweet, didn't know it was his own blood, running now from both nostrils. Moving awkwardly, jerkily, pushed on by something he could no longer identify, he put the truck in gear and fought the wheel over so the truck was going down the road to his right, having chosen that direction for no particular reason except perhaps instinct.

He had gone only a few yards when he was suddenly blinded by bright white light that shone deep into his eyes, piercing to the center of his brain, adding its agony to the others already there, joined by the deafening pain of sirens and klaxons and alarm bells. Logan pulled at the wheel, trying to get out of the path of that burning light, only to be faced with another one, the twin of the first, that sprung up in the new direction. For a few seconds Logan collapsed at the wheel, and the truck, deprived of a foot on the gas pedal, stalled and jerked to a stop.

Logan looked up, into the again intolerable light, groped for the handle of the door and struggled out of the truck, holding in one hand the rifle he had not let go of for hours, it seemed, and dragging, somehow, one of the cases of dynamite in the other.

He lurched away from the truck, trailing a thin, brown line of dynamite sticks that tumbled from the open case as it bumped along the ground. He tried to find a direction away from the horrible burning lights, which, now that he was out of the truck, seemed to come from every direction but one, the one toward which he stumbled desperately. He was struck by an attack of coughing: violent, wrenching coughs that ended in his standing bent double, retching and spitting blood.

The soldiers approached him slowly, spread in a wide circle on the new-mown grass of the parade ground. They were men of the Special Detail, all officers, and a select group from Major Cooper's security detachment. In the bright, blue-white light of the three huge banks of searchlights, they could see a lone man holding a rifle in one hand, doubled over in what looked like a position of great pain.

One of the soldiers held a walkie-talkie. It crackled and buzzed and he heard Lieutenant Colonel Lieberman's voice say, "Is he taking any action?"

The man with the walkie-talkie said, "No, sir. He's standing up but he isn't moving."

The coughing and retching passed. Logan, standing with his back to the lights, could see nothing, even in the patch of brightness the lights made beyond him. He had the sense, though, that there was something menacing him, that out there, where he couldn't see it or reach it, there was something terrible. He leveled the rifle and fired.

At the first shot, the approaching soldiers fell to prone positions, their rifles aimed at Logan like the deadly spokes of a huge, watchful wheel. Logan's shots went wild, over their heads.

The walkie-talkie crackled. "This is Command," Lieberman's voice said, attenuated and tinny. "Hold your fire. Repeat. Hold your fire. Remain in your present position until ordered to advance." The soldier with the walkie-talkie acknowledged the order and passed it down the line.

The soldiers waited.

After a time, they heard the helicopters. The first one swept low over them, its passage bringing a cold wind and the loud beat of rotors.

At first, Logan was aware only of the noise, then he

was whipped by a violent wind, cold and harsh, snatching at him, pressing him down. A light burned down at him. He tried to look up, but the light struck at him, and the wind. He pressed the trigger of the rifle and did not know whether it fired, or where.

The rifle slipped from his numb fingers and he slumped to his knees, fighting to stay there, to hold himself against the wind and the light that bludgeoned him forward onto his hands, crawling on all fours to be away from it until he fell onto his side.

He tried to roll over, to push himself up, but he had no control of his muscles. Thcy bunched up and released for reasons of their own, uncoordinated, uncommanded. He found himself stretched out on his back, one hand hammering the ground, and then he was arched into a bow and straining for the sky, his eyes wide and staring into the light. He collapsed into a limp heap.

Again he was pulled into stiffness, his limbs jerking, his head grinding into the grass. His mouth strained open and he bellowed his agony into the night.

Hovering above him like a giant malevolent bug, the helicopter watched.

5

By the time Roy Cardwell reached the perimeter of Fort Howard, the first light was ringing the horizon with blue. At the side of the dew-moistened road, a small sign pointed the way to Gate A. Cardwell made the turn and drove slowly toward the small side gate of the Fort, the one closest to the Logan ranch.

He was still more than a hundred yards away from the fence that marked the actual boundary of the Fort when he became aware that there was a lot of activity at Gate A. The road in front of the gate seemed to be crowded with soldiers and vehicles. As he speculated on the meaning of so much activity so early in the morning, he was passed by an ambulance leaving the gate area.

He realized suddenly that his fears had been justified. Something had happened here. But he was afraid that he was too late to do anything.

He was about ten yards from the gate and slowing down when a soldier in fatigues and combat boots stepped out in front of him. The soldier was holding an M-16, and Cardwell was amazed to see that it was pointed straight at him. He stopped the car.

Another soldier, this one carrying a riot gun, came up to the driver's-side window. Cardwell wound the window down and said, "I'm Roy Cardwell." He was going to say more, but the soldier, whose collar bore the insignia of a captain, cut him off.

"You'll have to leave," he said.

"But I've come to see . . ." Again, Cardwell was cut off.

"You'll have to leave immediately, sir."

Cardwell was angered by this unequivocal dismissal. "You don't understand," he said. "I'm here on important business."

The captain barked at him: "Now."

"Damn it, the man's my patient," Cardwell said. He opened the car door.

The captain hit the door with the butt of his rifle, slamming it, almost catching Cardwell's hand. In the same motion, he pumped a shell into the chamber of the riot gun and pushed the gun toward Cardwell's face. Behind the gun, the captain's expression was hard and unyielding.

Cardwell realized that if he pushed the matter further, he would run a real risk of being shot. Shaking his head in frustration and disbelief, he backed the car around and headed slowly down the road, away from Gate A.

Before he reached the perimeter road, he let the car coast to a stop. He sat there, confused, defeated, saddened. Ahead of him, the sun was rising in red and gold splendor into a pure blue sky.

Cardwell stared at the sunrise, unseeing. He thought about Dan Logan and about Chris. He thought about his own life and the lives he had brought into being. He thought as well about the lives he had seen end, the ones he had been unable to preserve. He thought about Logan and himself and he put his head back against the seat and cried for the helpless, ceaseless vanity of the world.

6

At the edge of the parade ground, Franklin stood looking down at Dan Logan. Next to him, Major Holliford was bent over the inert form of the rancher, feeling his neck for a pulse.

Holliford looked up at Franklin and shook his head. "He's dead."

Franklin nodded. "They're going to want him in Denver as soon as possible," he said, his voice flat and emotionless.

Franklin stood there for several minutes, oblivious to the activity around him, as Holliford drew a sample of Logan's blood and a stretcher was brought up. The enlisted men carrying the stretcher put it next to the body and waited.

After a moment Franklin nodded to them, and they put Logan on the stretcher and carried him to the waiting helicopter. The helicopter took off slowly, carrying Logan's blanket-shrouded body in an open metal basket strapped beneath the glass bubble of its cockpit.

Franklin watched as the helicopter climbed over the Fort and flew into the rising sun. Then he turned and walked to the jeep that was waiting to take him back to his quarters.

EPILOGUE

1

CONGRESS OF THE UNITED STATES OF AMERICA

HOUSE OF REPRESENTATIVES

ARMED SERVICES COMMITTEE
SUBCOMMITTEE ON
CHEMICAL AND BIOLOGICAL WARFARE

#AS–92–4937CBW–41–P
REPORT SUBMITTED BY REP. MICHAEL PAINE (ASC–CBW–8) (WISC) TITLE: EVENTS RELATED TO THE DESTRUCTION OF THE DEPARTMENT OF DEFENSE RESEARCH AND DEVELOPMENT FACILITY AT SINCLAIR, WYOMING.

THIS DOCUMENT IS FOR THE PRIVATE USE OF MEMBERS OF THE ARMED SERVICES COMMITTEE. IT CONTAINS CLASSIFIED AND SENSITIVE MATERIAL.

DISSEMINATION OF THIS DOCUMENT IS PROHIBITED BY LAW.

TOP SECRET

(EXTRACT)

14. CONCLUSIONS.

. . . What is amazing to me, and the thing that I think bears the most serious implications, is the extent of the subterfuge, indirection, and even outright falsification of which I found evidence. I am not proposing here that any conclusion be drawn with respect to the ultimate advisability of these programs as a whole. Rather, I am raising the question of the proper conduct of such programs if, indeed, they are deemed to be necessary. The foremost issue raised by the events of the past month in and around Sinclair, Wyoming and Fort Howard is that of the undermining of our most important asset: the faith of the American people.

. . . We are presented with a man whose fundamental loyalty cannot be questioned, because when he was given the opportunity to demonstrate it, he did so unstintingly. The image of the disillusioned hero has come to be a popular one in our contemporary gallery, but it is not appropriate to Daniel Logan. Once he had demonstrated his willingness to give his life in defense of his country, performing with notable distinction, he returned to his ranch and toiled hard and unquestioningly. . . . His reputation in the community was one of goodness and honesty and uprightness. Yet he was driven to commit acts of awful destruction against the very army with which he had served so valiantly.

. . . Much of what happened in his final days will never be known. Much of the evidence has been obscured. Many of the participants have retreated behind the shield of official privilege. But there remains the sense of what he did.

. . . What I believe we have to fear is not only the wanton disregard of human life that is apparent in this incident, because we have too often seen how easily that can be explained away or disguised to appear to be something else. The thing that carries the most danger to the fabric of our lives is the trifling with human dignity, the attitude that no manipulation of life or belief or truth is too great if the end it serves is important. No doubt the officers and civilian scientists involved in this incident thought that they were acting in a good cause.

. . . The tragic thing is that there is a poison loose in the country today which is far more insidious and far more dangerous than the experimental nerve agent that leaked accidentally beyond the boundaries of Fort Howard. It is the poison of fear and mistrust and hopelessness; the fear and mistrust of the people for their government and institutions, and their hopelessness to maintain their self-respect and dignity in the face of the uncaring, overpowering forces they face daily, and toward which they feel this growing fear and mistrust. . . .

I believe that a full and public investigation of this incident is both advisable and necessary. There is no way to calculate the harm that will inevitably result if we do not remember the basic principles upon which we operate and from which we derive our greatest strength. I believe that this disclosure is especially important in view of the key appropriations bill that is currently being considered by this committee. I appreciate the action of the committee in postponing its vote on that bill until I could complete this preliminary investigation, and I respectfully request the members of the committee to pass a further postponement so that we, and the people, may have an opportunity to learn the whole truth of this matter. . . .

It is time, I believe, for a reappraisal of the attitudes and policies that have led us to the point where something like what seems to have happened in Wyoming could come to pass. There is no group better suited to lead that reappraisal than this committee, which is enjoined to function as a prime guardian of the public interest in military matters. . . . It is our duty to lead in the establishment of a responsible policy which, with the proper regard for the defense needs of this country, will nonetheless uphold the primary principles of human dignity that are the foundation stones of our democracy. . . .

Whatever is the final determination of this committee, I feel that it is my duty to my constituents and to my fellow citizens of the United States of America to make known the facts of this incident as I understand them.

Respectfully submitted,
Michael Paine
Wisconsin

2

CONGRESS
OF THE
UNITED STATES OF AMERICA

HOUSE OF REPRESENTATIVES

ARMED SERVICES COMMITTEE

Minutes of the Thirty-Eighth Plenary Session

(EXTRACT)

49. #AS–92–4937CBW–41–P
Report by Rep. Michael Paine (Wisc.)
MOTION: No action
VOTE: aye 26; nay 8; n/v 6
FUTURE ACTION: None